✓ P9-CAD-759

THE Dreadful
TALE OF
Prosper Redding

THE Dreadful TALE OF Prosper Redding

ALEXANDRA BRACKEN

Disney • HYPERION

LOS ANGELES   NEW YORK

WEST HARTFORD
PUBLIC LIBRARY
4687

If you purchased this book without a cover, you should be aware that this book is stolen property. It was reported as "unsold and destroyed" to the publisher, and neither the author nor the publisher has received any payment for this "stripped" book.

Copyright © 2017 by Alexandra Bracken

All rights reserved. Published by Disney • Hyperion, an imprint of Disney Book Group. No part of this book may be reproduced or transmitted in any form or by any means, electronic or mechanical, including photocopying, recording, or by any information storage and retrieval system, without written permission from the publisher. For information address Disney • Hyperion, 125 West End Avenue, New York, New York 10023.

First Hardcover Edition, September 2017
First Paperback Edition, September 2018
1 3 5 7 9 10 8 6 4 2
FAC-026988-18201
Printed in the United States of America

This book is set in Adobe Caslon Pro, Caslon Antique Pro, Edlund/ Monotype; Bad Neighborhood Badhouse Bold/House Industries; Blossom/Fontspring

Designed by Marci Senders
Library of Congress Control Number for Hardcover: 2016058799
ISBN 978-1-4847-9010-6

Visit www.DisneyBooks.com

SUSTAINABLE FORESTRY INITIATIVE   Certified Sourcing
www.sfiprogram.org
SFI-00993

THIS LABEL APPLIES TO TEXT STOCK

J
BRACKEN
ALEXANDRA

For the Garrett–Geyster–Bracken clan

A Word from the Malefactor

Light a candle and step close to the looking glass. Time is short, and we cannot delay.

In another time, in another world, you would not have been worth the slightest flicker of my gaze. However, even I cannot break the terms of our contract. So if you find yourself still foolish enough to follow, there are three things—three things—you must know. Three lessons that must be heard, obeyed, remembered. These may one day prove crucial to your survival, human. Whether you choose to pay attention is entirely up to you. I've never had time to suffer fools.

The first is that you can never trust a Redding. The family will whistle lies between their teeth and beg for mercy until their wagging tongues tire. Do not give in. Cover your ears, your eyes, and block out their cowardly stench. These are the humans that broke a contract written in blood the moment they feared for their fortune. Their tradition is one of foolishness. They are no family of yours.

Listen. Mind me well, for the light grows dim and our hour approaches. The Reddings will tell you they were wronged, misunderstood. They will tell you I am a liar, a cheat, and a scoundrel. But do not forget that even as I slept, they feared me. As should you.

For the second thing you must understand is that *my* tradition is one of revenge.

And the third: anything I give you, I can—and will—delight in taking back.

Which, in the case of the Reddings, is everything.

Founder's Day

See, here's the thing.

In the big scheme of life and planet Earth, the town of Redhood is a tiny speck. An itty-bitty speck of a speck. Don't even bother pulling out a map, because the town isn't on most of them. It never held a witch trial, wasn't responsible for starting any kind of revolution, and the Pilgrims landed on a rock about two hundred miles away. To most people, the only interesting thing about Redhood is the family that founded it.

Well, *you* might be interested to know that there is nothing interesting about us Reddings. I mean, okay, my great-great-great-great-great-whatever came *this close* to signing the Declaration of Independence but got held up by a sore throat that killed him two days later. A *sore throat.* Which, sorry, is just about the lamest way a guy could go. I don't think he should get points for *almost* signing. That's like me telling my parents I *almost* got a perfect score on my math test—a D is only four grades away from an A, right?

Anyway, the point is, my family has been around forever and doesn't seem to be going anywhere. The walls of the Cottage are stuffed with portraits of frowning ancestors in black coats and bonnets. Every day is like a bad Thanksgiving play over there.

Just below those are pictures of a few dozen four-star generals, important congressmen, and some CEOs. Grandmother likes to say that if any one of us decided to run for president (aka her), the country would be so in love (with her), they'd get rid of "this pesky democracy" and name President Redding (her) a monarch (queen).

The faces of my family changed with each generation, but you couldn't say the same about Redhood. It never changes, not really. Probably because it takes years of town meetings and vote after vote to get anything done. I mean, it became front-page news when my grandmother, the mayor, finally allowed them to bring high-speed Internet to the town. Before that day, I don't think Grandmother had ever touched a computer in her life.

Redhood was like a page that had fallen from an old history book and was stuck, forgotten, under a desk. It was still around collecting dust, but if you weren't looking for it, you'd never find it. Families came and went, but they always seemed to return eventually. And the worst was that everyone was constantly all up in each other's business—especially my family's. The place felt smaller every year.

Which was why it was so weird that no one else noticed when a stranger came to town.

On Founder's Day, the only place to be was on Main Street, under the ropes of warm, twinkling lights draped between Peregrine S. Redding Academy and the courthouse.

The steps of the two redbrick buildings were littered with straw-stuffed cushions and folding chairs, every last available spot claimed by the town's residents for the evening's Candlelight Parade. The tourists who wandered into Redhood to see its famous festival were too entranced by everything to know they needed to reserve their own seats long before sundown.

Most of the time, I would do just about anything to get out of this place. Founder's Day is the exception. It's when the town wakes up from summer's sweaty sleep and exhales some strange magic stirring inside it. You feel it shift, transforming a place as stiff as a book's spine into a maze of haystacks, wreaths, and garlands. The air crisps and sweetens, and breathing it in is like taking the first bite of a freshly picked apple.

In the dark midnight hours of October, the trees of Main Street set themselves ablaze with color. They lean over the streets and create a canopy of dazzling gold when the sunlight hits them just right. I *still* haven't found the right blend of paint to capture it, and maybe I never will. Most of the fallen leaves are then rescued and stuffed into scarecrows that guests can take home with them from the celebration.

The best part of it, though, is the morning mist that creeps along the streets, glowing just enough to mask everything secretly ugly and rotten about this place.

A chilly breeze suddenly slipped up beneath my school uniform blazer, ruffling the edges of my notebook. I slammed my fist down to keep it from flying away with the fluttering leaves.

I should have sharpened my pencil before I left school. When I tried to sketch the nearby kids tossing rings over pumpkin stems, everyone came out looking like one of those troll dolls. Their parents watched from a short distance away, gathered in front of the white-and-orange-striped tent that the local café, Pilgrim's Plate, had set up to sell pie, cobbler, and apple-cider doughnuts.

I think that's why I noticed him then. He wasn't standing in one of the parental unit clusters, sipping hot cider. Instead, the stranger stood on the opposite side of the street, by the cart selling sugar-sweet-smelling roasted chestnuts. He was broomstick thin, and if I had to draw his face, I would have started first with his long nose. He sneered as someone tried to pass him a piece of paper to use for the growing bonfire at the center of the square.

He was dressed like a Pilgrim, but sad as it was, that wasn't actually weird. A lot of people in Redhood got dressed up for Founder's Day, especially the old people. Old people love those big black buckle hats and billowy white shirts, I guess.

I glanced at the wide-brim straw hat he wore, then down at his shoes. Unpolished and missing buckles. He was lucky Grandmother wasn't around. She would have tossed *him* into the bonfire, instead of a slip of paper that listed her regrets she was hoping to burn away.

The bonfire was the whole point of the Founder's Day festival—the time we could let the fire eat up every bad feeling, thought, or secret we had and be free from it. That's what Grandmother says. I think most people just came to make their s'mores.

The guy, whoever he was, waited until the man running the cart turned to help another customer before snatching some chestnuts for himself. He must have felt me staring, because he turned with a crooked grin and a wink.

Okay, then, I thought, and turned back to my drawing—only to immediately jump up to my feet. "Aw, *crap!*"

A glob of maple syrup had dripped from my Silence Cake onto the notebook page, and slowly made its way down onto my pants, where it pooled in the worst place imaginable. Awesome.

With a small sigh, I popped the rest of the treat into my mouth and tore out the ruined sheet of paper. A whole hour's work, reduced to use as a napkin to wipe away sticky pumpkin leaf crumbs.

That's right. Some towns get caramel apples. Others get a special chocolate treat as their claim to fame. We got fried pumpkin leaves.

Some backstory: way back, and I mean *way* back, before Redhood was even named Redhood, the small group of settlers that arrived with their terrible hats and frowns experienced an endless string of crop failures. During one particularly bad season, the wife of our town's founder, Honor Redding, was left with nothing but the leaves of their sad, dying pumpkin field. Her name was Silence, which probably tells you everything you need to know about what was expected of her in life. Anyway, legend has it that she saved our fledgling town from starvation by sharing their pumpkin leaves and finding different ways to prepare them to survive the winter.

Since no one wants to eat a plain pumpkin leaf if they aren't starving, we now fry them and dunk them in honey, maple syrup, or chocolate and slide a stick through a line of them to munch on. And we call them Silence Cakes in her honor because her husband, actually named Honor, gets credit for just about everything else.

The *bong, bong, bong* of the bell in the clock tower tolled. I looked up, frantic, checking the time—how was it already five o'clock?

Climbing onto the bench, I searched the heads and hats of the milling crowds, the volunteers who were beginning to light the thousands of candles that would eventually be added to floats or carried by the school choir as they sang during the parade. Prue had been pulled away by her group of friends, each dressed in the Academy's navy blazer and plaid skirt, and my heart started hammering in my chest, just a little, when I realized I'd been so focused on my own stupid sketch I'd lost track of her completely.

But—there they were, by the haystack maze. I leaped down, charging through the line of tourists waiting for their chance to paint pumpkins.

There was a quartet of string musicians playing some dead composer's song in the white gazebo, under a banner that read CELEBRATING 325 YEARS OF REDHOOD HISTORY. Just as they finished and people began to applaud, the black iron streetlamps flickered on. I tripped over one of the jack-o'-lanterns lining the sidewalk.

Crap. We'd have to run.

I shoved my way through the crowd around the gazebo, fighting through the sea of elbows and baby strollers.

"Watch it—"

"*Hey!*"

I ignored them. That is, until a hand gripped the back

of my neck and yanked me so hard I dropped my backpack. One whiff was all I needed to know who the hand belonged to. Mr. Wickworth smelled like lemons and dry-erase markers. My stomach turned into a knot of wriggling worms.

"Mr. Redding. Would you care to explain this excessively rude behavior?"

Did you know that human beings can, in fact, cluck? I didn't, not until Mr. Henry Wickworth found me dozing off in class on the first day of seventh-grade English at the Academy. His face turned a shade of purple not normally found in nature, and me and the rest of the class had to sit through a ten-minute rant about *respectful behavior* and *rudeness*, and how he'd be expecting an essay outlining the difference by the end of detention that same afternoon.

Yeah, detention on the first day of school. Detention every day for the entire first week of school, actually. So far, I'd written papers on *disrespect, inconsiderateness,* and *honor.* I thought he was actually going to take his ruler and break it over my head when he asked for one defining *wiseacre,* and I only wrote one sentence: *I prefer smart aleck, sir.*

The truth was, Mr. Wickworth spent more time watching those survival reality-TV shows on his school computer than he did teaching us. The walls of his classroom were decorated with quotes from famous authors I'm pretty sure he made up (*"School is important. Pay attention in class."* —Ernest Hemingway). Trust me, if I had the choice between listening to an hour of TV static or sitting through one of his lessons, the static would be about a hundred thousand times more interesting.

"Well?" he said, fingers pinching my shoulders. "What do you have to say for yourself, Prosperity?"

Sometimes I wished I could be reprogrammed to think before I opened my mouth. "Since when do I have to say anything to you outside of class?"

You know when you try to cook an egg in the microwave, how the yolk starts to wiggle, then puff, then explodes all over the walls? I was pretty sure Mom would have had to take my uniform to the dry cleaners to get Mr. Wickworth's brains out of the fabric if Prue hadn't suddenly appeared.

"There you are, Prosper!" she said, brightly. Her friends trailed behind her, glaring at me over her shoulder. "Oh, hi, Mr. Wickworth! Are you enjoying the festival? Grandmother asked me to pass along a hello and to thank you for all your hard work."

Mr. Wickworth's hand lifted off me. I turned just in time to see the amazing change come over his face. His lips parted, and the face that had been as red as Prue's firebright hair took on a delighted, rosy kind of pink. "Oh. Miss Redding. Forgive me, I didn't see you there."

He, along with everyone else standing nearby, created a path for her. When she reached me, she put a hand on top of my head and gave it a little pat—a stupid habit she'd developed since she shot up three inches taller than me over the summer. Clearly we weren't identical. With my black hair and dark eyes, and her red hair and blue eyes, we didn't even look like we shared the same parents.

But I remembered how it used to be. I remembered all the hospital rooms. I remembered having to go to school without her, and then coming home and showing her all the pictures I'd drawn of it since we weren't allowed to turn on our phones to take photos. I remembered the way my blood turned cold each time she looked pale, or her breathing became labored.

I remembered, when we were really little, getting out of bed in the middle of the night to check on her. To make sure her heart was still beating.

A Spell of Bad Luck

Grandmother called Prue's heart condition the only bad luck the family had had in centuries. That's true. But even on the worst of days, I could make her laugh with a dumb story, watch a movie with her, help her get around the house, or make her lunch when our parents were traveling. I knew all the emergency numbers for her doctors, and still do.

But Prue was a Redding, and she survived, even when doctors said she probably wouldn't. Our parents founded Heart2Heart, an international charity dedicated to raising funds for underprivileged children with heart defects, and Prue became the face of it. The whole country was pulling for her with each surgery, and the most recent one, two years ago now, made her healthy and strong enough to do the things she'd never be allowed to before.

Prue enrolled in the Academy with me. She made friends who weren't related to us, and those friends happened to be the kids I never told her about, the ones who would fill my backpack with dirt or steal my homework.

And then, like all of the pent-up Redding good luck previously denied to her hit at once, she became president of our class, and set three consecutive track, horseback-riding, and archery records, and won a statewide essay contest about the need for better access to clean water in underserved parts of India. The one time she had brought home a report card that had a single A- on it, the teacher actually apologized to *her* for failing to teach up to her standards.

Prue is amazing, anyone will tell you that. It was just . . . now she knew the truth about me. I couldn't hide what other people really thought of me when she could see it for herself.

We came from a family of winners, record-setters, and firsts, and there wasn't a day that went by that our grandmother let me forget that I wasn't one of them.

Well, I, Prosperity Oceanus Redding, was proud to report that I was the first to set the record for the most times of dozing off during class in a single year, winning me some disbelief from parents and teachers, and twenty-four straight trips to the headmaster's during sixth grade. The only reason they hadn't kicked me out of the Academy was because my great-great-great-great-grandfather had literally built it with his bare hands.

You think it stinks to be named Prosperity? Try being named Prosperity when you get straight Ds in school, and everyone in your family starts hinting you should consider trash collecting instead of college. I don't know what's wrong with that. Trash collectors are nice people, and they get to ride on the back of trucks all day and do the important work of keeping the streets clean. That sounded pretty good to me.

But from the moment I'd first fallen asleep in his class, Mr. Wickworth had decided that *I* was garbage that needed to be disposed of, and Prue only proved his point when she swept in and acted like she had to clean up my messes, no matter how small.

"You know how Prosper is," Prue said sweetly. "He's, ah, well . . . he's Prosper. But clearly he needs glasses."

The girls behind her snickered.

"Glasses don't fix stupid," one of them said.

"And they won't fix his face either," said another.

I flinched as Prue coughed to disguise her laugh. A few of the adults nearby chuckled, craning their necks to get a better look at us. This was what it was like to be a Redding: when we were in Redhood, we were no better than zoo animals. I was surprised no one interrupted to ask for a selfie.

"Please excuse us," Prue continued. "We're due back at the Cottage for a family dinner. Will we see you tonight at the Candlelight Parade, Mr. Wickworth?"

The man couldn't help himself. He actually bobbed his head, like he was giving her a little bow. "I will see you there, Miss Redding."

"I'll see you too," I said between my gritted teeth. "After I get myself a pair of glasses."

"You do that, young man," Mr. Wickworth said. "Perhaps then you'll also be able to spot your manners."

I had something to say to that, but Prue tugged me away, leading us off Main Street. Behind us, the bonfire roared to its full size, sending sparks up into the shadows of the evening sky. People applauded and cheered, lining up to begin to toss in their regrets. I looked back, just once, to see the way the light made the nearby statue of Honor Redding glow so I could commit it to memory and sketch it later.

Once we were out of sight of the square, Prue finally let go of my arm.

"Why do you always have to stick your nose in everything?" I asked. "They already think I'm an idiot without your 'help.'"

Prue rolled her eyes. "If I don't play hero, who's going to rescue you? Besides, we're already late. You-know-who's going to kill us as it is."

Prue slowed down to let me catch up to her, digging in her bag until she pulled out a blue notebook. "Here—I accidentally picked this up instead of mine."

Heat rushed to my face, even as my shoulder slumped in

relief. I snatched it out of her hands and stuffed it into my bag, like that would be enough to bury it forever. *Of course* she found it. How could I have been so stupid? She probably had gone through all the old sketches with her friends, making fun of every single one. She should have just thrown it away when she realized it didn't have her class notes in them. My breath locked in my throat.

"Some of those are pretty good," Prue said, keeping her voice casual. "I mean, you're no da Vinci, but they're not half bad. I didn't realize you still kept a sketchbook and drew those . . . characters."

From the stories I used to invent to make her laugh, back when she was stuck in her hospital bed. Why did I still draw them? I don't even know. Maybe in the hope she might want to hear the stories again. The way she looked at me, then, lips pressed together to keep from laughing, told me that was going to be the day after never.

I gripped the strap of my backpack. *You don't know anything about me,* I wanted to say. *This is the first time we've talked in a week.*

"Are you ever going to show them to someone? What about Mrs. Peters?"

Here were a few things I would have done to avoid showing my drawings to the crusty art teacher at the Academy:

1. Cut off my toes.
2. Eat my own liver.

3. Walked the length of the United States to swim
   through shark-infested waters to Hawaii so that I
   could throw myself in a volcano.

The other kids at school already had enough ammuni-
tion against me without knowing I liked to sketch pictures
of them, not to mention benches and gardens around
Redhood.

"What about Mom? Or Dad? He likes museums, I
guess."

As crazy talented and smart as my family was, not a
single Redding could call him or herself an artist. The only
exception was maybe Nathaniel Redding, a second cousin
once removed, who wrote the *New York Times* best-selling
book *The Lost Longship*. It was an incredibly popular story
about time-traveling Vikings and the conspiracy to cover up
that they had killed off the real Pilgrims from the *Mayflower*
in a bloodthirsty rage.

I thought it was pretty awesome, but Grandmother just
about went supernova when she read the first few chap-
ters. Dad had bought a copy for Mom as a joke, and they
had laughed together as he read passages of it aloud. And
laughed. And laughed.

So I didn't need to imagine the look on my parents'
faces if I were to show them my sketchbook. I didn't need
to tell them I liked art. I already knew what their reaction
would be. *When you and Prue are old enough to help us run*

the Foundation, Dad would say, *then we'll really change the world.* Then Mom would smile, and talk about how the most important thing in the world was to help others. And then the only thing left in my head was the realization that art was something *I* loved, but it didn't do anything for the world, did it? It just made *me* happy.

So I kept my sketchbooks closed, until I was sure no one was looking.

I shook my head, my face turned down. "Can we just hurry? We're already late."

"Then let's go this way." Prue turned off the leaf-splattered road, and I felt a chill slither down my spine.

There was a small patch of dark forest between Main Street and the Cottage. I knew it pretty well, seeing how I'd spent all twelve and a half of my years trying to avoid it. It might have been a good shortcut, but it didn't make me feel any better as I slid down the soggy hill.

The woods made me feel like my skin was shrinking around my bones. There was a strange light there that turned the bright fall leaves to gray mulch. A little less than four hundred years ago, a terrible fire had torn through the area, and it was clear the trees never really recovered. Their trunks had grown a splotchy bark to hide the scars, but their bodies were twisted. They leaned away from the center of the forest, like they had tried to pull up their roots and run from the flames.

Sometimes, when the rain cut through their bare limbs,

I thought I could hear the echo of the trees screaming. *Don't be stupid*, I'd think, but the sound stayed in my ears for days. The place was damp, freezing, foggy, or some combo of the three, even in the summer. Even squirrels didn't like it, which is saying something.

"Prosper," Prue said suddenly. "Why does Wickworth give you so much detention? I thought you were feeling better. . . ."

I shrugged. "I just doze off sometimes."

"Pros—"

"I don't want to talk about it, okay?" I picked up my speed, running harder, pulling ahead of her. Anger and frustration made my head feel like it was boiling inside. "My teachers are just boring. I hate school."

That wasn't really true. I sort of liked school, aside from homework and tests. It was just that every few nights I had these dreams. . . . This enormous dark cat would come stalking toward me, eyes glowing like emeralds. Sometimes it would just watch me from behind a flickering line of fire, pacing back and forth and back and forth, teeth clattering in anticipation. Other nights, it would be cleaning meat off bones, licking the blood off its teeth. And always, just before I woke up, I'd hear the same words snarled over and over again: *Awaken the singing bone.*

I'd read that dreams, even nightmares, are our brains' way of trying to work out a problem, or remember something we've forgotten. So clearly this was my brain trying to tell me that my grandmother was going to try to peel off my skin and eat me one day.

It was nothing. Compared to what Prue had gone through, it was *less* than nothing. I didn't want my parents to have to worry about me even more than they already did.

Prue opened her mouth to say something, but closed it again. She reached over and punched me lightly on the shoulder. "Whatever you say. I'm always up for a rescue."

That was the problem. I didn't want her to rescue me. I just wanted her to like me again.

"We're here," I announced, tucking my chin down against my chest, waiting for her to lead. As always. Prue darted forward, only to stop dead in her tracks.

"What the—?" The words seemed to drop off my lips.

At the base of the hill was the start of the Cottage's long driveway—and dozens upon dozens of people, familiar and strange, were waiting there.

For us.

A Worrying Welcome

It wasn't that me and Prue hated our grandmother. It was just that we thought she might be the Devil in a dress suit.

She was our only living grandparent after Mom's parents, Grannie and Pa-Pa, were killed in a terrible car accident, and Grandpa Redding died of a heart attack. You think we'd all be super-close since we only lived a few streets away, huh?

Yeah. Right.

She didn't try to hide the evil lurking beneath her jewelry and expensive clothes either. She would skin a puppy if she thought it would make a good hat. Besides handing out fake money to the homeless, electing herself mayor of Redhood for ten consecutive years, and once forcing a gardener to continue pruning her roses after he had fallen off a ladder and broken both arms because she was hosting a party that night, Grandmother was *also* responsible for my name.

In the 325 recorded years of Redding family history, there had only ever been two sets of twins: Prosperity Oceanus Redding and Prudence Fidelia Redding in the seventeenth century, and Prosperity Oceanus Redding and Prudence Fidelia Redding in the twenty-first.

I don't know how she talked Mom and Dad into it. Maybe Mom was still out of it or something, or Grandmother bribed the doctor and nurses to let her fill out the birth certificate? And, okay, I get that there are worse Puritan names in the family we could have inherited. Be-Thankful, Help-on-High, Diffidence, and Obedience, to name just a few of the awesome options. Let me tell you, though, there is a special kind of awkwardness that comes from being surrounded by cousins with names like David and Josh.

And both David and Josh were waiting for us on the driveway below.

"What the . . . ?" Prue squinted down at them.

It felt like someone had head-butted me in the chest. "Oh my God," I said, dropping my schoolbag. "Something happened to Mom and Dad."

That was the only explanation. Founder's Day always brought out weirdo distant cousins, but not this many. The last time I had seen this kind of a crowd was when my second cousin once removed had croaked. Half the family showed up at the Cottage to see if they had made it into her will.

"No," Prue said, shaking her head. "No way. They would have told us in school. I don't even recognize half of these people—she's just having a special party and forgot to tell us, as usual."

Okay, that wasn't impossible, but why did it feel like they were waiting for *us*?

The wind whistled through the dense trees around us, stirring up the whispers of the leaves on the ground. I felt it nudge at my back, pushing me forward down the steep path, toward the cobblestoned driveway. The wild ivy that grew alongside it stopped at the exact point where stone met dirt, as if too frightened to grow in the direction of the house. The birds in the trees stopped their chattering as they fluttered down to the wrought-iron fence that guarded the estate like the barbed back of a serpent.

"Is that . . . ?" I began, squinting.

It was. My grandmother was standing in front of the family, holding a silver tray of chocolate chip cookies.

I almost didn't recognize her. Grandmother, who only ever wanted to be called *Grandmother* or *Grandmère* even though none of us were French and had no plans of becoming French, was a lady with sharp features. Her hair was the same shade of gray as an overcast sky, always kept in a tidy little bun at the base of her skull. Grandmother was tall and always rigid—and I mean *rigid*. Sometimes, when she wore a gray dress suit, it felt like I was talking to a frosty streetlight.

"Ooooh, children!" she sang out. "Hurry, won't you? We've been waiting for you."

That was it. I whirled around with only one goal: to run back up that hill, through the creepy forest, and straight out of Redhood. If she was giving us sweets and talking in that strange, drippy voice, it could only be for one reason. She was going to poison me.

Prue caught my elbow. "I'm so sorry we're late. Mrs. Marsh's orchestra was playing in the gazebo and we were enjoying ourselves so much we lost track of time."

There was a slight twitch at the corner of the old lady's right eye, but she recovered quickly. "No matter, my darlings." She handed the tray of cookies to one of my aunts and motioned for my other one to take our schoolbags.

A drop of sweat ran down the back of my neck despite the cold air. Everyone, at least fifty people, was staring at us. Even Great-Uncle Bartholomew, who had been engaged in bloody warfare with my grandmother over the Cottage for years. He was missing his left eye, which Grandmother swore was because he had an "unfortunate run-in" with a fireplace poker. Personally, I think she was aiming for his heart, and had missed.

Grandmother ushered Prue into an awkward hug. Her

arms were stiff as twigs, and one hand came up to pat Prue's back, like she was burping a baby.

I took a step away, but my cousins swooped in.

"Prosp, it's so great to see you," said David, who once locked me in the Cottage cellar for ten hours to see if the mice down there would eat me.

"It's been too long! What's up?" said Josh, who spread the rumor at the Academy that I still wet the bed.

Sarah, who had stolen one of Grandmother's diamond bracelets and dumped the blame on me, asked, "How is school going? I hear you have Mr. Wickworth this year. . . ."

And Charlotte, the oldest of all of us, the one responsible for *throwing me off a second-floor balcony* to see if I could fly, only smiled and wrapped an arm around my shoulder. They all looked like my aunts: tall, extremely blond, and tan, even in the dead of Massachusetts winter.

The rest of the family came at us like ants swarming a piece of candy on the sidewalk. We were crushed in a sea of white suits, silk dresses, and fur coats. I was passed up through a line of family members, half I didn't even recognize. They didn't let me go until I reached the foot of the curved marble stairway that led into the Cottage's grand entry. My grandmother stood at the top step, staring down the length of her nose at me.

She clapped her hands three times, summoning silence. The lights flickered on behind her, the candles in the hanging lanterns sparking to life like magic. I glanced up at the dark sky and felt my chest tighten. Behind us, the curls of fog from the nearby woods were rolling down the hill, spreading like curious fingers along the grass. Trying not to shudder, I turned to look for Prue.

I caught the spark of her red hair at the other end of the crowd. But standing beside her, like he belonged there, was the stranger. He glanced toward me, bright eyes narrowing. I shifted on my feet and looked at the ground.

"Good evening," Grandmother said finally. She handed her apron to the servant that had popped up like a daisy behind her. "We've awaited this night for a very long time, and it warms my heart to see so many of you decide to travel back to your ancestral home. Rest assured, we will put this all behind us tonight and finish our great ancestor's work. We will be free of the last chain holding us back."

I snorted, the sound deafening in the silence. Grandmother turned to look at me. Her light eyes slanted with the tight smile that spread over her face. "Welcome home."

A Family Reunion of Sorts

Let's get one thing straight—the Cottage wasn't really a cottage. It wasn't a little wood house, with flowers and vines climbing up the white walls like you've seen in fairy-tale books. No. A better word for it would have been *estate* or *palace*.

New England Architecture magazine called it a "castle," but that was kind of a stretch. Sure, if you went around back you'd find stables for horses and an acre filled with nothing but my grandmother's garden, but it wasn't like there was a moat and drawbridge. As my dad tried to explain to the reporter a good ten times on the tour, the Cottage was only called that because it sat on the site of the original Redding family cottage, from when they had first settled in Redhood.

The building is somewhat difficult to describe, the reporter had written, *being a mixture of the kind of stone castle you would expect to see in Europe and the grand tradition of colonial estates. The overall effect is sturdy, imposing, and hideously wealthy. What had once been a dark wood one-room cabin now contains thirty-eight fireplaces, marble imported from Spain, an indoor pool, a wine cellar, a front portico the size of a normal home, fifty guest rooms, a private spa, and a series of towers capped by finials, gables, and turrets.*

Grandmother glowed like the moon when she read that. But, frankly, I thought it made the Cottage sound like a hotel for rich people to come get murdered. The kind you sec in scary movies. Where the halls are haunted by ax-wielding monsters.

With one hand on Prue's shoulder and one hand on mine, Grandmother guided us into the largest room on the first floor: the Louis XIV drawing room. I had no idea who Louis XIV was, but someone seriously needed to have a talk with him about his sick obsession with gold naked-baby-angel statues.

A great-aunt, an interior decorator for Lilly Belle, you know, from *Southern Comfort,* was explaining why I was supposed to care about the scene of lambs painted on the ceiling when the first tray of food appeared. The waiters glided around the room, their crisp red uniforms blazing against the pool of white.

There's this feeling you get when you know someone has their eyes on you, like they're jabbing two needles into the base of your skull. I turned, glancing over my shoulder, only to see my aunt quickly look away, staring into her wineglass. Beside her, my uncle did the same, only he turned toward the portrait of Silence Redding on the wall and acted like he was trying to start a conversation with her.

The creaking of the house's old bones was drowned out by the high wail of the violinists (second cousins once removed) in the foyer. Each note seemed to slice against my skin. I started to slip out of the room, but there was a sudden, hard poke at my back—hard enough to knock the breath out of me, and back toward my great-aunt. Great-Uncle Phillip. His white fluffy mustache twitched, still wet from his cider. One matching overgrown eyebrow arched up as he jabbed two sharp knuckles toward me again and nodded toward his wife, who was so still so mesmerized by the ceiling she hadn't noticed my escape.

"—to be a true replica of Versailles, though, Mrs. Redding"—Mrs. Redding is what everyone called Grandmother—". . . well, she would have to do what Lilly Belle—you know, from *Southern Comfort?* She would have to do what Lilly Belle did and install mirrors. Panels of them. I haven't the slightest idea why she refuses to keep any."

Well, the reporter from *New England Architecture* had wondered the same thing. Dad had only shrugged and explained that the house had never had mirrors because of our town's weird—excuse me, *unique*, as Grandmother insisted—superstition about ghosts and bad luck. Something like, if you didn't cover your mirrors when the sun went down, it was inviting a whole host of evil to come in. Believe it or not, plenty of people in Redhood, the old families especially, still covered what few mirrors they had at night.

As I glanced around for an exit strategy, my eyes found the stranger again.

He crept along the back of the room, moving around the busts of dead poets and ancestors and shelves of old books. Whenever the trays of food skirted close enough to him, one bony hand would reach out and snatch a snack off it. Then he'd disappear into the shadows again. *Poof.*

"Oh, Bertha, I wanted to thank you again for the work you did on our gazebo—" A second cousin caught my great-aunt's elbow and turned her away from me. I didn't miss my chance. I ducked my head and all but ran out of the room, dodging furniture, annoyed looks, and serving staff.

Where was Prue? I'd lost track of her when we'd come in, Grandmother pulling her off to the side to brag to her sister about Prue's latest achievement. Every now and then I'd think I'd see her, only to realize I was seeing Heart2Heart advertisements and framed magazine covers of her.

I got no more than five feet into the hallway when my aunt caught the collar of my blazer and tugged me back into an awkward, rose-perfume-soaked hug. That was a first.

"Now where are your . . . *darling*"—her mouth twisted as she choked out the word—"parents off to this time?"

"China," I said. "They're setting up the charity's office there."

"How positively . . . charming."

Don't sprain your arm reaching for that compliment, I thought.

"Doesn't it bother you," Aunt Claudia began, licking her fingers to smooth down the back of my hair, "that they're spending all of your money on other children?"

"I'm sure there are a hundred dictionaries in this house if you need to look up the word *charity*," I muttered, pulling out of her reach. I'd had ten thousand variations of this conversation before. My parents gave most of their money away, which automatically labeled them as deranged to the rest of the family.

"Yes, well, charity is a sickness not easily cured," came Grandmother's voice behind me, "but one day your father will see that. Oh—there you are, Prudence. Don't you look precious."

I followed her gaze up, to where Prue had appeared at the top of the curved stairway's second-floor landing. She had changed into a long black velvet dress with a lacy white collar and was totally aware of how stupid she looked. Her face matched the color of her hair.

I tried to get her attention, but Grandmother clutched

my arm and all but lifted me onto the first step. "Up you go, Prosperity. I've laid out a change of clothes for you too. And do wash your face, please."

For the first time in almost an hour, I finally squeezed out the words I wanted to say. "Are we going to Main Street together? The parade's going to start soon."

"We're having a family reunion of sorts first," was her low reply. Her fingernails dug into my sleeve. "This is a very special Founder's Day. Now, be a good boy and . . ."

The young new maid, Mellie, appeared at Grandmother's side, fiddling with the edge of her black uniform.

"What is it?" Grandmother snapped.

"Ma'am, it's the phone again. Your son says it's mighty urgent that he speak to one of the children—" The maid cut herself off when she saw me. The shade of white that washed over her face made her look half-dead with terror. Grandmother's face hardened until she looked like one of the gargoyles on the Cottage's roof.

"Is that so?" she murmured through a tight-lipped smile. "Kindly inform him that we're busy, won't you?"

It wasn't a request, it was an order. One I was definitely going to ignore.

The two of us took off at the same time. The maid headed back toward the kitchen, but I bolted up the stairs. I'd only have a second, maybe less—

I threw the door to my granddad's old study open and dove across his enormous dark wood desk for the old phone.

I gulped down a deep breath when I heard, "—sorry, sir, she says they're busy—"

"Can you at least tell me why they aren't answering their cell phones?" I had never heard my dad sound that way before. His voice was higher than normal, like he was barely keeping himself from yelling. I leaned back from the edge of the desk, patting around my pockets, only to remember I had left my phone in my schoolbag. There was a shuffling on the other end of the line, like he was about to hang up.

"Dad—Dad?"

"Prosper?"

Mellie blew out a deep, shuddering breath. She knew, I guess, what Grandmother could do to any hope she'd have of working again in the Commonwealth of Massachusetts, never mind on planet Earth.

"Mellie, I won't tell," I swore. "Just let me talk to him, please."

The girl's voice dropped to a low whisper. "But Mrs. Redding . . ."

"I'll handle her," Dad said. *"You won't lose your job."*

I saw it out of the corner of my eye, a rare gleam of silver in the dark office. A framed photo. In it, my own dad was proudly holding up his new diploma from Harvard. My aunts had hooked their arms through his. It was embarrassing, but just seeing Dad's grinning face made me feel a little better.

But there was something weird about the photo. Aunt Claudia had her other hand on another boy's shoulder. This one stood off to the side of the group, his hands shoved into the pockets of his jeans, a Harvard cap pulled down over his head. He had been photographed from the side and his face was turned down, but it could have been . . . it *could* have been my uncle.

The line clicked as Mellie hung up the phone in the kitchen. Before I could ask him what was going on, the words flew out of Dad's mouth.

"Prosper, listen to me—you have to get your sister and get out of the Cottage right now. Right now. I can't believe she'd do this, that she'd be so—" The connection flickered. *"Mom and I are trying to get home, but—"*

A milky-white light flooded the room as the door behind me was thrown open. I dropped the phone in shock, which gave Grannie Dearest an opening to scoop it up off the floor and slam it back down on the receiver.

"Hey!" I protested. "I was talking to—"

My grandmother stood staring at me for a moment, her chest heaving and her face flushed with rage. "You," she began, hauling me out of the office with surprising force. "You have been the stone in my shoe since the day you were born."

"Yeah, well, you're no diamond either, Grannie."

Dad read a mythology book to us once that had a story

about a monster called Medusa, the one with a nest of snakes for hair that could turn any person into stone with one look. Well, she might have lacked the snakes, but the fury burning in my grandmother's eyes turned my limbs into cement. I couldn't even swallow.

"I only hope it's you," she hissed, grabbed the collar of my shirt, and dragged me toward the stairs.

The Test

Rayburn, the Cottage's spidery butler, met us on the landing between the first and second floor with Prue. His cane stomped out an impatient beat on the rug, right by her foot. For a guy that personally raised three generations of Redding kids and saw—literally—hundreds of Reddings come and go, he had a surprising amount of hate for anyone under the age of forty.

He had been opening the front door for so long that no one knew which came first, the house or Rayburn. He didn't work in the Cottage—he haunted it.

"Madam." His voice was hoarse and crackled with age. "The others will meet us downstairs."

Prue, who had been watching the line of family members

shove their way down the hall below, whirled around. "What's going on?"

Prosper, listen to me, Dad had said, *you have to get your sister and get out of the Cottage right now.*

I could grab Prue and we could run. Sure, she was bigger than me, but I wouldn't need to carry her. Everyone was heading toward the back of the Cottage, but we could head out the front door. It would be easy, but I needed to get her attention—

The stairs behind me creaked as Great-Uncle Bartholomew and Great-Uncle Theodore came down behind us. Granddad's brothers might have been in their sixties, but they were tall, with the huge shoulders of former football players. Bartholomew held out his arm to Prue, who—stupid, stupid, stupid!—took it without question, and began chattering with him as he led her down the stairs.

I started down after her, my feet thundering down the first two steps. I tried to squeeze between them, stretching out my hand as far as I could to catch hers. But I was moving too fast, and my balance was all wrong. I gripped her fingers hard and yanked both of us back to keep from stumbling forward into Bartholomew. My vision flashed to black as we fell against the stairs in a tangled mess.

"Sorry," I gasped out. "Sorry, but, Prue—"

She pushed me off her and stood, her face bright pink with anger. "What's your deal? I don't need you to hold my hand anymore—I don't *need* your help. God, can you just *grow up?*"

I took a step back, feeling the sting of her words right down to my guts, but she only glared and turned away. My whole body jerked as Great-Uncle Theodore wrapped one arm around my shoulders, squeezing me hard enough to make my spine crack. I sagged against him, looking at the family-crest pin he had on his ivory jacket instead of the back of Prue's hair.

Which was why I didn't notice we were heading to the dungeon until we were already there.

When I was little, I used to think the Cottage had its own secret voice. One that would slither up to you when the lamps were switched off and you only had a night-light to protect you from the darkness. It whispered about the people who had lived within its bones, died in its beds; it groaned under the weight of the centuries it saw. *Come downstairs,* it would hiss, *come down, and down, and down, and down . . .* Down the hidden servant passages, down past the darkened kitchen, down to the basement where things were left to be forgotten. Down to the heavy door that was locked every day, every second, always.

To the dungeon.

It was supposed to be a joke, but why did it have to stay locked all the time if it was just for storage? What did

Grandmother put down there that she didn't want the rest of us to see? In the long, long, long life of the Cottage, I wondered how many people had actually been down there, and how few had ever held its heavy iron key.

Rayburn had a weird sixth sense about that locked door, and he had the totally terrifying habit of jumping out of the shadows whenever anyone got within breathing distance of it. And even if he wasn't there, there were four—count 'em, four—steel locks on the door, each needing a different key. David liked to tell me about all the torture devices that were down there that Grandmother was only waiting to use on me. *She'll pop you into the armor that's filled with spikes. She'll see if you can lie down on the bed of nails without them sinking into your guts. She'll strap you in and turn a wheel until your limbs are ripped off and blood is splattered across the walls—*

I really hated the Cottage. And I extra-hated David.

Great-Uncle Bartholomew grunted as he shoved me through the door. I tried to catch the frame with my arms, but he was way bigger and *way* heavier, and I didn't want my arms pulled out of my sockets. I might need them in the near future.

The steps were uneven and slippery soft, like they'd been ground down by a steady stream of feet. But that didn't make sense, did it? Unless—*unless* . . . this was part of the original foundation of the house. Back when it was growing from just a little seventeenth-century cottage to what it was now. The simple candle sconces on the wall seemed to back up that guess. No electricity. Or heat, apparently.

The damp chill passed through me, icing my bones. As we reached the landing, voices rose from below, flickering in strength like the candles on the wall. My throat felt swollen with the smell of wax and dust and something else—something like rotten eggs—I was gulping down. My thoughts scattered through my mind like spiders, too quick to catch.

But in the end, the dungeon was just an empty, windowless room with nothing more than a small table and fifty of my relatives. With so many people crammed down there, there was barely room for shadows, never mind me and Prue. I watched, my heart thumping painfully in my chest, as one of my great-uncles, the creepy one who never stopped smiling, helped her forward. He cleared a path through the tightly packed room. Great-Uncle Bartholomew nudged me forward until I was directly behind her. I tried to ignore the press of everyone's eyes, the flicking of their fingers as they twisted away to avoid so much as brushing me.

Get out, get out, I thought, I need to get out—

A small, velvet-draped table had been positioned at the front of the room. I turned back toward the rest of the family, trying to read their faces. The warm orange glow of hundreds of candles caught on the white clothes around us.

If I'd had the time to draw the scene, I would have sketched them in lightly, like ghosts floating at the edge of your vision.

Prue elbowed me hard in the ribs to get my attention and pointed to the strange lump on the table in front of us. The silky black fabric could have been a spill of ink.

Oh, crap, I thought, trying to take a step back. My family really is a cult.

That guy with the website had been right.

"Now," Grandmother began. "Our family's tradition has long held—"

"Just get on with it!" Great-Uncle Bartholomew snarled behind her. "We all know why we're here. There's no sense in putting things off any longer."

"Perhaps you would like to hold your tongue while I cut it out for you?" she hissed. The raised blue veins on the back of Grandmother's hands pulsed as she moved her fingers over the black cloth. "No? Then be silent."

I swallowed hard.

"Our family's tradition has long held," she began again, her voice colder than before, "that we would be called upon to do a great service to the world. This evening we take the first step toward doing just that."

Grandmother yanked the cloth off the table. I took a startled jump back, bringing Prue with me. I kind of expected whatever was under there to pop up and eat my face.

But . . . it was only a book.

A really, really old one, and much bigger than any I used in school. The brown leather cover was cracked and stained with age. At one point, it looked like there had been some kind of a lock on it, but that had been cut away. The stench of smoke rose from it, as if the pages breathed out a memory of fire.

"Grandmother?" Prue couldn't seem to decide where to look, and neither could the others. Great-Uncle Theodore was sweating behind me. I felt a drop fall on top of my head.

Grandmother used both hands to carefully lift the front cover of the book and set it aside. The binding was coming apart. There were hundreds of heavy yellowed pages inside. Most of them were loose.

"Prudence, child," Grandmother said, "please read the first page."

My hand came up to tug at the collar of my shirt. The room had become sweltering. The longer I stood there, the faster my heart beat, until it was galloping.

Prue leaned forward, so close to the page that her hair brushed against it. Her face twisted like she was upset. I stood on my toes to look over her shoulder—and just about fell over.

I rubbed the sweat out of my eyes, then rubbed them again. The page, at first blink, was blank as a new sheet of paper. Now blots of crimson ink were rising to the surface of it like they were soaking up through hundreds of pages.

Rivulets of the ink slid around like tiny snakes, twisting around each other. The stains squirmed and stretched, one end finding another as they formed cursive scrawl.

Spirits of Wickedness, ye Devils of Night,
Shall bear no Entry to this Book of Might.

"But . . ." Prue began, looking up at our grandmother. "It doesn't say anything. It's blank."

"What are you talking about?" I asked, reaching over to turn the book toward me. "Look right here, it says—"

There was a sharp pain in my chest, like someone had stabbed me straight through with a burning rod.

A shrill scream, half pain, half fury, pierced my ears. I reached up to touch my throat, stunned. It hadn't come from me; my lips hadn't moved. The hurt in my chest changed. The air choked out of my throat. It felt like I was being ripped down the center, bones tossed to the relatives nearby, panting like dogs. I fell onto my knees hard, knocking my head against the edge of the table. The whole world jerked, rocking the Cottage around me. There was another scream, this one louder. I forced my eyes up.

The book on the table burst into sudden, white-hot flame.

Stranger and Stranger

I still don't really remember what happened next.

My memory turned black and soggy at the edges, like a poisoned pond. Now and then a flash of an image would rise up through the sludge of uncertainty, but everything felt like bits and pieces and maybes. I thought I heard Prue scream my name, and I thought I caught a glimpse of her bright red hair, glowing with the light on the table. My grandmother threw the black cloth back over it, beating out the flames before they could jump up and catch the edges of her white jacket.

I couldn't tell if I was breathing fire and smoke out, or if I was dragging it into my chest. Every inch of my skin sparked with heat. The rumbling started deep in my chest. A rattling that made my teeth chatter and fingers twitch.

My bones felt like they were rearranging into spiky, crooked lines.

Ahhhhhhhhhhhhhhhhh, yawned a voice in my ear.

A stampede of feet thundered toward the staircase, shaking the floor pressed against my cheek. But a pair was moving toward me, not away, pristine high heels *click-click-clacking* against the stone, the toes pointed like knives.

Get up, I thought, get up *now.* With a grunt, I flopped onto my back, trying to get my arms under me. A wave of dizzy sickness washed from my head down to my numb toes, blurring the darkness. When it finally cleared, I saw Prue for real, standing on the stairs. Her face was as white as the wax dripping from the candles.

"Prosper! Prosper!" She tried to dart toward me, but Great-Uncle Theodore wrapped his enormous arms around her middle and hauled her kicking and screaming off her feet.

"No!" I choked out. I had to help Prue, I had to protect Prue, that was my job—but Great-Uncle Bartholomew was coming toward me, something long and silver clutched between his hands. The curve of the blade caught the winking candlelight from above, and I knew what it was.

A knife.

Rayburn slammed the rubber end of his cane against my shoulder, pinning me to the floor. I tried to kick at his knobbed knees, to take the old geezer down with me, but it was like the rest of my body wasn't listening to my brain.

Grandmother's tight face was swimming in front of mine. A look of total disgust, worse than what she normally wore when she looked at me, slipped into place. She took the knife in her hand.

No! a voice bellowed in my ears. *Not this night, nor any other!*

A ferocious wind came ripping down through the open door at the top of the stairs. It threw a shrieking Aunt Claudia halfway down the stone steps and devoured every candle flame. We were in darkness.

Everyone was screaming now. Feet pounded the ground in rolls of thunder, making the floor shiver and moan. Something wicked sharp drew across my left arm, just below my elbow, and I let out a scream of pain that sent the dogs upstairs into a howling rage. Agony filled the wound like hot wax, burning my skin, my veins, my bone.

There was this explosion of movement over my head. The reeking smell of sweat and pine flooded my nose, just as a blur of white went flying two inches from my face. The collision sent Rayburn and Grandmother down into a knot of wrinkled old limbs.

I kicked my feet out, using them to roll away. The knife skittered off, clattering against the tile. I stretched an arm out, reaching for it to fend off the other monsters, when a pale hand darted down to pick it up.

In the dark, I couldn't really see the stranger's face. I only recognized him from his stink, and the way his oversize white shirt puffed out around him like a dandelion. The heat came off him like an overworked lamp. I pushed myself up onto my hands and knees to crawl away—because it's one thing when it's your family that's trying to put you six feet under, but I wasn't about to let a stranger gut me. Not when I needed to find Prue.

Instead of the stab of burning metal I expected to feel through my spine, two hands came down to grip the back of my uniform blazer. That was the only warning I got. Next thing I knew, I had been tossed over the stranger's shoulder like a sack of rice.

"You okay, kid?" The words made the man's narrow shoulders vibrate. I couldn't speak and the guy couldn't see me nod, but the fact that I was breathing seemed to be enough for him.

The smoke detector and sprinklers switched on at once, turning panicked yells into gasps at the sudden attack of frigid water.

"*You!*" Grandmother yelled through the hiss of the sprinkler. I couldn't see her face, only the family members stupid enough to still be standing around on the stairs, staring. I didn't see her at all, not until the man turned back toward the stairs and began to run.

Rayburn was knocked out. Grandmother struggled to shove his weight off her. Every hair on her head was standing straight up. The water had stopped, but the hissing hadn't. And I didn't understand why, until I looked down.

I was losing it. My brain had up and left the joint. It must have, because I was literally smoking. The water on my clothes evaporated, rising up from my skin and jacket in white steam. It was like someone had cranked up the temperature to a thousand degrees. I was breathing in gulp after deep gulp of air that smelled like cooked meat, smoke, and rotten eggs.

Flee, the same prim voice rang out in my mind. *Flee, Maggot. I will aid thee this once.*

I think the stranger must have heard this—he had to have—because he launched himself forward at cannonball speed. Several hands reached out only to scream as soon as they touched me. Their palms were blistered, as if I'd burnt them.

By the time we reached the top of the stairs, the smoke in the dungeon hid most of the wreckage. Faces floated into sight, only to be swallowed again by drifting gray swirls of it. The very last thing I saw before the emergency lights cut back out was my grandmother, fighting to get to her feet on broken high heels, her white dress nearly black with soot and filth.

"Do not take that child!" she screamed.

The buzzing strength seemed to go out of me with the next deep breath I took. All of a sudden it was impossible to keep my eyes open. They felt so heavy. . . . I felt so heavy.

Wake up, I commanded myself. *WAKE UP!* The stranger's grip on the back of my knees went tight as he kicked a door open. My lungs flooded with cold, clean air, and my eyes stung with tears. I needed to find Prue, I couldn't leave without Prue—

No. The voice was echoing and sleek all at once. Definitely not older than me, even though his vowels all curled and rolled in a strange way.

No, the voice continued. *Now we shall rest.*

And it wasn't like I had a choice about it. The words boiled up between my ears, locked inside my throbbing skull, and I dropped into a deep, dark sleep.

Bone-Tingling

The enormous black cat, a panther, paced toward me, each claw ticking against the ground. *Awaken the singing bone, awaken the singing bone,* it purred into the darkness, tail curling like a question mark. Green eyes tracked me, but I couldn't move, couldn't so much as flinch. It felt like I was caught in someone's damp fist, and it squeezed tighter each time I took a breath. And then the cat did something I didn't expect, something it never had before: the light inside the creature's eyes flared to a vivid, molten green.

And then it fled.

What is the singing bone? I tried shouting, but my mouth felt like it had been sewn shut. I couldn't move. Just tell me. . . . Just tell me . . . just—let—me—*wake up!*

WAKE. UP.

The words bellowed through me, bouncing off my brain and shooting awareness through me. My left arm felt like it was covered in open sores, and moving it a little—waking the sleeping limb back up—made me taste puke. I kept my eyes squeezed shut, trying to take in one deep breath after another, but the scratchy blankets were wrapped too tight around me. I kicked them off, twisting to get away from the smothering heat.

The breeze coming through the window was blissfully cool and dry, carrying a hint of smoke from a nearby fireplace. Mom must have been baking a pie downstairs again, because cinnamon mingled with a hint of lavender, spicing the air. Somewhere nearby, kids were laughing, the wheels of their passing bicycles crunching a path through fallen leaves. A dog barked after them, but was drowned out by the sound of a passing car.

I breathed out a sigh as I turned over onto my stomach, pressing my face into the pillow. The knot my stomach had tied itself into finally released.

I was home.

Safe.

Okay.

It had been the nightmare to end all nightmares. But it had only been a nightmare.

And then, I opened my eyes.

And stared into the perfectly round, enormous yellow eyes of a black ball of fluff.

"What," I wheezed out, "the crap?"

It hissed, flashing two vampire-sharp teeth as it sank two sets of claws into my chest.

"Ow!" My body reacted before my brain, jerking in surprise. The fluff ball—a kitten?—darted to safety beneath the couch, quick as a shadow. I crashed to the floor a second later, sending up an explosion of dust as I hit the rug. In between trying to hack up my lung and sneeze out my brains, I waited for the black blotches in my vision to clear and the unfamiliar room to appear.

I pressed my hurt arm tight to my chest, trying to breathe through the pain. My breath whistled in and out through my teeth as I looked around me.

Crap, crap, crap. Not a nightmare. *Not* a nightmare.

The ceiling above me was low and slanted upward sharply at the center. I wouldn't be able to stand at the edges of it, but that didn't matter much, considering all four sides of the room were crammed with furniture. The dark wooden beams loomed over old, broken furniture—all of which had been repurposed into something else. A table leg had been replaced with a stack of thick old leather-bound books. The back of a wooden chair hung from the wall, various vines draped over it like dark velvet ribbons. An old armoire's drawers were pulled out and stuffed with dirt and small herbs, while bottles filled with murky yellow and brown mixtures and copper pots spilled over the upper shelves.

In the far corner, just beside a desk overflowing with

books and sheets of paper starting to curl like fingernails, was a spiderweb-ridden spinning wheel.

A pop of orange unknown to nature caught my eye, and my gaze drifted down, slowly, until . . . Yes. I was wearing a bright orange shirt—one I *definitely* didn't own. I pulled it out farther with my right hand, trying to see what was printed on it.

An enormous grinning jack-o'-lantern face. I didn't know what was worse—that, or the fluffy knit socks protecting my toes from the chill. TRICK had been stitched on the right foot, TREAT on the other. And boxers. Boxers that drooped down to my knees, with hundreds of little green witches flying around on their broomsticks printed all over them.

More important, though, was the white bandage, wrapped neatly around my left arm, just under my elbow. An angry cloud of blood had soaked up through it, just like the red ink had through the pages of the book.

The night came back in flashes of smoke and light: The book. The knife. The voice. The stranger. And—

Prue! I dragged myself to my knees. I held my throbbing arm to my chest, and tried really, really, *really* hard to stay vertical. This wasn't my house, and it wasn't the Cottage either. And if I was here, where was Prue? Had the stranger grabbed her too?

My legs shook, but I got them under me, leaning back against the powder-blue couch I'd fallen off of. Wild ivy sidled its way through the open windows and cracks in the wall from the outside, as if seeking warmth. Their leaves curled as they withered with the turning season, the branches spread out like veins against the dark wood of the walls. For a second, I just stared at them, trying to match their colors to the paint I had hidden in a box under my bed. The late-afternoon sun flushed the room with pure cider-colored light, almost enough to brighten the soot on the old candle-crammed fireplace.

There was a cracked full-length mirror at the other end of the room, rimmed with a dusty gold frame. I hobbled over to it, tripping through piles of clothes and overflowing black trash bags leaning against the walls. When I was finally standing in front of it, I needed a full second to realize I was staring at myself.

It wasn't just the bruise down the side of my face, blue and black and almost green in places. I poked a finger at the center of it and immediately wished I hadn't. My dark hair was standing straight up, like tufts of raven feathers. I turned around, searching for a comb or water to try to pat it down, before remembering I had no idea where I was, and what I looked like and was wearing shouldn't matter because of the real, looming chance I could be murdered.

Every Redding is known for *something*, you see. It would be just my luck to be the Redding Who Died While Dressed as a Giant Pumpkin.

I needed to get out of here, wherever that was. I limped over to an old rickety broom. It had been left leaning against a bookshelf that looked to be on the verge of vomiting up a thousand sheets of crumpled and torn pages. The knotted, curving wood of the handle was smooth to the touch, but the bristles themselves looked more like old straw bound together with twine. Thinking twice about hitting an attacker with what basically amounted to a dried-out twig, I picked up one of the copper pots instead.

There were two skinny beds pushed together in an L shape on the other side of the room, just next to where a stack of old leather trunks were piled up, separating that space from the small kitchen next to it. Actually, could you even call one sink, a metal cart, a mini fridge, and a microwave a kitchen?

From beneath the couch, the ball of fluff hissed again. All I could see were its big, round glowing eyes.

"Yeah, well," I said lamely, "I don't like you either. So . . . there."

It cocked its head to the side, and for a second, all I could think of was the enormous panther stalking through my dream. This kitten was so small, so overwhelmed by its own coat, it looked like a fur ball the nightmare creature had coughed up.

The unpolished floors creaked under my bare feet. Once my nose got past the sweet smells of the crisp outside air and the herbs and flowers hung up to dry over the desk, new stenches blossomed. Dust, mold, and sour milk. A single red leaf scurried across the unpolished floor, dancing with a loose newspaper clipping around the stained woven rug.

What was this place? *Where* was this place?

I didn't notice them before, not when everything in the small space seemed to be piled onto something else. But the next breeze forced its way through the window, and I saw where the small cutout article had come from. There were rows of them tacked up across the wall, over one of the beds. I hugged the copper pot to my chest as I took a few steps forward. The wind ruffled them, and they rose and fell together as one, making it look like the walls were breathing. Mixed in with the articles were photographs, dozens of them, but not of the stranger or anyone in his family.

Oh no, they were pictures of *my* family.

Photoshoots from magazines. A super-stalkerish picture of me and Prue from last year's Founder's Day, just before I was pushed off the school float into the mud. Five years' worth of family Christmas cards. Even snaps of Mom and Dad when they were younger—only a few years older than me.

REDDING FAMILY SETS NEW RECORD

ONE FAMILY'S FORTUNE IS A TOWN'S TREASURE

THE COTTAGE OF REDHOOD

All the newspaper and magazine clippings were either about someone in our family, the Cottage, or Redhood.

I crawled onto the unmade bed to get a closer look. Just to the right of them, pushed to the edge of it all like an afterthought, were drawings. Prints. All black-and-white, maybe ink—no, I recognized what they were now. The Redhood Museum had some just like these. They were colonial engravings. Only these didn't depict happy little settlers planting crops or raising families. *These* engravings were almost creepier than seeing a photo of my grandmother back in her beauty-queen days. Men and women in bonnets and hats and long dresses and black coats stood around a fire, their arms raised. In another, a woman was huddled over a book, one hand clutching a broomstick.

I reached up and pulled one off the wall. Dread ran down my spine like a claw. The people in that drawing were hanging from a tree branch like dead geese, ropes wrapped around their necks. And . . . I pulled the others down frantically, spreading them out over the bed in disbelief. In every single one was this little devil with horns, a spiked tail, a pitchfork, and bat wings.

My eyes drifted back up, landing on the handwritten family tree at the center of the mass of shivering articles. It started all the way back at Honor Redding. The red line that snaked down the center of it ended at my name.

Frantic, I searched the room for a phone or computer, something I could use to try to get in touch with my parents. I found none.

Of course. If I had been kidnapped, they wouldn't want

to give me any sort of means to escape. Sweat slid between my shoulder blades, leaving a trail of goose bumps behind it. Panicky noises rose in my throat, squeaking out a little with each breath. Even worse, the smell of rotten eggs was back. It was thick enough that I could taste it on my tongue.

I looked for my coat, my shoes, *anything* that would have helped me escape or at least figure out where I was. But just when I had given up and had one foot dangling out of the window, I heard the girl.

"—*it is my name! Because I cannot have another in my life!*" Her voice was hoarse, like she was on the edge of tears. A random burst of thoughts fired off in my mind, trying to figure out where I had heard those exact same words before.

I reached for the small metal doorknob, and I was twisting it open before my brain could stop me. One deep breath in, and I stepped out into the dark hallway.

And it *was* dark. Long and narrow too, with only a sliver of light peeking through the black curtains hanging over the window at the opposite end of the hall. I felt something soft tickle my cheek and jerked back away from it, stumbling foot over foot. I flapped my arms, trying to keep my balance, but I only got more tangled in the long white cobwebs that drifted down from the ceiling.

"—*Because I am not worth the dust on the feet of them that hang! How may I live without my name?*"

I saw her then. Unfortunately, I saw the rest of the hall

too. The walls and doors were decorated with axes and bloodstained swords, all pointing in the direction of the coffin and the girl standing in front of it. She was shaking her fist in the direction of the gleaming bones of a skeleton, and the thing was staring straight back from black, eyeless sockets. Its jaw was unhinged, and the bottom row of teeth hung open, as if it had been shocked into a scream.

"I have given you my soul!" the girl continued, dropping her voice into a low, dangerous growl. *"Leave me my name!"*

She flung herself onto the ground, almost bringing the skeleton down with her. Then, after a moment of silence, she sighed and stood, muttering, "No, too much . . ." and got herself back in front of the coffin, like she was going to go through it all over again. She flicked her hand, and it almost seemed like . . .

No. I was imagining things. The skeleton's jaw didn't clack shut. Its hand didn't come up under its chin, like it was contemplating her. In any case, I had no idea how she could have missed the idiot in the flaming orange shirt, tangled up to his neck in cobwebs, still holding a copper pot.

"Uh, a little help here?" I gasped, twisting to get away from the humongous spider hanging from the ceiling.

The girl spun around with a yelp. Her hand lashed out and it was like a hundred invisible fists flew through the air and barreled into my chest. The spider-webbing tore away and I was flying, flying, flying—and then crashing,

crashing, crashing through the plastic ghosts and blackout sheets. The pot rolled away, disappearing under enormous plastic spider legs.

"Don't you know," the girl fumed as she stormed over to me, "not to sneak up on a witch?"

Nell and Barnabas

"A *what?*"

For a second, I was sure she had said "witch." The wind that came bursting through the open window behind her must have knocked my brain loose or something. I clutched my bandaged arm to my chest, counting the black stars floating in my eyes again. It screamed in pain as I untangled myself from the plastic pumpkins and black sheets, and I tried not to do the same. But before I could even stand up, a small streak of black zipped through the open door and came flying for my face. Claws out.

"Toad, *no!*" the girl cried.

I ducked, throwing myself onto the ground. The kitten hit the wall with a *thwack!*, hanging there for a moment by its razor nails. Its tiny bat wings fluttered in annoyance as it freed itself.

Its . . . tiny . . . bat . . . wings.

"Oh my God," I said, backing up, tripping, falling. The girl was coming toward me, cooing at the furry demon, her cloud of curly dark hair threaded with a hundred little glow-in-the-dark star-shaped beads. "What is—*what is that?*"

It flew—*literally flew*—into her open, waiting arms.

"That's a good Toad, who's my good boy?" she said, bopping it on its small black nose. Ignoring me. "We talked about this. No attacking our guest, remember? Guests are friends, not fiends."

The kitten licked its paw indignantly.

"What are you staring at?" she demanded. "You're acting like you've never seen a cat before."

"That's not a cat, that's a *monster!*" I said, trying not to meet its big eyes.

"Monster?" she shouted over Toad's hissing. "The only monster I see around here is the Redding standing in front of me! Wait—" The girl held the small cat out in front of her, letting it extend its wings. "You can see these?"

"Uh, yeah."

"Oh." All her anger seemed to deflate. She set the animal down and reached up to push her bejeweled rainbow glasses back up the bridge of her nose. "So you *can* see through glamours. I told him you probably could."

"Told whom?"

"Told *who*," she corrected.

"No, it's *whom*," I insisted. The one grammar lesson I actually remembered, thank you very much.

The girl and cat glared at me, eyes narrowed. "Come on, let's go downstairs. Guess I'm stuck explaining things until he gets home."

He? The stranger?

"I'm not going anywhere with you," I said, backing up. I cast a quick look around. There were windows at either end of the narrow hallway, but we had to be at least one or two stories up. I would *definitely* be the Redding Who Broke His Neck in a Pumpkin Shirt. The wood floor dipped at the center of the hall, buckling slightly. There were two doors—the one I'd come out of and another, blocked by her skeleton. Both were cut at a crooked angle in the bare, dark wood wall. "I don't even know who you are!"

"My name is Nell Bishop," she said, hands on her hips. Her sweater had been sewn together from three different floral patterns and was big enough to droop over her jeans. "I'm your . . . I'm your cousin, I guess."

Awesome. Just what I never wanted: another cousin to hate me.

"You guess . . ." I repeated. "Can you not guess? And just tell me?"

Her eyes narrowed. "You're as annoying as I thought

you'd be. Fine. Stay up here for all I care, and stew in your questions. I need to start setting up for the show tonight."

Nell spun toward the stairs, unclipping a small chain with the sign PRIVATE, and thundered down them. The whole roof rattled with the force of it. And rather than sit there and be the Redding Who Had a Ceiling Dropped on Him, or the Redding Who Got Mauled by a Mutant Kitten, I followed.

If I had sat down at my desk at home, opened my spiral-bound notebook, and tried to draw my perfect nightmare . . . it would have been adorable compared to this house.

It turned out that I wasn't on the second floor—I was on the *fourth* floor. The attic. The stairs wound down the center of the old house like a rickety spine, revealing one terror after the other.

There were three open doors on the third landing. The one to the left was completely pitch-black, save for an amazing light show that made it seem like thousands of ghosts were fluttering around, swirling like a tornado at the center. The air it breathed out frosted my skin with flecks of snow and ice. The center room looked to be a dark forest filled with nightmares, where the trees were crawling with spiders and draped with mirrors of all sizes.

My feet came to a crashing halt when I caught a glimpse of me—but not me, not really—in the largest one. An ancient man, a hundred years old, who had my eyes and mouth, stared back at me, screaming—banging on the glass, as if begging to be let out.

Bam! I all but leaped over the banister to get away from the door on the right, where something was bumping around behind the gleaming wood like a frantic heartbeat.

On the second story, all I needed to see was a room full of tombstones and the ghostly apparition of a weeping woman in old-fashioned clothes before I felt my blood turn to needles. She looked up. Her voice sounded as though she were whispering in my ear. *"Are you my baby? Are you my sweet boy? Won't you come to me, sweetling? Your mama loves you dearly—"*

Somehow, there were clouds floating above her. Somehow, those clouds opened with thunderous, bloody rain.

I spun toward the stairs, but Nell was there, standing in my path. When I tried to get past her, she blocked me, laughing. "It's not real, brainiac. Look."

She held a hand out into the room, and though it looked like—it *sounded* like—blood was splattering over the graves and the ghost, none of it coated her hand. It was all an illusion.

But I could have sworn that, when I finally pushed past her and continued down the stairs, she quickly leaned forward into the room and drew a hand across her throat, and there was an annoyed *"Harrumph"* in response.

Keeping one hand gripped tight to the banister, I forced my eyes to stay on my feet, not on whatever was waiting on the second floor.

"What is this place?" I muttered when we got to the first floor. In the place of a living room set, a TV, or a kitchen, there were walls covered in smears of fake blood. The words THERE IS NO ESCAPE were scratched into the biggest patch of it with what probably were fingernails. Propped up two feet away was a dead body—*fake dead body*, I thought, when the buzzing in my ears got too bad—on a stainless-steel gurney, its mouth open, its plastic intestines dangling over the ground. They looked like they were soft to the touch. Even the mannequin's skin bristled with wiry, lifelike hair.

My stomach squirmed uncomfortably as Nell jumped up and sat on the gurney beside him, idly twirling the fake large intestine like a lasso.

"You're in the prime destination for nights of fright and magical mayhem!" Nell said, throwing her arms out wide. Behind her, a zombie-nurse puppet shot out of a hidden panel in the wall with a screech that, unfortunately, didn't drown out my own.

"Will you chill out?" Nell said, laughing. "Wow. You really are not okay, are you? It's *alllll* fake—okay, at least ninety percent is fake, and the other ten percent isn't going to bite you. We would never put you in real danger." Her voice dropped as she said, with what I had to admit was a pretty great dramatic flourish, "Unlike the *true* monsters in your life."

She hopped off the gurney and held out a hand toward the stairs. Toad (The cat? Bat? CatBat?) came fluttering down the steps, as light and airy as a stray feather. It caught her hand and crawled up her arm to perch on her shoulder. I backed up toward the wall, fingers touching the holes the creature had already torn in my shirt, eyeing Nell.

I thought of the Impressionist paintings I'd seen in museums with my dad. From a distance, they looked like a typical scene of people or landscapes. But, up close, you could see the thousands of tiny strokes of paint that made up the image. Nell was like that in a way. Up close, she was like a kaleidoscope of color and motion. Her skin was a warm bronze, a shade or two lighter than her black hair, which I saw now she'd pinned into two high buns. It looked as if she'd reached up and plucked the stars out of the sky, scattering them in her hair. They twinkled as she moved, as iridescent as the many colors of her sweater.

There was nothing stiff or cold about her. You could never paint her the way artists had done with my ancestors, all flat, pale, sickly, and glowering. Nell was about my height, and I'd guess my age, but that was where the similarities ended.

"This is Toad," Nell said, bringing it closer. "I think you need to meet again on better terms."

"You named your mutant kitten Toad?"

The creature sniffed, adjusting its position so that its legs dangled over Nell's shoulder and it could cross its furry little arms, the way a human would. Panic began skittering around my brain again at the unreal sight. I was hallucinating. Clearly.

"How rude," Nell said, pulling a small piece of carrot out of her pocket. The creature snatched it between its paws and fluttered off to devour it on the dummy corpse. "Toad is over a hundred years old. And he's not a kitten. He's a *changeling.* This is the form he's decided on for now. I just enchanted him so any human would see him as a plain black cat—including B, so don't tell him, you hear me? Toad has been known to turn into chain saws when angry."

I slid down the wall, narrowly avoiding the zombie nurse as she swung out with a handful of syringes filled with bubbling crimson syrup. Pressing my face into my hands, I tried counting backward from ten to keep from throwing up. Or worse.

But when I opened my eyes, Nell, the CatBat, and the zombies were all still there.

"Okay, seriously—where am I, who are we waiting for, and why is the skeleton in the corner doing the Macarena?"

"The Macarena?" Nell spun round. "I said the Danse Macabre! *Listen to my voice as I say to thee—* Oh, never mind, I'll fix it later."

She snapped her fingers and the fake skeleton's shoulder seemed to slump a bit as its bones clattered back into an open, waiting coffin.

"What is happening?" I moaned. "What is my life right now?"

Nell cocked a dark, unimpressed eyebrow. "You're more dramatic than I am, and that's saying something. You're in Salem. In the House of Seven Terrors, a haunted house show. And it's all going to be okay."

Salem? *Salem?* Redhood was over two hours south of Salem, on Cape Cod. It might as well have been in a different country for all I knew of how I'd be able to get back.

Nell crouched in front of me, peering at me through her strange glasses. I couldn't help it. My cheeks flushed with embarrassment and anger. It felt like my insides were boiling, and I was sweating again despite the cold, dry air coming through the front door. I had the stupidest urge to cry.

"Okay," I repeated. "*Okay?* Of course I'm not okay! My entire extended family tried to murder me, my parents are stuck in China, and my sister—"

A surge of energy burst through me at the thought of my family. My real one. Not the cousins, or my grandmother, or any of the other strangers I just so happened to share DNA with. Where were Mom and Dad? Where was Prue?

Nell turned her back to me for only a second, but I took my chance. I jumped to my feet and shoved her out of the way, bolting for the hallway door. I heard the sound of a clap, and before I could take another step, something hooked around my neck and dragged me back. I went sliding through the fake dried blood on the floor, yanked right back to where she stood. Nell let out a huff and gave me an unimpressed look.

"Yeah." Nell rolled her eyes. "Like *that* was going to work."

I tried to sit up, but her finger flicked toward me, and I was none-too-gently shoved back down. I brought my hurt arm up against my chest, ignoring the way it burned.

"Can't . . . blame a guy for trying . . . ?" I wheezed out.

"You're a bit clumsier than I expected, given your father," said another voice. "But I see you've perfected the Redding cower."

A pair of dusty boots came steadily toward me, parking inches from my nose. My eyes traveled up the man's stockings, to his old-fashioned trousers, to his billowing shirt—right up to his ponytail of blond hair. The stranger, even stranger now.

"No," I said, finally breaking free from whatever had been holding me down. I lurched away, stumbling. "Get away from me!"

"Prosperity—"

"I'll take care of him—" Nell began.

"No!" the stranger said. "No more magic, you've frightened him enough!"

I tried to run again, but I didn't make it half as far. The

guy grabbed me by the scruff of the neck and held me tight against his chest. I kicked and stomped my feet, trying to aim for his toes like one of the security guards at the Cottage had taught me. But the guy might as well have been made of stone. He took all my hits like I was throwing feathers at him. I dug my feet into the carpet, trying to keep him from dragging me out to the back of the house to murder me, until, with a sigh, the stranger reached down and threw me over his shoulder. Again.

"What did you do with Prue?" I shouted, pounding his back with my fists as we made our way back upstairs. "Hey! *Hey!* Let me go!"

Nell trailed behind us, watching me with a look that said, *Are you two years old?*

By the time we got back up to the attic, all of my limbs felt like they had been turned into lead. I was exhausted, and as if that wasn't bad enough, it felt like I was burning up again. The fire started in my belly, pulsing and crackling through every single vein. To add insult to injury, Toad came prancing in behind us, just as I was dumped back on the couch. The creature flicked his tail and shut the door behind him.

"You're safe," was the first thing the stranger said. The cushions dipped as he sat down next to me. "Cornelia and I got you out of there just in time."

"*Nell,*" the girl got out between gritted teeth. She was

right about that—she was definitely more of a Nell than a Cornelia.

"They—" I began. "Wait . . . that actually happened?"

Instead of answering me, the stranger took my left wrist and lifted my arm. The bandage was redder than before.

"Iron," the man explained, setting my arm down. "A cursed blade did this to you. The wound may never fully heal, but we'll work on it."

"Who are you?" I demanded when I finally found the words I was looking for.

"I'm your uncle Barnabas," the man said with a sad smile. "Though I don't suppose you've ever heard of me?"

Not only had I heard of Uncle Barnabas, I had spent pretty much all twelve or so years of my life trying to figure out how he managed to get himself pruned off the family tree. Dad had only mentioned his brother once or twice that I could remember, and usually only as a slip. He didn't have any stories like, *When my brother and I were little, we used to fish in the stream behind the Cottage.* There were no questions like, *I wonder what your uncle would think of this?* There weren't even calls on birthdays.

No one dared to breathe his name in front of Grandmother. Mom claimed that Dad loved his brother very, very much, but I wasn't sure I bought that. If you really loved someone, why would you let anyone else tell you how to treat them?

"Oh."

"Oh yes." Barnabas shook his head. "The rumors of my death have been greatly exaggerated."

"No one said you had *died*," I assured him. "Just that you're a waiter in a casino in Las Vegas, trying to get an audition to be a dancer in that Beatles show, and selling self-portraits of you in elf costumes on the Strip."

Which, to Grandmonster, was probably a fate worse than death.

Uncle Barnabas's face went pink around the edges at that. "How . . . imaginative."

I got a good look at him in the silence that followed. Barnabas had a long thin nose that was at odds with the rest of the family line. Thick eyebrows. High cheekbones, a square jaw dusted with the beginning of a pale, scratchy beard. Me and Prue were in no way identical, but it was a little surprising that Uncle Barnabas was so different from Dad. Not just in the way they looked, but the way they carried themselves. Percy—Dad—had several inches on his brother, dark hair, and the same brown eyes as me. He had a natural confidence to him that, in comparison, made this guy look like he was walking around with an army of fire ants in his underwear.

But I had only gotten a quick look at the picture in Granddad Redding's study. This guy . . . It *could* be Uncle Barnabas. It had to be.

"If he's him," I began, turning to look at Nell, "who are you?"

She opened her mouth, but Barnabas was faster. "Nell is my daughter. She and I . . . recently became acquainted after her mother's sad passing."

I was glad I was looking at Nell when he said that. The smug expression on her face seemed to dissolve into one of pure pain. It vanished just as fast, but it had been there.

Of course she was upset. She lost her *mom*. What was worse than that? I hadn't seen my mom in three days and I missed her—I couldn't imagine never seeing her again.

Toad began to weave between her feet, as if trying to soothe her.

"All right," I said, "but what am I doing here?"

Uncle Barnabas nodded in Nell's direction, and a strange looked passed between them. Some kind of silent communication. Without a word, she stood and went toward the beds, hopping up on one to pull down the large Redding family tree.

"With stories like these, it's best to start at the very beginning," Uncle Barnabas said. "Tell me, Prosperity, what do you know about the family curse?"

The Malefactor

"I know that she was born in 1945, despises puppies, and enjoys trying to kill her grandchildren with daggers in dungeons."

Uncle Barnabas stared long enough that I started thinking he'd inherited Grandmother's No Laughing Unless It's at Other People's Pain gene.

Then his face broke out into a huge grin. He laughed from deep in his belly, shaking the couch. Beside him Nell just crossed her arms and stared at the wall.

"Nice of you to take this seriously," she muttered. "But what did I expect? You are a Redding."

"Got your old man's sense of humor, I see," Uncle Barnabas said, snorting.

And pretty much nothing else, I thought, feeling a little

miserable. As if to echo the thought, the breeze from the window rattled the bottles on the shelf, making them chatter and shiver. I crossed my arms over my chest, struggling to get the words out. "My mom and dad—they don't know where I am! They don't know what happened!"

You have to get your sister and get out of the Cottage right now!

I couldn't even do *that*. I pressed my face to my hands, ignoring the hot stinging in my eyes. They were going to be so mad at me. If anything happened to Prue . . . I would never forgive myself.

Uncle Barnabas put a warm, comforting hand on my shoulder.

"They're aware you're with me and that you're safe," he said.

"You don't know that," I said, pulling back and trying to stand. "I don't know you, you don't know me—I don't even know if anything you're saying is the truth!"

"You don't remember me, Prosperity, but I remember you. Even when you were a baby, I'd come to Redhood to catch a glimpse of you from afar. The last time I did it was a few days before Christmas when you were five." He spoke softly, his hand tightening on my shoulder. "I brought your sister a set of books and you a paint set. I had to leave them outside, because I was too nervous to try coming in, and, anyway, you were all at the hospital with your sister."

"That was you?" I asked, shocked. I had found the paint

set a few years later while rummaging through a supply closet. There had still been a large red-and-green ribbon on it, along with a gift tag with my name. For whatever reason, maybe knowing it had come from Dad's brother, my parents had kept it instead of tossing it like I'm sure Grandmonster would have wanted.

Uncle Barnabas nodded, smiling gently. He turned toward the girl. "Cor—Nell, would you be so kind as to get the letter?"

She stared at him for a moment, confused. Toad had wandered off and nestled in one of the open armoire drawers, chewing idly on the herbs growing there. At that, he let out a loud purr, his tail pointing repeatedly at the desk. It was only then, when Toad's wings started fluttering and Uncle Barnabas had no reaction to it, that I remembered what Nell said about normal people not being able to see through . . . what did she call them? Glamours?

So—that made CatBat a secret, I guessed. When the man looked at him, I wondered if he saw only a tiny black cat.

Nell let out a small noise in her throat and nodded, venturing over to the desk. She dug through the rolled-up scrolls, the books with their warped pages, until she pulled out an envelope and retrieved a letter inside. When she thrust it at my face, she didn't even meet my eyes.

Prosper, the letter began. With a jolt that zipped straight from my heart to my brain, I recognized my dad's handwriting. The neat, usually uniform letters were messy, as if he'd written this quickly.

I'd hoped it wouldn't come to this, but your grandmother refuses to see reason. Your mother and I have taken precautions to ensure that you or Prue, whoever it might be, will be safely out of her reach. Please be good for your uncle Barnabas, and listen to what he tells you. As hard as it will be to believe, it's all the truth. He will do everything in his power to see that you get the help you need. Until then, it's too dangerous for us to come to you, or for you to come to us. Do not call us. Do not e-mail. Do not tell anyone your name. Be patient. Be brave.

And then he'd signed it . . . with his business signature. Not a *Love, Dad*. It could be that he wanted to prove, in case I had doubts, that it was really him. I traced my finger over the loops of *Percy Redding* and wondered why it felt like my heart was pumping ice.

"Why . . . why did he send a letter?" I asked. "Why didn't he tell me any of this in person, or call, or e-mail?"

"Because of your grandmother," Uncle Barnabas said. "Because he knew that your grandmother was now watching the lot of you, and had men assigned to monitor your e-mails and phones. I don't have either, for my own safety and now yours. This was the only way."

All of that, unfortunately, sounded plausible. When you

had more money than Bill Gates and plenty of time on your hands, you could achieve a whole new level of meddling. My grandmother had bypassed evil and gone straight for supervillain.

Nell had begun pacing but stopped suddenly, cutting off whatever I was about to say next. "Can you just skip all this babying and get to the part where you tell him he has an ancient demon trapped inside him?"

I rolled my eyes. "Oh, like the way you're a witch? Come on. Be real."

But even as the words left my mouth, I remembered how hard those invisible fists had shoved and punched at me. And when a faint crackle of light seemed to travel over Nell's skin and hair, her eyes turning to slits, I sat as far back into the couch as I could.

She *was* a witch.

Oh, crap.

"Prosperity—"

"Call me Prosper," I begged. "Please."

"All right, Prosper it is." My uncle cleared his throat explosively. "What I'm about to tell you may be shocking, too fantastical to be believed, but you have to hear me out."

Listening. I could do that. The curtains fluttered around us as a breeze moved in, carrying with it a scattering of bloodred leaves. I smelled the faint cinnamon again, the smoky scent of autumn, and forced myself not to think of anything or anyone I'd left behind in Redhood.

"Your—*our* family, I mean," Barnabas said, glancing at the family tree. "We've had dealings with a devil."

Yeah, and what else was new? "I know," I said, holding up my bandaged arm. "Her name is Catherine Westbrook-Redding."

But this time, Uncle Barnabas didn't laugh. "I wish I were joking, but believe this if nothing else—the Redding family's fortunes in America were no accident. All of this wealth and power and influence came to us because Honor Redding made a contract with a demon—a fiend, as they're really called—in 1693."

"*Oooookay*," I said, suddenly thinking of the gallery of stalker photos and articles on the attic's wall. The engravings. "A fiend."

"This kind of fiend is known as a malefactor. They draw up contracts with humans to give them whatever their heart desires. In exchange, upon their death, the malefactor will come to claim their soul." Uncle Barnabas paused, but I wasn't sure if he was trying to be dramatic, or just making sure my brain had time to catch up. I could barely hear him over the *thump, thump, thump* of my heart. The scratching of the racks of drying herbs against the wall. "Honor Redding leveraged the souls of his family and every settler in Redhood for a guarantee that the Reddings' fortunes would not fail."

Now that it was autumn, I knew to expect night to sweep in earlier, coating the room. In the silence that followed, it seemed to arrive all at once. With the dark wood all around us, the cramped nooks and crannies, it started to feel less like an attic and more like a coffin. And we were just waiting for someone to close the lid over us.

Nell snapped her fingers, and the three lamps in the room turned on. It startled me out of my thoughts. I blinked.

"Like I said, it's a bit of a shock, but . . ." Uncle Barnabas's gaze flickered between his bony hands and my face. "Do you need something for your nerves? Tea? I have a little brandy—"

"I'm twelve," I reminded him.

"Right, well . . . right . . ."

Nell began to roll up the family tree. I watched the names of my family disappear branch by branch, until, finally, my name slipped by with the rest of them.

"It's true," she said. "It sounds absurd because it *is* absurd. I don't think anyone ever gave you the full story. Like the Bellegraves. They sound familiar?"

Uncle Barnabas's lips went white as he pressed them together. "Ah. The Bellegraves."

"I do know about them," I said. "We had a unit on Redhood's history last year. They were the big family that followed the Reddings from England and settled Redhood with them back in 1687."

Uncle Barnabas nodded, obviously pleased. "The families were great rivals. Honor Redding tried everything he could to destroy Daniel Bellegrave—sabotaging his crops, spreading malicious rumors about him, stealing correspondence.

And still, the Bellegraves flourished. Back then, you know, the town wasn't called Redhood at all."

"Yeah," I said, trying not to give him a "duh" look. I'd only had to hear about this every day of my life since birth. "It was called South Port."

"Right. Once the Bellegraves were finally out of the picture, Honor renamed the town in . . . well, his honor."

"And he drove them out by making a pact with a demon?" I said, not even bothering to hide how stupid I thought that sounded.

"A *fiend*," Nell corrected.

"Okay, sure, a fiend," I said, trying to ignore the way that word tasted like ash on my tongue. "So what does this have to do with me and Prue?"

"I'm getting there," Barnabas said, standing. He made his way over to the corner functioning as the kitchen and began rummaging around in the boxes of tea. He kept me waiting until he had a mug of water spinning around in the microwave. "In order to outmaneuver the Bellegraves," he called finally, "Honor used a very ancient kind of magic, one he'd only heard about in the stories passed down in his family for centuries. He summoned a malefactor."

When Uncle Barnabas came back toward us, it was with one of the computer printouts that had been hanging over the bed alongside the newspaper clippings.

I took it with an uneasy feeling in my stomach, almost afraid to look. Three men and a woman were gathered around a fire, their hands thrown in the air—toward the winged, split-tongued devil floating above them in the cloud of smoke.

"Back then, anything that frightened the colonists was labeled witchcraft and devilry. They were never quite able to understand that the Devil—religion, for that matter—has nothing to do with this. Magic has been around for much longer than any of us could know, and flows from a place that exists between ours and whatever might lie beyond."

"Like . . . the Internet?"

Uncle Barnabas choked on his tea, coughing. "More like another world or dimension. The souls sent there obviously do not return, and fiends are forbidden to talk about their home. So there are no first-person accounts to give us a sure answer."

Nell jumped in here. "There are four worlds—four realms—in all. The human world at the top"—she held out a hand, then slid her other hand beneath it—"the fourth realm. The fiend world is the third realm"—she moved her hand again, creating another layer—"the world of ghosts—*specters*—is the second realm. The first realm is the realm of Ancients, the mysterious race of creatures that created magic and balanced the world when it was very young and full of darkness."

"So they live in Earth's crust, or something?"

"No!" she said, rolling her eyes. "*Dimensions*, Prosper. Worlds that exist layered beneath ours."

Uncle B waved a hand between us, interrupting the conversation. "No one knows who or what the Ancients are. Ancient civilizations believed them to be gods, but their kind no longer leave their realm. The only thing we know for certain is that they were the first occupants of this world, and to ensure life would survive, they created a new world for the fiends who were ravaging ours. Humans and fiends cannot coexist without destroying the balance between the realms and causing each world to collapse in on itself."

"Uh, okay," I said. My brain felt like mush. "That's really cool and all, but can we go back to the malefactor thing? Why are they in our world if they're fiends or whatever?"

"When an evil human dies," Uncle Barnabas began, "their spirit—their *shade*—is guided down to the realm of specters. Unless, of course, they formed a contract with a malefactor during their life. Then, upon their death, their shade goes to the fiend realm and serves the monsters there in eternal servitude."

"There are hundreds of different fiends," Nell said, "but malefactors are the only kind of fiend that can make the contracts."

"What are the contracts for?" I asked, not liking where this was going. This was unbelievable . . . but then, so was everything that had happened in the dungeon.

"I've heard of different contracts requiring different things, but I know the one Honor Redding signed with Alastor required eternal servitude for the entire family in exchange for the lasting success of the Reddings and an influx of wealth," Uncle Barnabas said. "In a way, you could say that they punish people by granting their wishes."

Nell jumped in. "It's like a fairy godmother with a catch. Or a genie with a price tag. Their real job is to collect souls to serve the fiends in their world. The malefactors influence other humans through magic, plant ideas, carry sickness—that kind of stuff. After the contract is signed, they not only get to come back for the shades, but they get to feed off the misery of the signer's victims."

Of course it had been Honor. The image of perfection, ingenuity, bravery, and resilience that had been shoved in our faces all of our lives. He was the standard we were supposed to surpass, or, at the very least meet. He was everything to my family, the whole reason they'd survived. I should have known no one could ever be that uncompromisingly perfect.

He got desperate. He didn't want to fail. If anything, it made him feel like an actual human, not just the grimacing, nearly colorless portrait hanging in the entryway of the Cottage.

Suddenly I had a very clear picture of where this story was headed. "What . . . what happened to the Bellegraves?"

"Half were killed in the fever that swept through the colony that first winter," Uncle Barnabas said, with a sharp tone. "The other half starved to death when their crops turned to ash one night."

"Jeez." It wasn't like I didn't know my family wasn't

going to win a gold medal for kindness, but that was seriously rotten. "But I still don't get why I'm here or what happened last night."

"I already *told* you—" Nell began, but Uncle Barnabas silenced her with a wave.

"Almost there." He took a long sip of his tea. "You know what happened here in Salem, of course?"

"Of course! Birthplace of the National Guard!"

Uncle Barnabas cocked his head to the side, giving me an unamused look. Man. Tough crowd.

"Well, it's true," I said, crossing my arms over my chest. "Yes, okay, I know about the Witch Trials. I also know they were also held in Danvers, Ipswich, and Andover, and not just Salem Town," I added, when it looked like Nell was about to correct me.

"For many years," Uncle Barnabas continued, still looking unhappy, "the Reddings benefited from their partnership with the malefactor, and there were no problems. Suspicions, though . . . those ran rampant. When those young girls in Salem began pointing fingers and accusing everyone around them of consorting with the Devil, you can imagine how uncomfortable it made those *using* witchcraft. And then the witch-hunt fever began to spread through all of the Massachusetts Bay Colony, and things took a turn for the worse."

I stared at the WITCH'S BREW logo on his mug, and the grinning witch there. Probably wouldn't have been so happy in the 1690s, swinging from a tree with a noose around her neck.

"The Reddings, who had never lost a crop, never seen their numbers reduced to nothing by fever, or even suffered bloody conflict with the Native Americans . . . they, more than any other family, felt the suspicions rise around them like unwanted shadows." Uncle Barnabas shook his head. "They did what they thought they had to do to avoid being caught, accused, and killed. They broke the contract."

It turns out that breaking a contract with a malefactor isn't as simple as tearing up a sheet of paper or snapping your fingers. You couldn't even bribe the fiend-demon-whatever into leaving either. You had to engage the services of an actual witch.

"Dangerous business, hiring a real witch during those times," Uncle Barnabas said, leaning back against the couch. It sounded like he was half-impressed by Honor Redding's cunning. "But they found the real deal in Goodwife Prufrock. She gave them the casting they needed to trap the malefactor in a human body."

"Why would they have to do that?" I asked.

"Malefactors exist in our world as spirits, which means they can't be harmed physically. To trap a malefactor in a human body is to render it mortal, and the only way to break a contract with a fiend is to kill it."

"So they got Alejandro—"

"Alastor," Nell corrected.

Well, excuse me for not knowing whatever fancy-pants name the imaginary creature had.

"So poor Al got trapped in someone's body? Whose?" I would be the first one to admit that most of this was sailing clear on over my head, but I got the feeling that if you were going to kill a fiend—hypothetically, since, you know, *not real*—you probably had to kill whoever he was trapped inside of.

Uncle Barnabas shrugged. "Some expendable servant girl."

Oh no.

"Ugh, are you serious?" I asked, instantly taking an eraser to every nice thought I'd ever had about Honor. Another small, awful thought slithered up to me and sank its fangs in. "But the girl . . . she survived, right?"

Uncle Barnabas shook his head.

"How did she die?" I whispered.

"How did they normally kill witches in that day?" Nell asked darkly.

Oh no.

"I mean . . . hanging . . . drowning . . . stoning . . . ?"

Don't say fire, don't say fire, don't say fire—

"They burned her at the stake," Uncle Barnabas said.

I put my hands to my face again, moaning, "Oh *nooooo.*"

Here's the other thing you need to know about Founder's Day and the bonfire: they don't really mark the day when

Redhood was settled, but when the family's luck turned around and the settlement was renamed. The legend that gets lost in the shuffle of pretty ideas about renewal is that Honor started the bonfire with some sort of object they believed was cursed. And once it was gone . . .

"Oh noooooo." Even the bonfire was awful. There was officially nothing good about Redhood except the Silence Cakes. And knowing the truth about my family, they were probably originally made from the hearts of babies, not pumpkin leaves.

"Don't pretend like you're actually upset," Nell said icily. "Aren't servants invisible to you people? Only good for how well they polish the silver?"

Anger flooded me. "You don't know anything about *my* family. And yeah, I'm upset! She was an innocent person, and she shouldn't have had to die because some guy got scared and made a terrible mistake—"

"Guys, guys," Uncle Barnabas said. "We're all in agreement. It was a terrible act. The important thing is what came next. Nell, perhaps you'd like to explain?"

She was still giving me a shifty eye, as if she was trying to find a lie in my face, but she nodded. "Somehow, the casting was messed up. When the servant girl and the malefactor were near death, Alastor warned the family that he would survive the fire and bide his time until he could return to this world, reborn inside of one of Honor

Redding's descendants. When he regained his full power, he would take back everything he had given them."

No, but this . . . this was too strange. This was *unreal*.

And what happened to that book wasn't?

"Wait, wait, wait," I said. "What do you mean, he could return? How could he do that?"

Nell shifted uncomfortably, and seemed reluctant to explain. "A witch's magic is tied to her bloodline, and a spell only lasts as long as the witch's descendants walk the earth. We think he fed on the servant girl's pain and fear and what was left of his power to retreat into the Inbetween, a shadow world between life and death. As long as one of Prufrock's heirs was alive, Alastor was barred from returning unless he wanted to die."

"How many are left?" I whispered. "How many of her descendants?"

"None," Nell said. "The last one died thirteen years ago."

"Oh, well, then, I'm only twelve," I said. "It can't be me."

"Your birthday is in two weeks, is it not?" Uncle Barnabas asked gently.

It was. *It was.*

My heart slammed against my ribs. Every inch of my skin shivered with panic, pricking painfully with realization.

"Goody Prufrock explained that it would likely take a full thirteen years of feeding off the energy of his host for the malefactor to regain his strength and escape whoever that might be to gain his vengeance against the Reddings. Have you felt tired over the years? Did you experience any unusual weakness?"

I couldn't breathe. I just nodded.

"Your grandmother went through and tested all of the extended family herself as they reached thirteen, checking to see if the curse was upon them, growing more and more certain that Prufrock's theory was correct, and that the timing would align the way she predicted. The family you saw in that dungeon all believe that destroying the malefactor will save them from ruin, and they're desperate to protect themselves and their wealth. You and your sister were the only ones left to be tested. Your parents had always refused, thinking the whole thing was an absurd myth, but the wily old woman knew she was running out of time before the malefactor might make an appearance."

"What was that book?" I asked. My palms were drenched in sweat, but I didn't want either of them to see me wipe them off. "That was the test, wasn't it? I could read it, and Prue couldn't."

"That was Goody Prufrock's grimoire—her book of spells. It was enchanted in such a way that no fiend would ever be able to open it, let alone destroy it."

"And when I touched it, and it caught fire—when the words appeared"—my mouth was racing faster than my brain—"it proved to them that—"

"You," Nell finished, "are one doomed Redding."

Conversations by Candlelight

I was no stranger to lies. In fact, I think if you were to line up all the lies I'd been told in my life, the ugly chain of them would probably stretch from Redhood to Jupiter. Every day I had to deal with little lies from my cousins, like when David convinced me that eating broccoli would make trees grow in my stomach. Big ones too, from Mom and Dad, like, *Oh, Prosper, of* course *your grandmother loves you, and you* will *get better, and the enormous panther you see in your dreams* isn't *real*. By now, I could spot a lie the second someone spat it out.

But the longer I stared at Uncle Barnabas, the longer I waited for my internal lie detector to start beeping, the slower the blood ran in my veins, until it seemed to stop completely.

"Is he going to faint again?" Nell leaned close, peering at my face.

"He won't faint," Uncle Barnabas said, patting my back. "Though I imagine you're very tired after your ordeal. We'll leave you now to—"

Ordeal. Try *nightmare.*

"Wait," I breathed out. *"Wait!"*

You know, I might not have been the sharpest pencil in the drawer, but I got what they were saying. Some part of my brain knew what they were implying, even if I didn't see how it was possible. My family had tried to destroy the malefactor by trapping it in a human body. They screwed up. The malefactor said it would come back for vengeance. They wanted to get rid of it again. To do that, they had to get rid of me before he could escape and ruin them. Human host. Dead meat.

"Does this mean that they're not going to stop until I'm dead?" I only had to see their faces to get confirmation on that one. "Oh. Great."

"You don't have anything to be afraid of," Uncle Barnabas said, putting on a fake smile. "Not while you're with us. Unlike the rest of the family, I've never believed that killing the carrier was the solution. Hence, why I'm no longer invited to the Cottage."

"How do you fix it?" I asked. "How do I get it out?"

The idea that I had some kind of pest . . . some *parasite*

crawling around inside me, hiding in my bones, made me feel like a million ants were roaming beneath my skin. I started scratching my arm, even though it didn't itch.

Uncle Barnabas stared at me for a second, smoothing a hand over his low ponytail. I got an answer—just not from him.

Ye might ask me yourself, came the cold, prim voice in my mind, *thou mangled sheep-biting scut.*

Over the past twenty-four hours, a few things about my family had finally started making sense.

Grandmother's hatred of me and all of my cousins, for one. Why she never wanted to talk about Uncle Barnabas. What exactly was in the dungeon. You know, typical family stuff.

And now that I was standing in front of the cracked floor-length mirror, its clawed feet near my own toes, I had a very new understanding of where that superstition about mirrors in Redhood had come from.

I followed the fiend's instructions exactly. Find a candle and light it. Find a mirror, and stand in front of it holding the lit candle. Continue to stand there. Easy enough.

"Is it him?" Uncle Barnabas asked, trailing behind me to the mirror. "He's speaking to you now, isn't he? What is he saying?"

Well, that was kind of the problem. It sounded like the

thing-creature-fiend-whatever was speaking English, but he was tossing in words and phrases I'd never heard before. Like "beslubbering tickle-brained mouldwarp." I wasn't sure what that one meant, but I *also* wasn't sure I wanted to repeat it out loud. Which worked out great, since it seemed like Uncle Barnabas was totally happy having a nice conversation with himself.

"Fiends travel between our world and theirs using mirrors," he was saying, his eyebrows drawn together, "but a powerful fiend like a malefactor has to be the one to open those portals between the realms. I assumed they only communicated through dreams—at least, that's what my research has told me. I didn't realize a mirror could be used for a conversation as well . . . *fascinating.*"

I let him ramble, staring hard at my reflection in the mirror. Nell had plopped a fat white candle into my hand that smelled of wax and honey. She lit the black wick with a snap of her fingers.

I jumped so high in the air, the flame went out and she had to relight it.

"Chill," she said. *"Of all base passions, fear is the most accursed."*

I rolled my eyes. "Sorry I don't speak Fortune Cookie. You're going to have to—"

"Well done! *Well done!*" Uncle Barnabas elbowed me to the side and beamed down at her. It was like a cloud finally moving away from the sun's face. Nell grinned back at him. "You've been practicing with elemental magic! Have you mastered any of the—"

The two were chatting in excited voices, flinging around words like "cunning one" and "pocket spells" and "charms."

Me? I was a little more interested in what was watching me from the other side of the mirror's filmy surface. Only Toad seemed to see it too. He half clawed, half flew to the very top of the armoire, spitting and hissing in disgust or fear.

The flame flickered between my hands, then caught the cracked glass with a brilliant flash of white. I winced and looked away. By the time my heart started beating again, our reflections had disappeared, and the mirror's surface had turned into some kind of window.

A white fox sat still and silent, its fluffy tail sweeping back and forth across the darkness that hovered around it from all sides. It was a tiny, pale thing, more bones than anything else. I felt the weirdest need to squat down and be level with it—just so I could get a closer look at its eyes. One was a bright, bright blue. The other was as dark as the center of the burning candlewick.

"Wait . . ." I began, finally catching the attention of Uncle Barnabas and Nell. They moved in unison, leaning around my shoulders. I almost laughed at the way Nell gasped and my uncle started muttering, "What? What? I don't see anything—"

"Are you . . . ?" I began, slowly cracking my knuckles to try to ease some of the tension building up in me.

"*I am,*" came the reply. The words fluttered around the attic, winding through the space like black, shimmery silk. Even Uncle Barnabas must have heard them. His face went a ghostly shade of gray behind me.

It was the exact same voice I had heard in my head both a few moments ago and at the Cottage. The accent was refined and all proper, but it sounded like someone my age, not an adult. Not to mention, the words were slipping out of a fox's mouth. "*I would say it's a pleasure to meet thee, Prosperity Oceanus Redding, but truly, I only anticipate the delights of destroying thy happiness.*"

A few steps to the right of me, Nell crossed her arms over her chest and narrowed her eyes at the mirror. "Is that right?"

The fox paid her no mind. It *smiled*, revealing a mouthful of ivory teeth, each sharper than the next.

"Why is he talking like that?" I asked Uncle Barnabas. "It sounds like he swallowed a Pilgrim."

But he only shook his head, his mouth opening and shutting with a little gobbling noise.

Nell took a step forward. "It sounds like . . ." She shook her head and said slowly, "What does thou know of . . . um . . . thy circumstances?"

"*Does the lass speak the good speak?*" The fox's tail swished again. *"Or shall I deign to use your fouled-up form of an already wretched language?"*

"The, uh, second option?" I said, scratching the back of my neck. "You don't have to talk like Shakespeare?"

"I have been awake as you slept this day past," Alastor said, his voice oozing with pride. *"I have listened, with great horror, to thy manner of present-day speech, and I have already mastered it, as thee can see."*

"If you say so, pal."

"How . . . how *fascinating*," Uncle Barnabas managed to squeeze out. He leaned in closer to the glass and poked at it. He jumped back, like he was all surprised to find it was solid. "Yes," he murmured to himself. "Yes, he would speak an old form of the language until he fully acclimates to ours. Fascinating."

I set the candle on the floor and sat beside it, crossing my legs. I was surprised that I felt so calm when I was staring at definite proof that Uncle Barnabas and Nell hadn't been lying.

I took a deep breath. This was going to be so much easier than Uncle Barnabas let on. The fiend *was* trapped inside me, which meant he had no chance of hurting Mom, Dad, or Prue for now. That made my legs feel a little more solid.

Not going to lie, it also helped to see a fox, not some slobbering brain-eating monster, watching me. His fuzzy little head was cocked to the side, and a small black tongue darted out over his button nose. It was actually . . . kind of cute?

Alastor wasn't anything like the drawings. He didn't have pointy wings, or a pitchfork, or a scaly tail that curled with his dark delights.

The white fox didn't blink as its eyes shifted back to me. This time, when he spoke, it was only to my ears. *Ye—you, rather, should see me in my true form, peasant. By the end of it all, you will accompany me Downstairs, and I shall show you terror.*

You can hear my thoughts? The blood rushed straight to my face. *All of them?*

I know everything about thee, Prosperity. Everything inside thee belongs to me. I am joined to thy shade. I know all of thy fears, thy desires, thy jealousy—where thou hides thy collection of small porcelain ponies . . .

I turned to look back at Uncle Barnabas. "Is there any way to shut him up?"

Uncle Barnabas picked up the candle and blew it out with a single breath. As the flame died, so did the image of the white fox. "That work?" he asked.

Behind us, Toad was mewling frantically, as if trying to get our attention. I heard a thud and assumed he had jumped down from his perch. The scratch of nails against the floorboards faded beneath the rumble of laughter in my ears.

Hear me, boy. I have heard the things you and that man have planned for me, but this thou—you—must know. I have lived for over eight hundred years, and nothing, save the end of this world, will bring me more joy than ripping thy family to shreds and scattering every bit of their fortune to the winds.

"Go ahead," I said. "*Try* it."

Test me, and you will learn precisely how fragile the human heart can be. But . . . you are already acquainted with this knowledge, are you not? Imagine how easy it will be to undo what healing has already passed.

Prue.

"What's that supposed to mean?" I demanded. Fear and anger slammed into me. I gripped the sides of the mirror, shaking as hard as I could until the shelves around me were rattling with the force of it. *"What's that supposed to mean?"*

Nell yanked me back. "Cut it out! What did he say to you?"

I tore myself out of her grip and stormed over to the couch and its nest of blankets. I snatched up the darkest, sturdiest plaid and stalked back toward the mirror to cover it. Before I could, Toad's yelping turned to a furious yowl. His tiny fangs flashed as he practically unhinged his jaw to snap them around Nell's foot like a trap.

"*Ouch!* Toad! What's the matter with you?"

His tail flicked toward the mirror, frantically pointing.

The stupid white fox was gone now, but the reflection of the attic still hadn't returned to the mirror's dusty surface. In fact, there seemed to be something else moving inside of it, something dark, growing closer and closer. The surface of the glass rippled like water, and even though my brain was screaming at me to stop, I reached up and brushed a finger with it. When I pulled it back, it was coated with what looked like silver paint.

But then the distant shadow wasn't distant at all—and it wasn't a shadow, not any longer. Its dark robes swirled as it spiraled up, as if climbing out of a dark well. I saw a flash of red mask. The thing bobbed, hovering just in front of me. Its head cocked to the side, curious.

"Hello?" I said.

"Prosper . . ." Nell began, her voice tight with fear. *"Duck!"*

"What are you—?" I started to say. But just as I began to turn the red mask flipped up, revealing five sets of teeth. And then, suddenly, the creature wasn't inside the mirror.

It was crashing through it.

Hag Bait

In art, there's something called negative space. It's the blank space around the subject of whatever is the focus of the work. Sometimes it creates its own image, one more interesting than the original subject.

This shadow wasn't even negative space, and its image didn't render the room around it into space either. It was a black hole in the form of a creature that looked like a pruned and shriveled human corpse. It floated silently in the middle of the attic, the shredded ends of its black cloak drawing patterns in the dust on the floor.

Being beside it was like that second just as you crest up onto a roller coaster, when you begin to fall. Everything was suspended, even my heartbeat. The mask remained up, and there was nothing else around me except the rows and rows of teeth. It inhaled sharply, a high, wheezing sound that had no beginning and no end. Every hair on my body stood as straight and sharp as pins.

Then I felt the tug. It started at my center as a spark, and erupted into fire beneath my skin. My vision blurred and I'm sure I was shouting something, because I felt the words leave my throat. I just couldn't hear them. When I looked at my outstretched hand, it looked like it was dissolving.

Flee! Alastor roared. *Go now, Maggot!*

It was too late. My legs folded under me like paper. A thin black tongue slithered out, whipping against my forehead, smearing black, stinking goop down the bridge of my nose.

Thou dares—Alastor's voice rang in my ears, crisp as morning air—*thou dares to steal from me? From* **me?**

The weight on my chest doubled as the creature leaned forward. Its gaping mouth hovered over my face, slobbering spit and ooze on my skin. The red mask split into two, then three, then four. I blinked, trying to focus. Black crept in at the corner of my vision. I went boneless. Weak, like it would take a year to lift a finger.

"Prosper? *Pros*—*!*" Was that Nell? Or Prue?

Foul, thieving miscreant! Alastor thundered. His voice rose with each word until I felt them forming on my own lips. *If thou think I will forgive this, thou are gravely mistaken! I*

will come for thee, and I will take back every ounce of power
thou stole! I will crush thee, smash thee until thou—

"Slip from the shadows into sight," Nell yelled, "reveal
yourself in the light!"

The light from the nearby lamps streamed out, swirling
together until a white-hot orb floated above us like a full
moon. The creature shrieked like metal scratching glass as
it flung itself toward the ceiling. But Nell wasn't finished.
She gripped a bucket in two hands and launched its contents
up. The spray of white exploded into the air with a loud
whoosh, clinging to the shadow like frost. I squeezed my
eyes shut as the remnants of the white stuff—*salt*—pattered
down around me. I didn't open them again until the shrieking returned.

The shadow flailed about the room, narrowly missing
Toad on the back of the couch when the CatBat tried to
claw at it. Before, its robes had moved as if the shadow were
underwater, silently, gracefully. Now each part of it hardened, crackling and squeaking as its limbs and cloak turned
to gleaming obsidian glass.

Nell dove over my legs for the bucket and swung it
straight up with a grunt. The plastic bucket smashed
through the creature's center, exploding it into a thousand—
a million—shards that hovered above us, spinning and
dancing. The empty red mask crashed down on my knee,
a second before the rest of the shadow came raining down.

But the glowing orb from her spell burned through the shards of glass, turning them into nothing more than black sand.

"Are you okay?" Nell asked, shaking the sand out of her hair casually, like she hadn't just destroyed a creature of darkness.

"Fine," I managed to groan, still unable to move my legs.

"I was talking to *Toad*. I can see you're fine." She swept down, grabbing the red mask and holding it up for Uncle Barnabas to see.

"Cripes," he said. "A *hag*."

"What?" My lips felt numb, but they were finally working. I inched my way up onto my elbows.

A leech, Alastor groused. ***Filthy, despicable creature. I had thought their numbers largely vanquished—a necessity, given their need to feed upon superior fiends. It would seem we did not stamp them out entirely. I will have to rectify this.***

"Some call them psychic vampires," Uncle Barnabas explained, hauling me forward so I was sitting upright. He tried in vain to brush the salt out of my hair. "They feed off the energy of fiends and . . . gifted humans. The malefactor must have opened a portal when he tricked you into looking into the mirror."

"I don't know," I began, trying to shake feeling back into my hands. "Alastor sounded just as angry and freaked-out to see it as I was. I don't think the hag was his invited guest."

What is this . . . "freaked-out"? I will have an answer, Maggot!

I ignored him. "I just mean that if it was feeding on anything, it wasn't me."

"Yes, that's true," Barnabas said. "Perhaps he's done us a favor and robbed the fiend of some power he's managed to regain. But we'll have to take the utmost care from now on. Nell, I need you to destroy any mirrors that we have in the house."

"Wait," I said. "Isn't that bad luck? Seven years or whatever for each one?"

"*You* are bad luck," Nell shot back. "If you think you can fight the Redding vanity and keep from admiring yourself, I'd try to avoid looking into any reflective surfaces for the time being."

I was getting very tired of being told what a Redding was by a cousin who clearly had spent no time with us. And, no, she wasn't wrong that some of our family was like that, but plenty weren't.

"You seem to forget you're a Redding too," I said.

Nell inhaled sharply through her nose, her lips parting. Uncle Barnabas cleared his throat, cutting her off.

He handed Nell the crimson mask and jerked his chin toward the window. "Go hang it up and put a line of salt on the sill. That'll keep them at bay for a while. Prosper is exhausted enough with the malefactor draining him. He certainly doesn't need any other creatures coming for a visit."

"Wait," I said, holding out a hand to stop her. I needed both of them in the room to get answers. "What's the plan, here? So there's a malefactor inside me—do I trap him in a mirror to get him out? Feed him to a hag to keep him from feeding on me?"

Ye assume incorrectly, hedge-born applejohn. Alastor sounded offended at the suggestion. *I do not feed off the filthy souls of humans. They taste of sunlight and peppermint. Blech.*

Uncle Barnabas glanced up at the ceiling, scratching at his head. "We are, uh, entertaining a few options for solving your predicament at the moment."

"You don't have a clue, do you?" I asked flatly.

"No, no, no," Uncle Barnabas said, waving his hands. "We are looking into other options, yes, but we believe our best bet is to finish what Goody Prufrock began. We'll transfer him out of you and into another living host—a spider, a frog, and—" He smashed his hands together. "The trouble is, of course, we've been trying to track down the necessary ingredients for the spell."

"Which are what?" I asked. "Can you just order them off the Internet?"

"Some," Nell said. "But the spell calls for three toes of a man hanged for his crime—"

"Wow," I said, "that's specific."

Nell shot me an irritated look, continuing, "Three toes of a man hanged for his crimes, a newborn eel's freely given slime, wings of a black beetle plucked midflight, two eggs of a viper stolen at night, a gleaming stone cast down from the moon, all boiled in a cauldron at high noon—with the right incantation, of course."

A dead man's toes, viper eggs, a moon rock . . . *really?*

"And that's going to work?" I asked, my voice pitching higher and higher. "What can I do to help? What's my job?"

Nell looked at me like I'd asked if I could grow six more legs. "You want to actually *do* something?"

"You think I'm just going to sit and twiddle my thumbs and wait for this . . . this *thing* to come and destroy my family?"

My parents had worked too hard to build their foundation to see it all possibly turn to ash. I couldn't get Prue out of the Cottage, but I could do *this*. The truth was, my family could stand to lose some money. But why did I get the feeling "vengeance" entailed more than just lost income—that it might involve lost lives?

Hmm . . . you are giving me rather intriguing ideas, Maggot.

"Your job is to stay put and stay out of trouble," Uncle Barnabas said. "The dead man's toes are proving to be, uh, a challenge. But I have a lead. Someone in Australia willing to dig up an old convict, and, well, snip snip."

I tried not to shudder. "How long is that going to take? Why can't we buy a ticket and fly over there to pick them up?"

But even as the words left my mouth, I wished I could take them back. A plane ticket to Australia was expensive—just because it was something my family could do, it didn't mean Uncle Barnabas could. And, sure enough, I was right.

"With what money?" Nell scoffed. *"Yours?"*

"My parents asked you to help, didn't they?" I tried again. "Maybe they can pay . . . ?"

"No, Prosper," Uncle Barnabas said sharply, only to soften his voice as he explained, "we cannot have any contact with them whatsoever. Your grandmother is watching them so closely now, and I have to imagine she somehow has access to view their bank accounts. We don't have your passport, and we also don't have the time to figure out how to go about finding another way to get you out of the country."

Logic really sucked sometimes.

"I could just make a quick call," I begged. "I could leave them a message from a pay phone or send an e-mail—"

"No!" Nell said, sharply enough to send Toad jumping into the air. Behind Uncle Barnabas, the CatBat hovered, its enormous eyes alert and unblinking as it looked for trouble. When Uncle Barnabas turned to glance back, it promptly crashed back down into the black dirt and herbs. "You can't have contact with *anybody*. I put a glamour spell on you the second we left Redhood. It prevents anyone who is actively

searching for you from being able to see you, but it only holds if you don't reveal your location."

"What about everyone else?" I asked. Most people were shameless about snapping photos of my family and sending them to magazines. All it would take was one person posting a picture online. . . .

"Everyone else sees the glamour I put into place, not your real face," she said, eyes glinting behind her glasses. "It's like a magic mask. Don't worry, I gave you a huge nose and beady little eyes."

I sighed. "Well, it can only improve my looks, right? Everyone always says I'm a dead ringer for my great-great-uncle Ichabod, and he basically had the face of a rabid squirrel."

Nell let out a sharp laugh, then caught her lip between her teeth, forcing herself to stop. She sat down again, this time on the far edge of the couch, keeping her distance.

"Please," I said. "I have to do *something*. Assign me anything." *Anything* to keep my mind off the fact I had an evil creature inside me.

"Well . . . all right. I suppose you could look for an appropriate vessel to contain him?" Uncle Barnabas said.

"That's it?" I asked. "What about the plucked beetle wings? I could try to do that. What do I need—a pair of tweezers?"

"We already bought those," Nell said. "*All's well that ends well*, so chill out."

My voice came out embarrassingly high. "Okay . . . but what happens if the fiend regains its full strength and escapes *before* my thirteenth birthday?"

"Well, that's a worry for then, I suppose," Uncle Barnabas said. "For now, I need you to believe in this plan and not contact your family, no matter what."

After a second I nodded, wiping a trickle of blood off my cheek. My face and hands stung from where a few pieces of glass had cut me.

"I believe I asked you to refill the salt," Uncle Barnabas said, turning to Nell. She had faded into the background with Toad, watching me from behind her glasses. "Grab the healing tincture off the shelf before you go, will you? We can't have our guest wandering around with cuts and bruises."

"But—"

"*Now*, Cornelia. And don't forget the mirrors."

With a noise of frustration, Nell jumped to her feet, clearly aware of the fact she was being dismissed. She plucked a small silver jar off the armoire shelf and all but shoved it at my chest. The top popped open on its own, and the smell of aloe and peppermint rose from it, curling pleasantly in my nose. I touched the pale pink cream and began to pat it on my face, hands, and arms. Within seconds, the aches disappeared, and my skin was pulling itself back together. My insides squirmed again at the sight.

Unreal. All of this was just . . . unreal.

Nell crossed the room and snatched the bucket up off the floor. For the first time, I noticed the stars had fallen out of her hair and had scattered onto the floor, forgotten.

"You're *welcome*," she hissed, clutching the blue plastic to her chest.

Oh man—what brand of jerk was I that I hadn't even thought to thank her for saving my life? Right after, the only thing I'd thought of was the fact she'd had to save me while I curled up on the floor like a shrimp. I have some pride, you know? Not a whole lot, thankfully.

Before I could try, she disappeared out the door with a fuming "Come on, Toad."

The CatBat started to fly after her, only to remember he had an audience. His flight turned into an abnormally large leap that Uncle Barnabas was completely oblivious to. But even after the two had disappeared downstairs, Nell's anger stayed behind, hanging like a thundercloud in the doorway.

I waited until the stairs stopped creaking before asking, "What will hanging up the mask do?"

"It'll ward off any other hags who might take an interest in you and the malefactor's power," Uncle Barnabas said.

"Do you really think we might have gained a little time? That the hag drained enough power from him to make a difference?"

"Hopefully. We should know more soon, I think," Uncle Barnabas said. "I know . . . I know I might not have any right to say so, given that we have only just become reacquainted, but . . . I'm proud of you for how well you're handling this."

I'm proud of you. When was the last time I'd heard those words?

Years. It had been *years.* When Prue had gone into shock at home, and I'd called all the right people, in the right order, and the 911 dispatcher taught me how to do CPR.

"Thanks," I said, meaning it. "I'm trying. It's just . . . *a lot.* And I'm worried. I don't really get how I can be both a host *and* a prison for the malefactor."

I wonder that myself.

"Shut up," I grumbled.

"Excuse me?" Uncle Barnabas blinked. "Oh. Is he . . . speaking with you, then?"

Like a flame which has already burned itself out, so is this man's wit. Were he any more loggerheaded—

"Guess what?" I said, cutting him off. "No one likes your fancy English."

"What is he saying?" Uncle Barnabas pressed. "Is he talking about the curse?"

Foul-tongued wretch! Alastor spat. *Thou will not speak to me in such an informal manner. I am thy lord and master! I am prince of the—*

"Well, thee is being a huge jerk," I said, then turned toward my uncle. "Seriously. Is there a way to force him to go to sleep?"

"None that I know of," Uncle Barnabas said, rubbing his

finger down the bridge of his nose in thought. "But there is one trick that always seems to work."

"And it is . . . ?"

"It's like with any bully," he said, reaching down to haul me up off the floor. "You just ignore them and they'll go away eventually."

Yeah. Because that trick had worked so well for me over the past twelve years.

The House of Many Terrors

About three hours later, I was wide-awake, staring up at the ceiling. All kinds of horrible screams and shrieks were drifting up through the cracks in the floorboards. I had the timing of the fright house's different animatronics down by the third tour group, though. The zombie nurse's cackling, the thumping from whatever was chained up in the room downstairs, the fake bats' shrieking, and, less than two minutes later—Nell jumping out at them from a hidden compartment at the top of the stairs with a deafening, *"Gimme brainssss!"*

One of the guests screamed so sharply I thought the glass windows would crack. Even Toad winced from where he was perched on the edge of the couch, watching me with such hawk-like intensity, for a moment I saw his button-like nose shift into a beak. His bulbous eyes were slits, unblinking as his tail swished back and forth, back and forth, like the arm of an old grandfather clock.

All that was *almost* loud enough to drown out the singing fiend in my head. He had composed a very special song for me, set to the tune of what sounded like "My Country, 'Tis of Thee."

Pull off their fingers and toes, he crooned, **bury them where no one knows—or roast them alive!**

The whole room was dark and freezing. When Nell and Uncle Barnabas had gone downstairs to finish setting up for the night's tourists and suckers, they'd left the window open. Apparently I needed "fresh air."

Here was a list of things I actually needed:

1. My hypoallergenic pillow.
2. A tall glass of skim milk.
3. Something sharp to jab into my ears.

"Are you sure you don't want to come down and watch?" Nell had asked. She was part of the show, but no one bothered to tell me that until she popped out from behind the couch in her skeleton costume. When I cringed, it wasn't because I was scared—it was because her makeup was just that bad. It looked like she had drawn a moon on her face and squiggled some black lines through it.

"I could help you with that . . ." I began. So far I hadn't done anything other than give Nell and Uncle Barnabas a headache and force them to smash the rest of the mirrors in the house. My fingers went numb at the thought of them laughing, or Nell mocking me again.

And, sure enough, her face screwed up at the suggestion, like I'd thrown up at her feet.

"It was just an offer, take it or leave it," I muttered, crossing my arms and looking away. What was her problem, anyway? Maybe if she had grown up within the family, she would have seen that my little corner of it wasn't nearly as awful as the rest. In fact, Mom, Dad, and Prue were the best of them.

Don't think about them, I thought. Not when that tightness was back in my throat, and all I could picture was my comfy bed back home, and the late-night snack Mom would have made me if she caught me still up at this hour. We would have watched a movie, just the two of us, or she would have told me a story I'd never heard before, about her scientist parents exploring the Amazon.

Where was she now—still in China? Had Mom and Dad come home once they realized what had happened? Maybe Prue was with them. . . .

"I could use your help, Prosper," Uncle Barnabas had said, offering me the palette of face paint. His costume was something like that of the undead ringleader of a circus, complete with a blood-splattered top hat. "Let's see if you put that paint set to good use over the years."

I studied his face for a moment, staring at his long nose and bright blue eyes. And, just to prove a point to Nell, I settled on a ghoulish skeleton face, mixing a bit of green into the white that covered him from forehead to chin, just to be that much more putrid. I patted black, ringed with a bit of purple, into the dips and dimples of his skin, added a tiny bit of red, like blood, to the stitches I drew along either side of his mouth.

Finished, I sat back. Since there were no mirrors, he turned to Nell for her assessment.

"How do I look?" he asked.

"Creepy," she had admitted, dragging the word out reluctantly, like it was coated in thorns. Wrapped up in her arms, Toad had lifted a paw and patted her hand.

Another scream. This time a girl, in the eardrum-piercing range. Uncle Barnabas's loud, booming fake laughter followed, then, like clockwork, the screeching sirens on the second floor went off, and another set of kids lost it.

"More satisfied customers!" His voice sounded deeper as it came through the microphone. And weirdly Irish.

—douse them with boiling tar, crack them o'er the head with a saw! Alastor was still singing in a cheery voice.

"That doesn't even *rhyme*," I growled, pushing myself off the makeshift bed. "Try *bar*."

When pacing did nothing but make my stomach churn and cause Toad to cling to my ankle by his teeth, I limped over to Uncle Barnabas's bookshelves and began to pull books down, flipping through them. The spines were all shades of leather—brown, black, blue—and soft from being handled so much.

I arranged them by color as I put them back, Toad watching me like the old nanny Prue and I used to have— the one that would slap the inside of my hand whenever I was *bad* or *silly* or *trying* so it wouldn't leave an obvious mark. The second Mom figured out how that nanny was disciplining us, she kicked her to the curb so hard that the old lady practically got whiplash.

Grandmother had hired her.

"Yeah, yeah, I'm putting them back, don't worry," I muttered, absently rubbing my hand at the memory. "Can't read them anyway, they're all in Latin. Oh—*crap!*"

The last book was so old and brittle, the binding all but fell apart in my hand. A chunk of the paper landed on the dusty floor with a *thwack* loud enough to make me jump. I glanced around, making sure Nell and Uncle Barnabas hadn't come back, accepting a swat on the nose from Toad in punishment.

My hand stilled. The pages had flipped open to another engraving, this one a circle of inky monsters with horns and tails.

"*Nominibus daemonum,*" I read from the title page. "*Nominibus . . . ?*"

The meaning is plain, if thou—you—possessed the smallest measure of wit. Thou clearly does not even speak thine own

ancient language, Alastor scoffed in disgust. *The names of—*

There was something in the sharp silence, the way he cut himself off quickly, that made me curious. Dangerously curious.

"The names of?" I pressed. "The names of . . . dae-mons . . . demons? The names of fiends? Why would there be a whole book listing just names?"

Alastor, for the first time in hours, remained strangely quiet.

I turned the page to a picture of a huge black snarl-ing demon and decided to shut the book. I'd have to ask Nell and Uncle Barnabas about it tomorrow, to see why my heart had given a little quiver, even though I wasn't nervous at all.

It took another hour before my brain went fuzzy enough around the edges to go to sleep. I was starting to drift off into dreamland when I felt the first twitch in my toes.

Then they curled and stretched and curled again. On their own.

I sat straight up, yanking the blanket up to my chin. The moonlight streaming in through the window was all the light I needed to watch my toes start wiggling.

"Could you not?" I hissed. *"Seriously!"*

Toad lifted his sleepy face from where he'd buried it in the blankets.

It felt like my feet were buried in a pound of sand. I

couldn't move them myself or make them stop as they tapped against the couch cushion. One-two-three-four-five, over and over.

"Holy crap—stop!"

Shall I? I think it best to explore my new habitat.

Alastor let out a low laugh and continued to play with each finger and toe. They were only little movements, but it felt like hot pins were streaming through my veins. My right arm burned like nothing else as it suddenly began to flop around on its own. The sensation was in my left arm, too, making the cut there hurt like you-know-what . . . but it didn't budge.

The fiend grunted with the effort.

Iron, he hissed. *That malt-worm dared cut me with a cursed blade?*

"Uh, last time I checked she cut me, not you," I said. I lifted the bandage so it was directly in front of my face. "Does that mean . . . if she had cut my other arm and my legs, you wouldn't be able to control them either?"

The idea that my icicle of a grandmother had done me a favor—whether she meant to or not—was too ridiculous for me to believe. I pushed the thought away.

Alastor was silent again, and I was starting to suspect this was a very bad thing.

Uncle Barnabas had asked me a million and a half questions about Alastor while we ate our cold pizza dinner. Each time I had to answer, the words felt clogged in my throat.

The truth was, I couldn't feel the fiend inside of me in the normal sense. He wasn't a little beetle roaming around under my skin. It was more . . . it was more like someone had forced me to swallow a thundercloud. It growled and rumbled and every once in a while felt a bit gusty. I could tell when he was frustrated or angry, because I felt frustrated and angry too.

It doesn't matter, I told myself. *I'll get him out soon.*

Alastor's voice came slithering out. **We shall see about that, no?**

I scooted down the couch and kicked off the blanket. I was hot and sticky with sweat. Feverish, almost. Even with the wind, the night sky was breathing in through the open window. I was miserable and wide-awake. It was a good thing there wasn't a phone or computer, because I'm not sure I could have resisted calling my dad's cell phone, just to hear his voice for a second. I would have broken Nell's spell in a heartbeat if it meant I could sneak off and hide back inside my own house and know for certain that Prue was safe.

"Did you always hate my family this much?" I asked him. "Do you have to hurt everyone? We weren't even alive back then to try to stop them."

Not that thou would have, came the rumbling response. **Every Redding heart is poisoned by greed.**

"Not my parents'," I said.

Are they not eager for praise from the world? Dost they not hunger to find the best care, not just for others, but for

thy sister? Alastor mused. *Thy parents did not make the contract, but they have cherished its effects, benefited beyond their dreams. And if it should all come tumbling down, if thy parents should lose thy good name . . . ahhhh, what a delight it would be.*

My heart thumped painfully in my chest. As if Toad could hear it, he fluttered over from the end of the couch, his wings flicking and snapping against my face.

"Don't do it," I whispered. "It wouldn't just hurt my family. It would hurt thousands of kids around the world—"

They will feel my pain. They will feel the agony of the girl-child your forefather burned alive. I swore I could hear the smirk in his voice. *And it will be all thy fault, Maggot. Who would accept you then, knowing you were the cause of such misery and misfortune? Who could love such a weak fool? But thou art well acquainted with scorn and mockery, art thou not? How certainly thou will prove their every suspicion that there is nothing remarkable, nothing worthy about you.*

He wasn't . . . I tried to breathe, to fight the sting in my eyes. He wasn't wrong. Everything he said was true. If I couldn't stop him, if I was the reason my own family failed, faltered, fell—

Thy misery tastes of pepper, Maggot. Delicious. But there is a way to save them, to ensure they will not hate thee. Thine own family—mother, father, sister alike. All safe, all cared for. You would only need to agree to a contract of your own. . . .

A tiny black paw pressed against the tip of my nose. Toad's gleaming emerald eyes glared at me, his claws out, just above my tender eyeballs. Rather than blind me, he removed his paw and leaned down, peering into my eyes. For the first time I noticed that his ears weren't as small as the rest of him, they were just folded down. Now one rose of its own accord, forming a perfect little triangle, listening.

"Can you hear him?" I whispered, wondering.

Changelings are nothing more than mice in my realm, Alastor said. *I see this fiend is no more than a lowly lap pet. Foolish. The only good use for them is to pickle them and roast them over a blazing fire.*

Toad answered my question, and Alastor's charming mental image, with a howl, drawing his claws back to strike. I seized him by the belly and launched myself up off the couch. "Come on, come on, buddy, you know *I* don't think that. He's just trying to get us worked up. Let's find a good distraction."

Since I couldn't read half the books on the shelves, and the other half would most definitely give me nightmares, that was out. I stood at the center of the attic, hands on my hips, orange pumpkin shirt glowing in the moonlight. The smell of sour milk seeped into the air, and, just as suddenly, I knew what I had to do.

So gross, I thought hours later, trying to breathe through my mouth as I tied off the rancid trash bags and walked them over to the open window. I squeezed and shoved them through, trying not to squirm as one of them started leaking mysterious liquid all over my hands. So, so gross.

Nell and Uncle Barnabas didn't seem surprised to find me still up, but they *did* seem a little confused by the fact I was in the middle of sweeping the floor.

"What?" I said defensively. "It was dirty."

I don't stress about things being clean, I swear, but I like to organize my clothes by color in my closet and for there to be no dust or crumbs on my desk at home. It wasn't like there's anything wrong with that. People shouldn't have to live with boxes and bags left out everywhere to trip over, never mind mugs crusted with days-old dried oatmeal. Or unmade beds. Or spider-infested curtains. Or the threat of stacks of books falling over and crushing them.

"It's . . ." Uncle Barnabas began, taking off his glasses to wipe them before replacing them back on his face. "Very clean in here."

You bet it was.

"Couldn't sleep?" Nell asked, raising an eyebrow. She didn't sound tired in the slightest, and I felt like I had taken cold medicine. I had to drag myself around the room. It was almost midnight—my parents usually forced me and Prue to be in bed by nine thirty, ten at the latest if we had family movie night.

Tonight was family movie night.

Don't think about it, don't picture it, don't miss it. . . . A whole lot of good telling myself that was going to do.

Still, a small, excited part of me recognized there was at least *some* good in all of this. No bedtime, no plain, boring food, and no Grandmother. In Redhood, you lived by the rules, or you couldn't live there at all. As much as I wanted to think my parents were different, they still had their own unique set of them. Here, with the exception of my two commands from the resident witch—no mirrors and no revealing my name or location—I was mostly free of them.

At least, as far as I could tell. But if Nell and Uncle Barnabas knew what had happened, that Alastor had been able to control my arm and toes . . .

"He—" I began, but stopped myself. Did I really want to tell them about the toe controlling? If they knew that, would they strap me down, or lock me in some kind of closet? "Alastor's like a baby. All he does is whine and cry."

"I might have something to help shut him up," Nell said. "I've never tested it before, but it could work. . . ."

Uncle Barnabas's hand came down on my shoulder and Nell's eyes locked on it.

"Is it a new spell," he asked eagerly, "or a hex?"

Nell grabbed her purple backpack and pulled out a sheet of notebook paper and a pen, bringing both back to the couch.

"It's just a pocket spell," she said.

"*Pocket spell?*" Uncle Barnabas grunted as he tossed his costume's hat off onto his bed. "This folksy stuff is beneath you, Cornelia. Your mother was a magnificent witch, and I have to think she would be disappointed you aren't trying to push yourself more."

Nell kept her eyes down on the paper. I thought I saw her hand tremble around it, but just as quickly, she handed it to me.

"It *could* help," she said quietly, smoothing back a loose ringlet of her hair. "What you want to do is write down the fiend's name. *A-L-A-S-T-O-R*."

"Why don't you write it?"

"Because you're the one seeking protection, not me, genius." Her eyes rolled behind her glasses. "Just do it, okay?"

Alastor stirred in my mind, like a pile of fallen leaves, disturbed by the wind. He let out a curious ***Hmmmm?*** as I wrote his name down.

"Now fold the sheet along the middle, right through his name. Keep folding it smaller and smaller. As you do that, imagine his power diminishing until it's nothing."

Not likely.

"Shut up, Alastor," I said. I looked at Nell, all of a sudden feeling very determined. I folded the paper over one last time, until it was the size of a pill. "What now?"

Nell stood, her shoulders hunched, and went to get a candle and a mug from the kitchen. She snapped her fingers and lit the wick. "Light it on fire and drop it in the bowl—yeah, like that. Now repeat after me. *Your control is slipping. I bind thee back.*"

As stupid as I felt saying it, repeating it, the pocket spell worked fast.

Like magic.

Nooooooo! Alastor wailed. ***Stop, curse thee, stop!***

I couldn't get the words out fast enough. I kept repeating that one line, *I bind thee back*, over and over, until the fiend stopped sniveling and hollering and the paper burned itself through. Nell leaned over the bowl and stuck a finger in the black ash. Before I could stop her, she swiped it against my forehead.

I have no clue what I was supposed to feel, but my stomach had stopped jumping around like a grasshopper and I couldn't feel the prickle of Alastor's presence inside me. Nell's bright eyes watched me from behind her glasses, Toad climbing up her back to perch on her shoulder. He gave her cheek an approving lick. She even smiled a little when I did. Maybe it wasn't real magic like Uncle Barnabas had said, but it had been *something*.

"Well, that's enough excitement for one night. It's time for you both to hit the sack." Uncle Barnabas stood and stretched. "You have a busy day tomorrow—"

"I know," I said, smiling dreamily at the thought of dusting the bookshelves and finding blank, clean paper to sketch the attic. A day at home with nothing to do but draw. Heaven.

"—a new school is always a challenge, but I have faith you'll do well."

It felt like he had reached over and punched me in the throat. "Wait—what—*why?*"

"Because one of us needs to keep tabs on you at all times, to make sure no one tries to take you, or the fiend starts acting up," Uncle Barnabas said. "I've been training Cornelia to handle such a situation, and since she is required by law to attend school, so must you. Besides, the local coven put a heavy protection spell around the school grounds. It's the one place we're guaranteed no fiend, or anyone with ill intentions, will be able to enter. *And* it'll go a long way in establishing a new identity for you here."

"Plus, they have a sprinkler system," Nell said casually, "in case we try any spells after school and they, uh, misfire."

I stretched myself back over the couch, pulling the blanket up to my chin. My gaze drifted over to Uncle Barnabas. "Can't I just go to work with you?"

"Spoken like someone used to always getting their own way," Nell muttered.

"I'm afraid not," Uncle Barnabas said. "We'll have plenty of time to experiment after I do some research in the archive. I have this under control."

Nell stepped out of the bathroom in her pink pj's. She passed by her father without looking at him, even as he told her he'd wake us up in the morning. I waited until Uncle Barnabas was in the bathroom and the shower water was running before I turned to face her bed. Nell braided her hair, glaring at the opposite wall. I tried to figure out what she was trying to kill with her eye daggers when the overhead light suddenly snapped off.

As I pressed my face to the pillow, I suddenly remembered the book I'd found. "Is there some kind of importance to a fiend's name?"

Nell had been arranging her blankets, but stopped at my question. "That's random. Why do you ask?"

"I just saw one of the books earlier, and Alastor had kind of a weird reaction to it," I said.

"You already know his name," Nell said sharply. "That's just . . . an encyclopedia of known and vanquished fiends. Don't try to pretend like you know anything about this world."

"I wasn't trying to," I shot back. Why did she have to make every conversation feel like walking through thorny brambles? "By the way . . . I thought the pocket spell was awesome. I don't care what Uncle B says."

I wasn't even sure *why* I felt like I had to say the words to begin with. It was just that I had seen her face earlier, when Uncle Barnabas mentioned her mother, and for that one single second, it felt like I had seen a secret corner of her heart. One that was very dark, and very sad.

"Did your mom teach you?" I asked. "Before she . . . ?"

"Yeah." I had to strain my ears to hear her. "She taught me a lot, but not enough to make him happy, I guess."

"Well . . . I think it's cool," I offered. "It's more than most people can do, right?"

The shower water cut off with a loud groan from the pipes. I could hear Uncle Barnabas muttering to himself, but couldn't understand a word of what he was saying.

"Prosper?" Nell whispered. "It will work. I promise."

I shut my eyes, waiting for Al's cackle or the humming sound of his breath in my ears. But there was only the silence of deep sleep, of the bright moon hovering high over us.

"It already did."

The Witching Hour

It did not, in fact, work, but Alastor couldn't blame the little witch for trying. Pathetic as the attempt was.

He had been worried that his little performance earlier had been too dramatic to be believed, but he was pleased to discover that his host was, as suspected, as dull as an old doorknob. The boy's spirit slipped down into dark sleep, and Alastor's rose up to its rightful place.

It might have been careless of him to reveal his ability to control the boy's body, but the temptation to frighten him into submission had simply been too great. Making him squirm, feeling his heart grow heavy with dread—truly, it was a delicious thing. He fed off the boy's misery to replace what energy the disgusting leech of a hag had taken.

Possessing a body had once been as easy as sliding a hand into a silk glove. Now it took far more concentration. He hated the solidness of the boy, the cramped quarters, his human stench. More than anything, he hated feeling young and weak again, when he still had his past lifetime's long memories.

Over eight hundred years old and trapped in the body of a boy who couldn't tell the difference between a tharborough and a theorick! The Fates were so unkind!

Still, it was intriguing to look through the boy's memories. Horrifying, however, to see what had become of the human world. He had learned much in a few short hours and almost wished he hadn't seen the truth at all.

Alastor swung the human's legs off the couch and planted them carefully on the ground, mindful of the sleeping figures in the beds across from him and the annoying changeling dozing upon the witch's chest. How easy, he thought, it would be to make a run for it, heading straight back to Redhood to finish the curse he had begun years ago.

But he needed these flea-bitten, witless humans. Alastor's powers were growing back to their full strength, but if the wrong creature were to find him even a day too soon . . . well, it was simply not an option.

Alastor moved across the room, darting from shadow to shadow. The humans were breathing low and steady, fixed fast into sleep. The changeling's ears twitched at the sound of his faint steps, but its eyes did not snap open—Alastor waited, and nearly crowed in triumph when the creature merely turned over onto its side and began to snore loudly.

There was a reason changelings were hardly better than rodents to be exterminated in his realm. He'd heard that witches in the human realm had taken to them for their unshakable loyalty. Changelings imprinted upon the first being they saw as infants, binding themselves to their caretaker. More than that, they did, he could admit, make fair guards, as they possessed all of the excellent hearing and vision of their betters. That is, if they weren't sleeping.

More importantly, changelings could alter their appearance into anything, including malefactors and other superior fiends. That simply would not do. Every fiend Downstairs had a rightful place in the order of things. Anything that disrupted it, whether it be a changeling or a hag, had to be brought in line or permanently dealt with.

Still, Alastor felt a strange curiosity about the witch. Something tickled and nagged at the back of his memory when the boy glanced at her—an unlikely resemblance. He not resist the opportunity to examine her now.

He leaned in closer, inhaling the next soft breath she released. Yes, Alastor thought, this girl would surely fetch a high price Downstairs at the soul market. Such salty courage, tinged with bitter sadness. An irresistible mixture.

But it was her face that struck him now, being so similar to the servant girl he had been trapped inside. The one who had cried and begged as the fire was at her feet.

Like a wart grown back on his heart, stubbornly resisting his efforts now to cut it off, Alastor could not shake the image of the girl. He thought that it was a terrible thing, to not know her name, but to remember that her fear tasted metallic, like blood, and her pain, like ash.

He was a fiend of logic, and no part of him was willing to deny that the girl's death had, in turn, saved his own life. Without her fear and agony, there would not have been enough power in him to escape to the Inbetween, sleeping, biding his time until the witch's bloodline no longer walked the earth and he could return.

Dreaming all the while of what he would do to the Redding descendants.

Alastor cast a look around the room. He did not mean to go far, only to assess his new surroundings. The glimpses he had caught of this world on the drive in the horseless wagon (*car*, he corrected himself, when he remembered what the little witch had called it) had rattled him. He remembered Salem from his last life; he had visited it once with Honor Redding.

Honor Redding. It had been nearly four hundred years, and yet . . . it only felt like days since they had last met. Perhaps it was because the boy himself bore such a strong likeness to the young man Honor had been. Surely, the resemblance would not stop there. His sister, it seemed, had been born with a faulty heart, but the boy's weak heart was inherited, passed down from coward to coward. Alastor knew it would only be a matter of time before the boy agreed to a contract, much like Honor had.

Honor Redding had not been a friend. He had not even been a partner. Humans were the lowest form of life, tolerated only for the service their shades could provide. This boy was Honor's legacy—if he could just get the boy to agree to a contract, the energy formed from the new bond would feed him, and provide the last push of power needed to escape the child early, before the little witch and her father could bind him to another life-form and kill him.

Alastor was a reasonable sort. He could sacrifice owning those four souls, the boy's immediate family, if it meant hundreds more from the Redding family were at his disposal. He could summon the long-dead ones from the shade realm, and finally put them to use building a new palace for himself Downstairs.

The boy's arm, cut neat and quick by the cursed iron blade, hung useless at his side as he passed through the door into the hallway. He poked at the bats hanging from the ceiling, wondering how they could sleep so deeply—and in the company of humans, no less.

The rest of the house was enchanted—ghosts moved between the floors, mostly unseen. The magic here bloomed against the boy's skin like deadly nightshade, its wild wickedness both tainted and tamed by the pure hearts of the witches who defended this realm. Alastor reached the window in no time, but took a moment to sniff at the skeleton hanging there. It had a strange smell. Not the earthy reek of most humans, but a sort of hollow . . . burned *something*, perhaps. One he had never scented before. Why would a human keep such ruined bones?

Well, humans *were* strange, and stranger now than ever before. He turned back to the window, and thrust it open with the boy's one good arm. Ah. Yes. There was a long black ladder attached to the ledge. It was tricky business slithering out through it—business that was clearly below a being such as himself—but he continued wiggling and worming until he was balanced at the very top of the ladder.

"Egads." He gasped, feeling the freezing metal rock. With a loud creak, the ladder shot to the ground. The malefactor cursed in every language he knew, and several he didn't. The feet of the metal beast struck the wet earth and threw him off.

"A pox upon this house!" he hissed, raising a fist and shaking it.

Then Alastor, First Prince of the Realm, Master Collector of Souls and Commander of the First Battalion of Fiends, took in one deep breath of midnight air, and was off, running.

There was something very peculiar about this Salem.

His memories of his time here were dusty, but Alastor could not recall quite so many human houses, their lanterns blazing. Fiends had clearly failed in their duty of human population control, but it looked as though they had decorated the town themselves, adorning it with enormous spiderwebs, skeletons, and gravestones. If only the buildings were built from bone as well as stone, and spiraled up into the moonless sky like the towering homes Downstairs. Then Alastor might feel truly at ease. These humans and their square homes and slanted roofs. *Honestly.*

The boy's breath fanned out white against the cool night air, each exhalation escaping like a tiny, glowing shade. As he walked, weaving and bobbing between the houses, grass and brick gave way to a strange gray material, one that was as cracked and stained as an old tree elf's behind. Mindful of the tall humans watching him from across the street, Alastor forced the boy's body down into a squat and took in a deep breath of the hard substance. Satisfied with the chalky smell, he poked it with a single finger. Solid. Good. Above him, great poles held black boxes that flashed green, yellow, and red, over and over.

What language was this, he wondered, and what secrets did it hold?

"Speak to me, great blinking being," he called. "Tell me your truths!"

He pushed a button on one of the poles and watched as the pattern repeated, *green, yellow, red* again and again, each of the one hundred times he pushed it. He walked down the street and pushed the button there as well. But the lights only flashed *green, yellow, red*.

"Foul, toad-spotted dewberry! Dost thou mock me?" he hissed, when it was clear the great beings above his head would not converse with him. As he turned away, continuing his path along the odd silver snakelike path, the black box-like face of the creature shifted back to red. Just to be sure they knew his fury, he punched each button along the way.

Red was a good noble color, he decided, running the boy's hand along a low white fence. The pain that pricked the battered skin only fed him that much more. Red was life. It was the drip of blood from his enemy's fatal wounds. It was the color of anger, the most powerful of all energies.

But orange was the most cherished color Downstairs. It was the color of royalty, of superiority, of nourishment.

And there was much orange to be had in the Salem of this time. Parchment streamers wrapped around poles and dangled from trees like swaying spider legs. Flags with pumpkins fluttered, twitching and bobbing. One such flag stuck out from a pole, just low enough for the boy's arm to reach up and rip it away. He used the strings to affix it around his neck, already feeling more regal. He relished the bite of the howling wind.

Alastor stood with his face to it, letting it bring a bouquet of beautiful scents: waste, left too long in the sun, rotting vegetation from the dying leaves, and a perfectly putrid fishy odor wafting up from the nearby harbor.

Orange streamed down from the lanterns that lined the streets, high above him.

As he explored, he grew hungry. The face of the wooden house behind him, painted a hideous shade of pure white, was darkened. But there were two small rows of candle-like lights along the path that led up to the door. Even with the boy's weak eyes, he saw the spiderwebs draped from one of its front pillars to the other, and the small black creatures that looked to be crawling over it. He leaped over the low fence and allowed the boy's body to dance up to them, cooing with glee.

He ran the boy's fingers through the silky—yet not sticky?—web until he found what he was looking for: a pristine black spider, which he promptly popped into the boy's mouth.

"Ack! Ugh!" He flicked it out of the boy's mouth with his disturbingly pink human tongue. It was hard through and through—no crunchy shell with gooey innards. It didn't move or twitch when he bit down.

Alastor tried the next one, then the next, until they were all crammed into the boy's mouth. He spat them back out into the yard with one furious breath, and spun away, stalking down the path past the human bones half buried in the ground. But his journey had not been entirely in vain: for, just beside the blue door of the house, there lay another small button. And, unable to help himself, he jabbed a finger into its little glowing center.

Ding-dong! Ding-dong!

"*Noooooo.*" He covered the boy's ears and fled from the horrendous sound of bells. The lights in the nearby windows flared. Alastor stumbled down the path, tripping over an old tree's protruding root before reaching another fence. He tumbled over it, just as the door to the house opened, and an old crone stuck her face out.

"Hello? Is anyone there?"

So. These bells summoned humans. He would make certain to avoid them.

Alastor glanced around him, wondering why the boy's body seemed to be slightly sinking. The black dirt here was nearly turned, soft to the touch. Accounting for, he realized, the graves proudly displayed in front of this particular house. Clever humans, keeping their dead nearby. It would make for fertile breeding grounds for blood vipers, which would in turn hunt for changeling eggs and fairies.

He examined the gravestones smugly. Humans lived for such a short time, blissfully unaware of the other realms.

Poor Little Susie, one stone read, *her death was a doozy.* Another read, *I was Ted. Now I'm dead,* and the one beside it, *Mummy B. Ware.* The stones were small, and when he knocked on one, hollow—not stones at all! Alastor kicked over the scythe leaning against the nearby tree as he moved toward the low brick wall that separated the other side of that house from the road.

Then he saw him.

The fiend was no bigger than a human infant and strongly resembled one. But instead of the rosy blush of new human skin, the vampyre's flesh looked to have been cast out of white marble. Two long fangs hung still below unblinking black eyes. Alastor rushed up to it, seizing its dangling legs before he could stop himself.

The vampyre came crashing down against him, its hollow head knocking against the boy's. Its body was light, almost as if it was filled with air, but . . . squishy somehow.

"Zounds!" he said, gasping. "Longsharp! Longsharp, what hast become of thee, friend?" He had known this vampyre—or one that had looked nearly identical—Downstairs. They had played Pickle the Faerie together many times, and had even traded tips on the best way to get a lucky cat's tail without being mauled by the uncooperative feline's claws.

And now, Longsharp was . . . dead? Un-undead? Alastor shook the little body, trying to spark a reaction. When that didn't work, he set it down on the ground, but the vampyre's legs collapsed beneath him.

Perhaps vampyres in this world slept during the night, rather than the day? No, that wasn't right. Downstairs it was always night, and they could come and go as they pleased. But that had never been the case in the human world. The sun scorched them to dust (which in turn could be made into a fine cake batter, but that was beside the point). How foolish this vampyre had been to leave himself out in the open, unprotected.

Without another thought on the matter, Alastor picked up the body and tucked it under the boy's arm. He started through the fence, only to stop. A pumpkin, carved with a face like a troll, sat just beside where Longsharp had been.

Sniff. Sniff.

Of course. Orange—the color of sustenance. Of *food*. He snatched the pumpkin under his other arm and skipped off down the street with his bounty. It was hollowed out, but already tender as it began to rot. Perfection.

He had worried that he wouldn't be able to find the common, but there were signs aplenty and the walk was quite short. With the salty breath of the harbor to his left, he made his way to Salem Common, stopping only to pick up one more carved pumpkin.

The park seemed to be the only surviving section of the original settlement. Four-hundred-odd years had not struck Alastor as a particularly long time until he had seen the changes they had brought. The houses were wider, painted—something that, he noted, only the wealthiest could have afforded in the old days—and the roads wider, and painted with lines too. The first roar of the strange carriage—*car*—speeding past him had been enough to send him diving into the nearby shrubbery.

So this was the present, then. Loud, crowded, and altogether too clean. And not one bleeding spider to eat!

The trees in the common were cloaked in vibrant crimsons and golds, frosted with the cold night air. He claimed a seat on a nearby bench, the one closest to the magnificently reeking garbage canister so he might relish it, and set a still-sleeping Longsharp beside him.

The boy's skin prickled, numbed as he lifted the first pumpkin and bit into its smooth skin. Chewing happily, Alastor glanced up, searching for the moon through the overhead branches, trying to figure out the time of night. He knew it was most likely past the witching hour, but was still surprised there were no fiends out prowling. Surely there were errands that needed to be run. Imps sent out to gather the bones from cemeteries for their masters and mistresses, the shivering white light of a fetch sent to warn a human of a loved one's death. There was not even a goblin running his mischief.

Well. He had bigger concerns on his mind. The whole truth of it was this: He had not gone out that night only to see how Salem had done for itself. He had not gone just to find an escape route back to Redhood either. He needed fresh night air.

He needed to think.

Alastor needed to figure out which of his wretched siblings had helped the Reddings break their contract with him. Which of them had revealed his true name to Honor Redding.

He'd nearly given up his own shade when the boy had asked about the names of fiends. He pulled his cape tighter around the maggot's shoulders, his pitifully thin skin. How dangerously close he'd come to revealing the one way a Malefactor could be controlled . . . and how foolish the boy had been to not put the matter together.

Cheered by that last thought, he used the boy's teeth to gnaw on the remainder of the pumpkin before turning to the next, smaller one. Soon enough, the human's belly was distended, and Alastor himself was finally full. He belched, interrupting the twittering of small creatures in the trees overhead, impatient for morning.

He leaned back against the wet wood bench and considered them. Downstairs, in his own land, he might have looked up and seen those pernicious little faeries chirping in the branches. Or brainless golems taking their halting steps down the crooked cobblestone streets running errands for their masters. The animals of this world were . . . cuddlier.

For one brief, terrible moment, Alastor allowed himself to wonder if his own realm had been as altered by time as the human realm had. Even fiends were not immune to changing tastes and improvements. Would the buildings still be made of shining black stones? Would they still lean, like hunched shoulders, over the already crowded streets?

Were the souls he had already collected still there, serving his father, the king?

Other questions came flooding in. Had one of his five brothers taken the throne that was rightfully his? He was the first son, but his younger brother Bune, the one born only a few years after Alastor, had always eyed their father's throne with eyes that gleamed like fire. Surely he was behind this, but how had he learned Alastor's true, secret name, and *why* had he betrayed his own kin to the humans?

"Thou knowest why," he muttered. It was no different from what Alastor himself would do, were *he* second in line to the throne of Downstairs. Kill the heir, so he was no longer the spare.

"I will crack thy toes," he swore, "and make boots of thy intestines."

Was his precious young sister still Downstairs, or had they sent her up to begin her own Collection? He sighed, unable to picture it. Bune and his three other brothers had tormented her, sliced at her every nerve, clawed at her honor, and haunted her courage. All because she could not manifest an animal form, and therefore could not travel into the human realm. His own, the fox, was said to represent cleverness, as much as Bune's great, snarling cat was strength.

It was the greatest of all disappointments to have a malefactor without an animal form in one's bloodline, because it spoke of a flaw. It was so dishonorable, so shameful, Pyra, and all malefactors like her, were locked away to save the families from disgrace.

But Alastor knew Pyra's situation was like an eclipse. Soon the darkness that shadowed her life in the tower would pass, and she would find that small glowing part of her shade that could transform, that could show to all realms her gifts. Perhaps it already had, and she walked among humans now, forming contracts, collecting human shades.

The idea of Pyra dealing with the ruckus and danger of the human world made him feel as hollow as the boy's limp, useless arm.

Finished with his meal, Alastor made the boy stand and flung his makeshift cape out behind him. Before he could take another step, something bright—something strikingly *orange*—caught his eye.

Near the edge of the silver, chalky path was the finest hat he'd ever laid his eyes upon. Its base was square, but from it rose a beautiful, dirt-splattered cone, rising to a magnificent point. Left, for anyone to find.

Left for *him*, as if by fate!

He was surprised to find that its coating felt so very . . . waxy, like a dead man's skin. The weight of it too was surprising, as was the rather large hole at its base. The boy had a tiny head to match his tiny brain, it seemed. As long as the boy's puny neck was strong enough to bear its magnificence, he would wear it with pride.

Alastor easily balanced it as he carried Longsharp to the other side of the street, crossing into a narrow brick lane—some sort of promenade? There were few like this Downstairs, strips of shops where one might buy wares and goods. That, at least, held true here. The moon was high and bright enough that he could even catch a hint of his reflection in the nearest window.

"Mortal *fools*," he scoffed, admiring himself in his new cap and cape.

Then, before he could accidentally summon another fiend, the way he had the hag, he moved on to the next shop, which displayed crates of hideously bright sweets.

It was something of a strange coincidence that he smelled it then. The boy's nose was inferior to his own, but the wind was fierce that night, prowling up and down the streets, stirring up memories and old dust. The fallen leaves suddenly swirled around him, rising toward the moon. It picked up traces of the hob's delightful vinegar smell and swirled them straight to Alastor.

He tucked his vampyre friend beneath his working arm once more, and began to sniff.

After nearly a quarter hour of searching, Alastor found the hob behind an alley of several glass storefronts. The boy's weak eyes skimmed right over it, but there was no mistaking that sweet, sweet stench of rotten fruit.

Hobgoblins were prized servants Downstairs, a race

trained to clean and care for their superiors. At the Black Palace, Alastor had his own army of them to tend to his clothing, carry his messages, and spy on his brothers.

Human shades were the true workers of the realm, cursed for all eternity to perform duties like scrubbing sewers, or picking fruit from the fields of razor-sharp ganglebushes. Hobs were cherished, trusted to perform their tasks without complaint. Hob families stayed with the families of fiends, including Alastor's own, for centuries. His own nannyhob had been the daughter of his father's nannyhob, who had been the daughter of his grandfather's nannyhob.

Hobs stood about the height of a human infant, their skin a delightful shade of ash gray. Alastor was particularly fond of their bright yellow eyes, which bulged out from above a handsome nose as red and round as a radish. The true mark of a hob, however, was the snarfing, snorting, wheezing breaths they took as they tried to sniff out filth to clean.

And so Alastor was quite surprised to find this one wearing a half-rotten pumpkin dangling from his long, curved red horns. There were no gold hoops in his ears to mark his years of service. Instead of the pristine white spider silk the hobs Downstairs preferred, this one wore a dress of sorts made out of newspaper and something silver. It crinkled as the hob swung a twig at a hissing feral cat. The hob, it appeared, was guarding a tower of tidied rubbish—boxes, bright containers, and cartons stacked to look like a castle.

"BEGONE!" The boy's voice squeaked, but it was enough to spook the kitten. It bolted farther into the alley and disappeared into the night.

Alastor stood, waiting to be formally addressed, but the hob only sighed and moved back toward his creation. With careful certainty, he placed his sword stick over the opening of a box that read HEINZ KETCHUP and crawled inside on bony hands and knees.

Surely this was all in jest. . . . Alastor cleared his throat. When the hob still didn't reappear, he coughed. Loudly.

Finally, just as he began to detect the faint wheezy snores of the blasted creature, he called out, "Servant, I require thy attention. Be present and willing, and, in exchange, I offer thee—erm." Alastor paused, glancing around. Longsharp was beginning to feel heavy in his arm, so he set him down and picked up a sickly-looking apple. "I offer you this rare fruit."

All he could see were the hob's eyes, glowing in the darkness of his home.

"Do you accept these terms?"

It was a long while before the hob answered. "I do not. I do not serve humans. Blegh!"

"Come out into the night," Alastor commanded. "For I am no human."

"No." The creature took a deep breath and, with a sound like a cannon explosion, plugged up one side of his nose and blew a wad of blue snot on the boy's bare feet.

"Hob!" Alastor cried. "Zounds! Would a mere mortal be able to hear thee? Speak to thee?"

The hob seemed to consider this. "I think not."

"Then it stands to reason I am no human, yes?" Alastor began to unwrap the bandages on the boy's arm. The cut itself was still a furious red, blood oozing past black scabs. The air bloomed with the metallic smell of it. He could hear the hob take one rattling deep breath, then another.

"M-milord?" came the small voice from inside the box. "You are . . ."

Fiends could tell everything they needed to know about another fiend by their smell. Though his own scent was dampened by the boy's disgustingly flowery one, it revealed Alastor for what he was: a malefactor, and a prince.

The hob shot out of its home and fell upon the boy's feet, weeping. "Forgive me, milord! I am but a stupid creature, I have shamed myself—you must take a horn, please! You must!"

When a hob displeased his or her master, the most common punishment was to remove one of the curved horns. For the first time, Alastor noticed this hob was already missing one.

"It would not please me to punish thee now, servant. Thou may, however, clean me."

The hob went to work immediately, licking his snot off the boy's toes, licking away the dirt there, working his way straight up until he reached the knee. Alastor stood with his hands clasped behind his back, enjoying the warm slime of the fiend's spit coating his skin. The smell of rot it left behind lifted his spirits somewhat.

"Now, pray tell, what is thy name?"

The hob kept his eyes on the ground. "It be Nightlock."

"Nightlock," Alastor repeated. "A fine name. Thou may refer to me as my lord and master, or My Eternal Prince of Nightmares that Lurk in Every Dark Sleep."

"My—my lord and master, I do not mean to be—to be rude, and yet this hob wonders," Nightlock began, his one ear twitching in fear, "how is it that you appear in the form of a human? Your magic is great, yes, but why, oh *why*, must you shame yourself this way?"

"I am in hiding," Alastor said. "None of my kind may know I am here. That is your first command."

He could see by the look in the fiend's eyes that Nightlock was attempting to figure out who he was—which one of the six siblings Alastor would claim to be.

"Tell me," he asked, "are there many of our kind left in this village?"

"Oh, milord!" the hob said, his eyes shining with dark blue tears. "A few, oh yes, a few, but this place is cursed. I and the others, we are hiding too."

"What news from Downstairs?" Alastor asked. "How do our kind fare?"

A look of deep sadness passed over the hob's face like a cloud over the moon. "I could not speak of it, even if I wished to. Not even under milord's command."

Alastor felt something icy pierce his chest. The boy's chest, rather.

"They have locked the gates and allow no one to enter," Nightlock explained. "And those who are cast out are banished, and shall never be allowed to return."

"That is—" Alastor swallowed hard, fighting against the tension of the boy's body. "That is preposterous. Who issued such a command? Who reigns on the black throne?"

The rotting pumpkin slid down over the hob's face as he bowed his head in shame.

"One," he said, "who has taken care to charm their name so that it may not be spoken in this world."

Of all the fiends, only a malefactor could have the kind of power needed for such a curse.

"Milord, *milord*," the hob wailed. "I be so very sorry. Ask this hob for anything else, to do anything, and he is your servant until the realms collapse!"

"Nonsense," Alastor said, turning to pick up Longsharp. His mind spun with possibilities. His father? No—why would he need a curse? Fiends feared him already. One of his brothers, then, or perhaps a family rival? It sounded like a witch's curse, but there was no way that could be true. When a witch traveled Downstairs, her power quickly waned to nothing.

When he turned back around, Nightlock was no longer crying or snarfing, and the adorable glob of snot dribbling from his nose had slowed to one long strand. Nightlock was no longer afraid to lift his gaze from the ground. He stared at Longsharp, his bright yellow eyes bulging out of his perfectly round skull.

"If milord requires a doll, I can craft a magnificent one," he said, practically trembling in anticipation of it. "My last mistress loved toys. It is one of my many skills."

A toy? Alastor looked down on the face of the vampyre again. The eyes, which had seemed so red and glossy and perfect before, now looked like nothing more than glass. He licked one to be sure.

"I see," Alastor said in a prim voice, letting the doll fall to the ground by his feet. The hob quickly and carefully set it aside, finding a new place for it.

"Are you hungry, Master?" the hob asked, filling the silence between them. He reached for a bag, labeled with the words KITTY LITTER, and offered Alastor a handful of shimmering, coarse sand. The malefactor licked it out of the boy's palm, humming thoughtfully.

"Now, servant, we must begin to plot a course of action. The boy whose body I reside in must agree to a contract within twelve nights. As it stands, he has refused."

The hob made a startled sound, his spittle flying through the air. "He has refused your offering? He has a will so strong? Your persuasion is legendary, milord—"

"Yes, yes," Alastor said, flicking a hand dismissively. "The urchin has not given in to fear, nor has he bowed to threats. Perhaps if I were to keep at it . . . make the threats all the more terrifying . . ."

"What does he desire, milord?" the hob asked, handing him another scoop of the crunchy kitty litter.

"One thing too pitiful to name," Alastor responded. *Acceptance.* Little did the boy know that the pursuit of such a thing would mean he'd remain forever unhappy.

"Then . . . maybe . . . does this urchin know what else you can give him?" Nightlock asked. "Is it not the case with these humans that they must be shown they desire something before they know they desire it?"

Alastor looked to the moon, thumping the boy's fist against his chest. He was a genius of the first order, a true prince. "The solution has just come to me, Nightlock. Dost thou—do *you* know that humans often do not know they wish for a worldly good until they see it?"

"No, milord," the hob said quickly, "this hob knew no such thing."

Alastor gripped his cap and set his cape to twirling as he spun back toward the little witch's house, a new plan spinning and swirling like a poison inside him. "Come, servant. The moon sets, and this fiend rises."

The New Kid

I woke up the next morning feeling like I hadn't slept at all.

For a few minutes I just lay there on the couch under a mountain of blankets, watching the sun reluctantly come out and brighten the attic. I closed my eyes, waiting to hear Mom's voice call up to me that it was time to get ready. The only sounds in the room were Toad's trumpet-like snores and Nell tossing around in her bed.

"Come on, get up," I muttered, thinking of what Dad always said. "The sooner you start, the sooner you finish."

Another first day of school. My stomach lurched at the realization as I stumbled toward the bathroom. I felt heavy at my center, like dread had planted itself inside me and was taking root with its crawling, dark limbs.

That's it, Maggot, the fiend said cheerfully. *Your sadness is all I require. Revel in it, drown in it . . .*

I locked the bathroom door and turned the shower on, icy water spraying my bare arm. It hurt, deep in my heart. The clash of frustration and sadness slamming together left a ringing sound in my ears. I pressed my fists to my forehead, filling my lungs with the moist, warming air rising from the claw-foot tub.

If I couldn't think of my family without feeding Alastor more of my power, then I would do everything to avoid bringing them to mind for as long as I could. And, really, any day that didn't start with a malefactor singing about all the ways he could pickle my brain was bound to be a good one, right?

I jumped into the water, quickly washing my hair and scrubbing my skin with an alarmingly black bar of soap peppered with tiny flowers and herbs. The tincture that they'd given me hadn't taken care of all of the thin, angry scratches on my hands and arms—unless Toad had clawed me at some point in the night, which didn't seem too far-fetched. Dirt and grime swirled off my feet, dancing down the drain. I squinted down at it through the misty condensation, wondering how it was possible for the attic floors to have been that filthy.

By the time I finished and dressed in the jeans, T-shirt, and hoodie I'd found folded at the foot of the couch, I wondered where and how I'd get a school uniform, only to realize there probably wasn't one.

No uniform. For the first time ever—*no uniform.*

Toad was the first to wake, yawning. Rather than stay under the covers, he flew over to the window and nudged it open, slipping outside and flying away. To do . . . his business? Find food?

The floor was freezing under my wet toes. I hopped from foot to foot in front of the heater, trying to wake the thing up to its usual warm grumbles. When it became clear Nell probably had to use some magic to get it working, I gave up and headed for the fridge, shivering.

Mom taught me and Prue a lot about cooking, so I did think I could whip something up. It was just . . . there wasn't a whole lot to whip. Three eggs and one yogurt that smelled like it had enticed a rat to crawl inside of it and die.

Most of the house's pots and pans were in use, either to grow some little plant or catch rain from holes in the roof. The ones that weren't were covered in a mysterious, sticky gunk. I picked up a few from the desk and sniffed them. They smelled like old, wilted vegetables. I ended up cracking the eggs, dividing them between three chipped mugs, and zapping them to maximum fluffiness in the microwave.

It was the machine's beeping and the smell of food that finally got the mole creatures out of their nest of bedding. I took a step back as they came stumbling toward me, their hands blindly reaching for the hot mugs like a matching set of zombies.

They collapsed down around the small coffee table in front of my bed-couch, shoveling egg into their mouths, glaring at anything and everything that moved, including the window curtains. They didn't start looking like humans again until after they finished eating.

"Neither of us is much for mornings," Uncle Barnabas said once Nell had swept her clothes out of the old trunk at the foot of her bed and slammed the bathroom door behind her.

"I couldn't tell," I said drily.

He straightened out his black polo shirt and tucked it the rest of the way in his pants. Uncle Barnabas had explained the night before that he worked two day jobs on and off throughout the week. Monday, Wednesday, Friday in the Witch History Museum. Tuesday, Thursday, and Saturday in Salem's Pioneer Village, a "living history museum" full of men and women dressed and acting like they were Puritans in the 1630s. Which . . . sounded a lot like home, actually. At least it explained Uncle Barnabas's strange clothes on Founder's Day.

"That's okay," I said, folding the sheets and straightening out the pillows on my couch-bed. Seeing that Nell and Uncle Barnabas hadn't bothered, I made their beds too.

"I'm sorry I can't take you to school myself, but Cornelia

will get you all sorted out," Uncle Barnabas said, pulling on a gray fleece with the museum's logo.

The tight fist around my stomach was back. "Are you sure I have to go?"

"You'd rather stay here?" Uncle Barnabas raised a brow and looked around. I saw his point. It would be freezing and kind of lonely, but it wasn't like I was a stranger to either of those feelings. "Believe me, nothing can crack the coven's protection spell. You'll be safe there, and the rest is up to you."

The bathroom door burst open, and Nell came strolling out. Her outfit had been downgraded from yesterday's radioactive rainbow to jeans, a yellow T-shirt, and a purple sweater. It was her *hair* that was wild—braided and pinned in every direction over the top of her head, like a futuristic milkmaid.

"That's an . . . interesting hairdo," Uncle Barnabas managed to squeeze out. His arm tightened around my shoulder.

Nell's hand floated up to touch the braid across her forehead, her smile falling. "Why? What's wrong with it?"

Uncle Barnabas looked like he'd realized he stepped on a piece of gum. He started shaking his hands, like he could wave his words away. "Nothing's wrong with it. Looks great, Cornelia. Do you have everything you need for your cousin today?"

She sat down on the floor to tug on a pair of slouchy

black boots, her chin tucked against her chest so we couldn't see her face. After a second, she started to unpin the braids, one at a time, shaking her tight curls out.

I started to say something, but she disappeared under her bed, pushing aside a small, clear tub of her clothes to grab a beat-up gray messenger bag and a black North Face fleece. She sent both of them sliding across the floor to my feet.

"Here," she said. "You can use these for now. I put some notebooks and pens in there, but we'll have to borrow books from the library."

Someone—Nell, obviously—had written the words *What's past is prologue* in black ink on the gray bag. I brushed both it and the fleece off, trying not to cough with the dust.

"Don't stay too late at work tonight," Nell said, sliding her backpack onto her shoulder. "We have the thing tonight, remember?"

Uncle Barnabas cocked his head to the side, staring at her.

"The *audition*," she reminded him. "The tour companies?"

"Oh yes, yes, I remember now," he said, waving a hand. "I'll be home by six at the latest."

"Why?" I asked. "What kind of audition is this?"

"Nell had the idea to partner with some of the local tour-guide groups so tourists are guaranteed to end their night coming through the House of Seven Terrors," Uncle

Barnabas said, sounding distracted as he gathered up a small pile of books and papers.

Meaning a steady stream of guests and revenue. I looked at Nell in admiration. It was beyond smart.

After saying good-bye to Uncle Barnabas, Nell and I went down the back stairs of the house, avoiding the monster floors. We barely made it in time to catch the yellow school bus at the corner.

Nell kept her head down, ignoring the way the conversations around us died as we walked down the aisle, heading toward the back of the bus. I was so distracted by the way the other kids stared at us, whispering, I didn't even think to look back at the outside of the House of Seven Terrors until we were pulling away.

It looked like one house had been stacked atop another and the two awkwardly nailed together. Both halves were crooked, and with its dark wood and nearly black exterior, it looked like a crow in the middle of a long row of doves. The hand-painted sign outside that read WELCOME TO YOUR NIGHTMARE really added to the dire look. Or maybe it was just the fake blood splattered on it.

But the sick feeling in my already tight stomach had nothing to do with the house and everything to do with the weight of the eyes on me, picking me apart.

Wait. For once, they weren't whispering about me.

"The freak has a new friend," someone said from across the aisle. "Or is it her *boyfriend*?"

Anger prickling, I turned toward the direction of the girl's voice, but Nell gripped me by the collar and turned me back toward the window.

"Just ignore them," she muttered. "They'll get bored eventually. Look—there's the House of Seven Gables."

Another dark wood house zoomed by in a blur.

"The inspiration for your haunted house?" I guessed.

"Mom's," Nell said, leaning her forehead against the window. "The haunted house was her idea. We had just finished the last rooms when . . ."

I knew what she was about to say: *when she passed away.* Her mother hadn't gotten to see the haunted house up and running. I bit the inside of my mouth, wondering what I could say to make it better.

"Do you know that story?" she asked. "*The House of the Seven Gables?*"

"Uh, am I supposed to?"

"It's an old Nathaniel Hawthorne book, all about one family betraying another and basically stealing their fortune and secrets. And revenge." The bus lurched to a stop, throwing us both against the seat in front of us. "They turned the real House of the Seven Gables into a museum, and it's a tourist's dream. We pick up a lot of business being only two blocks away, and the people there even let us leave flyers to advertise. The haunted houses near the common are a little more successful, but I think we have a good word of mouth going. If we can seal the deal with these tourist agencies, we'll be set for years. We might even be able to redo the attic so we don't feel like we're nesting up there like owls."

I nodded, turning more fully to watch the town stream by. On first glance, Salem looked a lot like Redhood. It was the same kind of colonial architecture, the same narrow roads that wound up and down and around the same fire-gold maple leaves. Even the view of the glittering water out on the wharf we passed, the dozens of small boats docked there, felt as familiar as the lines of my palms.

I closed my eyes, trying to commit it all to memory for later, wondering how I would ever be able to capture the way the golden morning light flickered against the silvery river water.

But there was one key difference between Salem and Redhood. When you drove through our part of the Cape, it looked like a living history museum. There were rules about the height of trees on the lawns, about what your driveway could be made of, about how many holiday decorations you could put out, and for how long.

But Salem looked *lived*-in. The kids around me were in sweaters and jeans, flicking through their phones or reading. No designer purses, or stuffy uniforms, or shoes expensive enough to feed a family for months. The homes were dressed in autumn glory, spilling over with the spirit of the season.

Piles of leaves had been gathered to be burned or carted off. Beyond them, though, fake skeletons paraded and danced around lawns, and stuffed witches clutched their wicker broomsticks. Jack-o'-lanterns invaded walls, porches, gates, grinning maniacally as we drove past them.

The center of town seemed to be where most of the tourist stuff was located, including the witch museum and some kind of cemetery—maybe where they had buried some of the accused witches? The rest was all residential, with a few plain, modern strip malls and shopping centers that would have made Grandmother clutch her pearls in dismay.

It felt warm and loved, like a favorite sweater. There was excitement buzzing through the air, lighting the faces of the tourists who were milling around in packs—none of the careful, reserved demeanor of the old families of Redhood. Salem looked like how I always pictured *normal*.

"Fiends wear hats like that," Nell said quietly, following my gaze to a house with black pointy hats dangling from the front lawn's maple tree. "Not witches."

Before I could answer, I heard someone snicker behind us. *"Witches?"*

I sat up and craned my neck around, peering over the green vinyl of our seat. Two boys who looked to be about my age were staring at the back of Nell's head. One brought up a hand, a small wad of wet paper pinched between his fingers. Poised to throw.

Having been on the receiving end of way too many spit-balls to count, I threw a hand out just as the boy launched it. It stuck to my palm with a sickening *thwack*. I looked at it and grimaced. Great. He'd laced gum in it, too.

"What's your problem?" I demanded, ignoring Nell as she tried to pull my arm down.

"*Oooooooh,*" the boys crooned back. One wore a shirt that read SALEM TRACK AND FIELD. Blond hair stuck out from under his baseball hat. The other, the one who'd actually thrown the spitball, had darker skin and hair, and was big enough to look like he was a year or two older than us.

Nell yanked me down with a furious look. "I can take care of myself!" she whispered.

"Really? That was taking care of yourself?"

The bus's brakes shrieked as the driver pulled into the drop-off lane. Nell glanced back over her shoulder once, and just as we were about to come to a complete stop, she tilted her head toward the boys.

They slammed face-first into the back of the seat in front of them.

"They really need to get the brakes on this thing checked," she said casually to me, standing to collect her backpack.

"Definitely," I agreed.

The bigger kid had blood spurting from his nose onto his plaid shirt. As he shoved his way up the aisle, shouldering kids aside, Nell said sweetly, "You should probably go see the nurse about that. It looks painful."

His eyes narrowed to slits as he spun away. His friend, the one in the track shirt, shot Nell a curious look.

"He hates that you ignore him," the boy told her, sounding at least a little apologetic.

"Whatever, Parker," she said. "You don't reward your dogs for their bad behavior, do you?"

Before he could respond, she tugged me up and off our seat. The cold morning wind tugged at us as we stepped off the bus and fell into the herd of kids shuffling toward the brick building.

Thump, thump, thump went my heart.

Twist, twist, twist went my stomach.

Ha! Ha! Ha! went the fiend, sounding like he was basking in my anxiety, rolling through it like a flower field.

I took a step forward, ignoring Nell's quiet, frantic *"Wait!"*

Too late.

It felt like I had walked into an electric fence. A white-hot current ripped through me, throwing me back a few steps. When I opened my eyes, I half expected to see my clothes charred.

"Wow, cousin," Nell said loudly, "you are *so* clumsy!"

The other students glanced down at me in alarm or ignored me altogether as she helped me back to my feet. The blood drained from my face, leaving it numb.

"The protection spell," she whispered. "You have a fiend in you. I have to invite you to pass through the boundary."

She maneuvered so she stood facing me, with her back to the school. I saw the perimeter of magic now, the way it rippled a faint green against the air.

"Come in, come in," Nell whispered, holding out a hand. *"And let our work begin."*

Glancing around to make sure no one had heard or was watching, I took a tentative step forward. This time, I passed through without so much as an errant breeze to greet me. "Do all spells have to rhyme?"

"No, they're just easier to remember that way," Nell muttered. "Come on. We're going to be late."

But my feet wouldn't budge, no matter how much I tried to convince myself to take another step forward. *The sooner you begin, the sooner it'll be over. The sooner you begin, the sooner it'll be over. . . .*

Nell glanced at me once, then led me off to the side toward a cement planter, out of everyone else's way.

"Can't we just ditch?" I asked finally. "I won't tell if you won't!"

Nell did not look impressed by the suggestion.

"Is that how you get out of things you don't want to do at home? You just skip out on them?" She shook her head. "Come on, *cuz*. As Shakespeare said, it's time to screw your courage to the sticking-place."

"What does that even mean?"

"It *means*," Nell said, yanking on my arm, "time to suck it up and put your big-boy panties on."

I glared and reluctantly followed her up the cement steps, my hand trailing along the metal guardrail. It seemed like there were two separate wings of the school, attached by these cool enclosed glass walkways; even now I could see kids walking through them. To my right was an official-looking man, tugging the American and Massachusetts state flags up the pole, barking at the students standing on the patch of grass marked with several signs that read DO NOT TREAD ON THE WINTER GRASS.

"Nell, hey!"

She and I turned as one. My eyes scanned the kids coming up the stairs until I landed on the boy who was waving enthusiastically at us. Nell laughed and waved back.

"You missed school last week, I was worried," he said, huffing as he jumped up the last two steps. I stared at him, eyes growing wider by the second. Every single bit of the clothing he wore—socks, shoes, pants, shirt, sweater, hat— was a bright shade of blue.

"Is everything okay?" he asked, then did a double take as he saw me. "Were you that upset about the play?"

"The play?" I repeated, and it was only then that the kid seemed to notice me.

"The school play," he clarified. "Who are you?"

"Why would you be upset about the school play?" I asked Nell, something tickling at the back of my mind.

She ignored me, as usual. "Everything's fine, Norton. And he's my cousin. He's temporarily enrolling for the next few weeks while his parents travel the world."

The kid stuck out his hand, gripping mine in a crushing shake. If he noticed that the other kids were giving him a wide berth, he didn't seem to care.

"Nice to meet blue—er, *you*," I said. "Um . . . sorry about that, it's just . . ."

He was . . . so . . . blue . . . ?

"Norton is participating in a performance-art piece," Nell explained. "He only wears one color a day, and it reflects his mood." She turned back to Norton, watching him dig through his brown lunch bag. "Why so blue today, Nortie?"

He dug a hand into the lunch bag and fished out a plastic sandwich bag. "Mom only had bread ends left."

"That does suck," I agreed.

"Anyway, nice to meet you—maybe we'll have some classes together?" he said, with hope curling in his voice.

"I have no idea," I told him honestly. "Nice to meet you, though."

At the top of the steps, just before we reached the door, Nell reached into her backpack and pulled out a red file folder.

"What's that?" I asked.

"Your new life," she said.

The first bell rang, but neither of us moved.

"Hey, I know this has been . . . *really awful* is kind of an understatement, isn't it? But I just want to say . . ." Her lips pressed together. "I just wanted to say that you should listen to what my dad said and see this as a fresh start. You aren't a Redding here. No one knows your name. Maybe it'll be easier for you to act like the person you want to be, instead of the person you think you are."

"So I'm just supposed to *pretend* to be something I'm not?" I demanded. "What if I don't know how to do that?"

"It's easier than you think," Nell said. "It's method acting—you *become* the character, living and breathing life into him, creating him from what bare-bones info we've given you. There are no mistakes, just constant creation." Nell opened the file for me to see. "Your name is Ethan White, and you were born in Portland, Maine, on December twenty-second to Mary and John White. The rest is up to you to decide."

The doors to the school opened with a burst of warm air, but I couldn't tear my eyes away from the file, even as Nell continued her lightning-tongue pace. "It's easy once you get used to it. And I'll be here to help you. Because, you know, it doesn't matter how great the lead cast is if the supporting actors don't back them up."

The folder was filled with a xeroxed copy of a birth certificate for one Ethan White, who was definitely not a twin. A fake list of vaccinations was stapled to it, along with fake report cards from some middle school in Portland, and copies of two driver's licenses—one for Mary Elizabeth White, a dark-haired woman with a too-perfect smile, and another for John Adams White, six-feet-two-inches and 220 pounds of pure stranger.

"You know, it's okay to pretend to be braver than you are," Nell said, stepping inside. "I do it all the time."

Of Myth and Legend

It was a good thing that I liked Nell okay for the most part, since we had *every single class* together—well, every class but one. An elective. Nell was enrolled in theater, but I was stuck with a study hour in the library during the last hour of the day.

"Ready or not," she said, handing me a printout of my schedule as we walked down the hall. "Here we go."

And just like that, I was shaking hands with Mrs. Anderson, my new science teacher. I had her first thing in the morning for homeroom to listen to announcements and do the whole Pledge of Allegiance thing, but I wouldn't be back until later that afternoon for real class. I sat with Nell at the very back of the classroom, staring at the two aquariums that lined the side of the bright room: one with swarms of rainbow fish, the other with an extremely large, extremely hairy tarantula named Eleanor.

Thinking of my task from Uncle Barnabas, I pointed to it, raising my brows.

Nell shook her head, writing down on her notebook, *Find one we don't have to steal, you idiot.* Then she added, *Eleanor isn't what you think. Try a lizard or frog.*

A frog! It was the first time Al had spoken since earlier that morning. His presence had turned into a hum of static in my body. Sometimes it intensified, like he was trying to listen or do something. Other times, it was so quiet I could almost forget he was there at all.

I walked through the day in an overwhelmed daze. I had the weirdest feeling that I was outside my own body, watching myself move through the yellow-tiled hallways and their red lockers. From door to door, class to class, hour to hour.

Second period was language arts, with Ms. Mell—a young, blond teacher who had the nervous habit of lecturing about pronouns to the floor instead of to us.

Then it was off to third period for pre-algebra with Mrs. Johnson, who called on me for every single question, either because she was trying to force herself to learn my name, or just to torture me.

Fourth period was humanities with Mr. Gupta. Redhood Academy had combined language arts and humanities into one class—English—so it was actually kind of awesome when I found out that the class was dedicated to studying all kinds of famous works: writing, poetry, mythology, and actual art. And no boring grammar rules.

Mr. Gupta drummed his hands against his desk. "It's time . . . for another round of It's All Greek to Me! Which team will reign supreme and ascend to the heights of Mount Olympus and feast on the ambrosia of a magnificent pizza lunch?"

Mr. Gupta really loved teaching his Greek mythology unit.

Around me, Nell and the other students were shifting their desks, reluctantly scooting them so there was a clear divide between each side of the room. My team was slumped in their chairs or sneaking looks at their phones in their backpacks.

"We never win," Nell explained in a whisper. "I know that'll be a change of pace for you, but try not to sulk."

A change of pace for me . . . ? The last thing I'd won in life was a Silence Cake–eating contest, and only because the guy next to me barfed in his mouth and was disqualified. But before I could explain that, the trivia battle began.

"Why did Athena and Poseidon compete with one another?" Mr. Gupta asked.

Hey—I knew that one. Dad and I used to pore over this amazing mythology book each night before bed. I started to raise my hand, but the guy from the bus, the one with the baseball cap—now hatless, thanks to school rules—shot his hand up into the air.

What art thou . . . you doing? Alastor demanded. *Answer the man, fool!*

Al clearly did not understand the rules of this game, if he understood the concept of "rules" at all.

"Yes, Parker?" Mr. Gupta called.

"When Athens was being founded, they competed to see who the Greeks would choose to name the city after," he said while his team pounded their desks in approval. "Poseidon could only give them salt water, which isn't exactly useful. But Athena gave the people an olive tree, which they could use, so they named the city after her instead."

"That's correct!" Mr. Gupta said, marking one point for Team Two on the whiteboard. "Next question, my demigods. Who searched for the Golden Fleece?"

That was easy. Jason and the Argonauts.

You must answer *the man, Maggot, not bask in your own brilliance!* Alastor growled. *The other team conquers yours!*

The girl beside me, Anna, was quick to answer. "Perseus?"

Ack, *no*—

"I'm sorry, that's incorrect. Team Two?"

It was clear that Parker was the key to their success. He smiled smugly before answering, "Jason and the Argonauts."

We do not like him. Alastor's voice was flat and cold. *Do not allow him to take your throne of . . . this . . . pizza.*

A sharp elbow jabbed into my side as I raised my hand to answer Mr. Gupta's question about Zeus's wife.

"Hera," I said. Finally, we were on the board. A boy sitting opposite Nell looked up from where he was knotting and unknotting his sweatshirt strings.

"Holy crap, we have a point," he said, ignoring Mr. Gupta's warning: "Language!"

It went back and forth between the two teams. A girl sitting a few seats behind me answered the next one, which sparked another girl into answering the one after that.

"Who completed the Twelve Labors?"

Another point for our team. It volleyed back and forth and back and forth until there was only one question left, and we were, of course, tied.

"And now . . . for the pizza party," Mr. Gupta said, deepening his already deep voice. "Who killed the Chimera?"

I knew this one. . . . I *knew it.* . . . Dad and I had read this story together a few times, but I couldn't pull the name out, it was on the tip of my tongue. It started with a *P*—no, with a *B*, didn't it? I glanced over at Parker, who was staring at the ceiling, squinting hard in thought.

Come on, come on . . .

"Someone must know this," Mr. Gupta said. "*Suuuurely* you all did your reading?"

There was the sound of uncomfortable shifting. Chairs creaking.

Then the memory rose, floating up like a feather. A voice at the back of my mind whispered the answer. I lifted a tentative hand, swallowing my nerves.

"Yes, Ethan?" Mr. Gupta asked.

Don't let me mess up . . . Nell's eyes bored into the side of my head. Everyone's did.

"Bellerophon," I said.

Mr. Gupta was silent for a beat.

Then he grinned. "That's correct!"

"Yessssssssss!" The kid beside me, Blake, pumped both fists into the air like I'd just won us a gold medal at the Olympics. Blood rushed to my face as my teammates pounded the top of their desks.

"Oh my God, we *never* win—no one can beat Parker! Good job, Ethan!" a girl—Sara, I think—said. On the other side of the room, Parker scowled in my direction, quickly looking away to stuff his notebook into his backpack.

It is a difficult thing, to lose, Alastor mused with a smirk in his voice, ***when one is so accustomed to winning. Soon your family will understand that too.***

Go away, I thought, irritated. *I'm having a moment, here.*

"We don't suck! We don't suck!" Blake's friends began to chant.

Each word, each new voice adding to it, jabbed at my own excitement, until it deflated completely. An uneasiness stirred inside of me, a flutter of unhappiness.

Congratulations, Maggot, Alastor said, sounding unusually pleased. *It feels rather tremendous, does it not—being a winner?*

Winning classroom trivia doesn't make you a winner, I told him. *It just means you've read a book.*

But he wasn't wrong. Some part of me—the part that braced myself every time I got a report card, the part of me that learned to tune my family out rather than speak up—felt like it was shining. I leaned back in my seat, releasing a long, deep breath of relief.

"All right, all right," Mr. Gupta said, clapping to get our attention. "I'll see Team One back here for lunch. Come hungry!"

The bell rang for the next hour, and we all quickly put the room back in order. On the way out, Nell punched my shoulder lightly.

"Pretty impressive," she said.

"Yeah, I mean," I said, keeping my head down. "I guess?"

I wanted to be happy that I'd done something right, for once. But deep down, past that small slice of happiness, hidden beneath the pride, was an ugly truth. A nagging doubt.

Who had really answered that question—me, or Alastor?

A Taste of Lemon

Lunchtime arrived, and with it, six steaming, beautiful pizzas oozing with cheese.

I hovered behind Mr. Gupta as he opened the first set of boxes and set them out for the team, darting around to snatch a plate and napkin. While I did the mental math of how many pieces I could take and not be a selfish jerk.

"Will you chill out?" Nell hissed behind me. "You're acting like you've never had a piece of pizza before."

I was practically bouncing with glee. "I haven't had one in . . . five years?"

"*What?*" Now it was my turn to hush her. A couple of the kids glanced over from down the single file line we'd formed.

"Grandmother forced the one pizza place in town to

close. She claimed it was a 'health hazard,'" I said as we made our way over to two desks in the corner. "And my mom is all about healthy food at home."

"Not even at school?" she whispered in horror.

I shook my head.

"What did you eat, then? A ton of hamburgers and chicken nuggets?"

"Mostly couscous, bluefin, *cozze in bianco* . . ."

"Are you speaking in English right now?" Nell asked. She put one of her slices on top of my pile. "Here, you'd better take this. Cherish the memory forever."

And what of my food? Alastor asked, but I was way too busy stuffing my face to care.

Nell must have seen the irritation in my face. "What's going on? What is he saying?"

"He's hungry," I muttered. "But I thought he fed only on emotions?"

That is incorrect.

"Fiends replenish their power from sucking out misery from those around them, but they eat spiders and bats to fill their stomachs."

That **is** *correct.*

"What should I do?" I asked.

"Nothing," Nell whispered. She stiffened. "You two aren't buddies, and you aren't his servant. If you give him an inch, he'll take a hundred miles. It's like Shakespeare said— *one may smile, and smile, and be a villain!* Nothing good can come from a fiend, just remember that. And if he starts to act up again, let me know and I'll put him back in his place."

Whoa. Her voice had gotten harder and angrier the longer she spoke. "That's . . . I mean, don't get me wrong, I appreciate the charm you worked the other night, but . . . if you guys are all magic . . . magical things, why aren't you on the same team?"

Nell looked horrified.

"Why?" she demanded. "What has the little worm been saying about me?"

Worm! Al sputtered. *That saucy urchin-snouted strumpet!*

"He . . . thinks you are very, uh, special," I said. That was my mom's go-to word for whenever a teacher or relative called me something I didn't understand, like stolid or taciturn.

"Witches are *not* fiends. Fiends, by definition, are creatures from Downstairs who meddle in our world to better theirs," Nell said, her voice so low I had to lean in to hear it. "They want servants, but more than that, they want the magic found on earth's surface to flow down to them. They do that by inflicting misery on us, or managing to get us to inflict misery on ourselves through wars. They can't create enough magic Downstairs. They have to steal it from us, funnel it down to run their world."

Al was suspiciously silent throughout her explanation. Which, you know, meant what she was saying was probably true.

"So what are witches, then?"

"Witches are just women who are naturally attuned to magic in our world," Nell said. "They can manipulate it, when others can't even sense its presence. Moms pass the gift down to their daughters, ensuring the line continues."

I was about to ask her why it was only girls, but she barreled on, adding, "Back in the old days—and I mean the ancient days, we're talking, like, Greeks here—when humans finally figured out that fiends were leading them to needless battles and revenge, they began to gather gifted women into a coven to fight back. The thing you have to understand is, witches and fiends are enemies. It's our responsibility to ensure that they don't meddle in the lives of humans—that they stay Downstairs, where they belong."

I was about to ask her another question, when a voice from across the room interrupted.

"Hey, Ethan! Come sit with us!" Blake jerked his thumb toward the lone empty desk beside him and his friends. An invitation for one. I glanced at Nell out of the corner of my eye, who suddenly seemed very fascinated with her pizza.

"I'm good," I said. "Thanks, though!"

Even if it hadn't meant leaving Nell to eat by herself, I wouldn't have said yes. In my experience, when people were nice to me, it's because they were planning to lure me close enough to a trash can to drop me into it. But Blake only shrugged and turned back to his friends.

Thou—you are surprised they embrace you? Alastor said.

They desire your company, for you have gained that which you desire: acceptance.

All I did was answer a trivia question right, I thought back. I wasn't about to crown myself the King of Popularity over it.

You gave them something they themselves desired; of course they welcome your company. You would be wise to accept it, should you like to walk an easier path for yourself.

You make friendship sound like a trade-off.

Every relationship is a transaction. Every so-called friendship begins with a promise that must be kept by both parties.

Like your transaction with Honor Redding?

He was silent after that. Silent enough that I could hear the cluster of girls a few seats over that Nell was plainly trying to ignore, even as she kept turning her head slightly to hear them better.

"—glasses are ridiculous, even my mom thinks so—"

"—just so weird that she lives in that house—"

"—and that she wants to play that part—like she ever would have gotten it—"

You know—here's the thing. If you were to ask Nell what she thought of me, she'd probably say that I was better off dead, or she'd say she wished she could curse me into having a monkey tail for the rest of my days. But it didn't change the fact that we had at least one thing in common. My Redhood Academy classmates and the kids at her school weren't exactly falling over themselves to befriend us. If anything, they were tripping over each other to get away.

The kid on the bus had called her that terrible word—*freak*. I wondered how much of it had to do with any witchy-related rumors about what Nell and her mom could do, and how much was simply because she didn't look or dress like anyone else. As my own mom said, being different—being simply *you* instead of what other people wanted you to be—was its own kind of bravery.

Her despair tastes of lemon, was Al's only comment.

I shook my head. *Despair,* he'd said. Not simple sadness, or merely being upset. *Despair.* The point beyond hope and loneliness.

In all the hours I had been at school that day, I had only seen Nell talk to two people besides me: our science teacher and Norton. At home, it was just me, Uncle B, and Toad. Did she have anyone else?

Was she just . . . alone?

I tipped my chair back, thoughts running laps around my mind. I was only going to be here for less than two weeks. In the end, it didn't matter what the kids thought of me, so long as they didn't hate me enough to try stabbing me like my grandmother. But it *did* matter what they thought of Nell. After I was gone, she would still have to deal with them.

"Those glasses look great on you," I told her, loud enough

to catch the other girls' attention. "My mom picked them out on Fifth Avenue, at . . . um . . ." What was the name of that store Grandmother owned a stake in? "Bergdorf Goodman."

A piece of pizza fell out of Nell's mouth. She stared at me like I'd just stripped off my pants and started wandering around the classroom.

"Bergdorf Goodman?" one of the girls said. "Wait—you got those glasses in New York City?"

Nell's dark brow furrowed. "No, you nit—"

I kicked her shin under the table, leaning back again to look at the table of girls. "Oh yeah. My mom travels there for business and is always finding cool new stuff for Nell to try. She says that it's hard for the average person to recognize amazing fashion when they see it. Some people are born with taste." I glanced over at them again. "Others aren't as lucky."

Nell actually choked on her food, thumping her chest to dislodge a piece of pizza.

"Are they still for sale there?" the girl asked, a new glint in her eye.

"No, they were made for her by the designer—"

I thanked every lucky star in the sky that the bell rang, interrupting me. Method acting could only take a guy so far when his idea of "fashion" was sometimes wearing patterned socks under his uniform.

"Oh, Ethan?" Mr. Gupta called as I headed for the door. I was almost outside before Nell physically turned me back around with a pointed look.

Right. *I* was Ethan. Ethan was my name. Ethan, Ethan, Ethan.

"I know you're only with us for a short time, but I'd still like for you to participate in the midterm project. I get the feeling that you might like mythology . . . ?"

I hesitated a second, saying, "The thing is . . . I mean . . . I'm not very creative, you know?"

Mr. Gupta had asked the class to come up with some sort of project that spoke to the idea of storytelling in ancient Greek society, or reinvented the mythology in a modern way. If it had been Mr. Wickworth, he would have assigned us a twenty-page research paper and marked off points if we didn't get the right punctuation in every footnote.

Do you not claim to be an artist? Alastor said. *Do you not spend all of your secret time scratching at paper?*

Do you have to say "secret time"? That sounds so creepy.

Not as "creepy" as the ponies, Maggot. You know the ones of which I speak.

The porcelain ponies. My grandmother gave me a new one every single year for Christmas because . . . well, I don't know why. I guess that's what she thinks guys want these days. Even though I pretended to hate them, I actually thought they were painted beautifully and kind of sweet.

Nothing creepy about them. But that knowledge would die with me and the fiend.

"Ethan? Everything okay?"

"Oh yeah," I said, quickly, reaching into my bag for my notebook. "I'm not—I'm not very good, you know, but I like to draw." I opened my notebook to a sketch I'd done of the House of Seven Terrors during earth science. "So you can say no, but I was thinking . . . maybe I could, I don't know, illustrate some of the stories? Like what you'd find in a book?"

Maggot. If a man desires respect, he must not frame his every sentence as a question. If you consider yourself to be an artist, then be that artist.

That was . . . surprisingly good advice from a creature likely born from a fiery pit.

You could reward my genius by feeding me, Maggot, Alastor hissed. *Feed me!*

"Well, hey, this is pretty great!" Mr. Gupta said as I tried not to die of embarrassment. My whole face felt like it had caught fire, even as excitement zipped through me. "I think illustrated retellings would be excellent, as long as they're done in your own unique style. What elective did they assign you?"

"Just—" I ignored the feeling of hot sand rushing through my good arm again. "Just, uh, study hall."

Feed me!

"Have you ever taken an art class before?"

What was Alastor doing? Why were my fingers twitching again?

FEED ME.

I looked up, remembering to shake my head. "N-no, I haven't."

"I'll talk to the art teacher, see if she can't let you sit in on a few of her classes—"

Without warning, without thinking, my hand shot out and snatched a small, palm-size pumpkin that Mr. Gupta had been using to decorate his desk. My arm jerked my hand up to my mouth and my jaw snapped down around the pumpkin. I bit into it hard, tearing a chunk away to chew and swallow.

Mr. Gupta stared up at me from his desk chair with wide eyes.

"I . . . mistook it . . . for an apple," I said lamely, trying to hand it back to him.

"I think you'd better hang on to that," Mr. Gupta said. "In case you need a snack for later."

The Head of the Pack

Coach Randall was all squeaking sneakers and whispery whistles. He wore a white Nike tracksuit with orange stripes and a matching baseball cap. Both were emblazoned with the school's logo. Which, you guessed it, was a witch riding a broomstick across a crescent moon. From the look of him, I didn't think he was the kind of person to let me off the hook for the day because I had an upset tummy—or because I hated physical exercise of any kind.

Fear is for the weak and meek. This is yet another opportunity to prove your excellence.

Yeah. That, or I needed to be on some form of asthma medicine.

I sucked it up and tugged on the sad gray gym uniform Nell handed me before I went into the boys' locker room. We joined the rest of the class in the gymnasium for stretching. Then we had to do a few warm-up laps around the badminton nets.

I started out by trying to keep pace with Nell, but it became clear pretty fast that it wasn't going to happen. *Physical education* in Redhood was learning to waltz or golf.

Nell left me behind wheezing, a look of pity on her face, her glasses bouncing on the bridge of her nose. If we were ever chased by a fiend, I now knew for certain she could and would outrun me, leaving me to be eaten.

Faster! Alastor commanded, like I was some kind of horse he was trying to steer. *Have you no pride, man?*

At that point, no. But what I did have was a crippling cramp in my right side and a desperate need for water.

Out of the corner of my eye, I saw someone come up behind me, slowing down to match my labored pace.

Parker, of course.

He wasn't even sweating as he lapped me, turning back with a shrug, as if to say, *What are you going to do about it?*

Do you not tire, Alastor began, *of always trailing behind, staring forlornly at the back of others' heads?*

"Of course I do," I snapped, ignoring the alarmed look Norton tossed my way as even he passed me.

It wasn't until the start of my third lap, and everyone else's fourth, that things below my neck started to go a little weird. That same prickling weight I had felt in my arm at lunch was back, only this time it was in my legs. It came on so fast that I stumbled, my toes catching on the polished wood court.

What are you doing? I demanded.

Batten down the hatches, knave! Alastor said. **This ship is about to set sail!**

To say that it's disturbing to no longer be in control of your limbs is like saying it's only a little weird to see someone dressed as a dinosaur eating frozen hot dogs on a bench made of pigeons.

I let out a sharp yelp as my legs began to move, clumsy at first, then faster and faster, and steadier when the malefactor finally got a better grip on them. The gym walls and championship banners hanging from them blurred into streaks of orange and black.

I didn't ask for this! I told him. *This isn't a contract.*

Of course not, you urchin-snouted miscreant. Were this a contract, you would have finished by now. Onward!

The surge of energy that pulsed through me was like sticking my finger in a power socket. But I didn't feel any kind of pain. Actually, I felt great. The warmth spreading through my chest ate away at the tight ache. My breath came back in a rush. I pretended I was clinging to the back of a speeding car.

I came up behind Parker so fast he only had one chance to look over his shoulder before I passed him by. The next time I got close to him, he started running faster, trying to keep his thinning lead. His sneakers pounded the ground, his arms pumping wildly as he wove through the other students.

I don't want to lose, I thought. I don't want to lose. . . .

My legs charged into an even faster sprint, finally passing him. My chest felt like it was cracking open, it was that overstuffed with bright, sparkling elation.

Victory!

Was this what winning felt like all the time—like you were flying?

Parker tucked his head down and charged forward, his shoes squeaking with the force of his movement. He was so focused on picking up speed he didn't notice that Norton was directly in his path.

"Watch out!" Nell called.

Norton looked back just in time to see Parker collide into him at top speed, slamming them both down to the ground. The soles of my shoes squealed as I dragged them to a slow stop a short distance away.

"Oh Lord," the coach said. He threw his clipboard into the air and ran over, blowing frantically into his whistle. Like that was going to do anything at that point. "Emergency! Emergency! Someone call nine-one-one!"

"Maybe we should start with the nurse?" Nell suggested, helping a dazed Norton sit up. Aside from some red blotches on his knees and palms from where he hit the ground, Norton was okay. Parker was another story.

"*Owwww*—my ankle!" he said, rolling onto his back,

clutching at it with his hands. The whole PE class gasped and gagged when he lifted his hands and revealed the unnatural angle his ankle was bent at. Parker's face screwed up, his mouth twisting in pain.

My heart was still thundering in my chest, so loud I could barely hear the voices around me.

I didn't do that. I didn't trip him, or force him to run faster to try to keep up with me.

No, you did not, Maggot. The blame rests heavy upon his shoulders. You were merely proving yourself.

"He came out of nowhere," Norton was saying as he stood on shaky feet. "I would have moved out of the way."

"I know you would have," Nell said, giving me a narrow, suspicious look. "It was pretty strange, wasn't it?"

Within minutes, a young woman—the nurse—arrived to assess the situation. Parker covered his bright red face with his hands.

"Good *God*, son," Coach said, pounding my shoulder. "Tell me you'll try out for track and field! You're a natural—a godsend—!"

You are very welcome, Al gloated.

But I wasn't about to thank him. *It doesn't count.*

Of course it does, Maggot. You won. You were the best—we *were* the best.

But it wasn't a race. And even if it had been, I wasn't a track star—an eight-hundred-year-old fiend was. Still, I couldn't forget how easily my legs had eaten up the ground, how the cool air had felt against the sweat on my face. Passing people, instead of being passed, had felt as natural and necessary as breathing.

But I felt that small pride start to deflate as I watched the nurse comfort Parker. The other kids watched in both horror and horrible amusement as the scene played out in front of them. Something heavy sat in the pit of my stomach, and I didn't think it was the pumpkin I'd eaten.

"Thanks, I wish I could," I told the coach, watching as the nurse pulled out her cell phone and finally did call for an ambulance. "But I won't be here for long."

Sulfur and Search Engines

The first slap on my back scared the living daylights out of me. Then Peter Fairfield held up a hand as he walked by, and it took me a full minute to realize he wanted a high five. I was ready for the next one, lifting my arm, but at the last second Brian Farrell turned away. He waved a hand in front of his face and stepped wide around me. He looked grossed out.

Not this again, I thought, feeling miserable. For the first half of the year, the kids at the Academy had pretended I had some kind of disease that they could catch if I stood too close to them. There was a whole set of rules and everything. The only loser of the game was me.

I turned back to the bulletin board on the wall. Most of the papers stapled up there were sign-up sheets for clubs and sports. Some were just laminated copies of the school rules. But there was a big school calendar for October, with the thirty-first, a Monday, marked with a pumpkin sticker.

Halloween on a Monday? This really was the worst year.

I leaned in. There was a star on the Friday before Halloween—the twenty-eighth. The Thirteenth Annual Production of Arthur Miller's *The Crucible*.

I skimmed the board again until my eyes landed on the bright orange sheet labeled CRUCIBLE AUDITIONS.

Oh, I thought. Huh.

Hmm. That, from Alastor. *This would be frivolous human entertainment, I presume?*

The Crucible was an old-ish play about this guy, John Proctor, set during the Salem Witchcraft Trials. One of the girls—one of the evil ones who start accusing people they don't like of being besties with the Devil—falls in love with him, and when he shoots her down, she accuses him and his wife of being witches.

I'd never made it through the play without falling asleep. It's basically a lot of people running around screaming, "I saw Goody So-and-So with the Devil!" which gets real old real fast.

But apparently not to Nell. Her name was right at the top of the auditions list—barely visible under where someone had marked it out with a pen.

Ooohhhhhh. My brain was rapid-firing now. That weird

speech she had been reciting when I first met her. *Because it is my name!* That had been from the play, I was sure of it. She had been practicing even though her name was crossed out.

When Nell finally decided to show up, I pointed out the sign-up sheet. She didn't say a word, only lifted a small spray bottle out of her bag and aimed it right at my face.

"Did you make a contract with him?" she hissed, still spraying. "Is that how you ran so fast?"

"Ack! *Ack!*" I sputtered. It tasted so bad, so gross, I tried wiping my tongue off against my shirt. Ugh. "What are you doing?"

"Answer my question!"

What foul treachery is this? Alastor wailed. *By the realms, you smell of roses and spring. Find mud, Maggot, and quickly rid yourself of this rotten stench!*

Nell moved the bottle down and sprayed the rest of me, not stopping until my shirt was so wet it clung to me.

"Stop, stop," I begged, trying to twist away from the torture. "Of course I didn't make a contract. He just—he just gave me a little boost! That's it. I would never make a contract. *Ever!*"

"Fine," she said, returning her weapon to her bag. "From now on you *have* to shower after PE, okay?"

"What the crap, Nell?" The smell of flowers was already giving me a headache.

"You—" The witch lowered her voice, pulling me away

from the girls' locker-room door as more of the girls spilled out. "You mean you can't smell yourself?"

"I can now!"

"All right, come on, I need to show you where the library is and I'll explain on the way." She raised the spray bottle again and gave it a little shake.

Do not let her douse us with such a vile concoction again! Alastor said, and I felt my speed pick up to dart away from her.

"It's just Febreze!" Nell wasn't even gasping for breath as she caught up to us. "I'm just trying to help you, but if you'd prefer to smell like rotten eggs—"

I skidded to a stop on the uneven sidewalk. *Rotten eggs.* Like the night of the test? I lifted my shirt, and noticed that there was a kind of gross smell cutting through even the flower-power stench.

"That was . . . me?" I whispered, horrified. Nell took me standing there as permission to spray me down again.

"It's bad," she said. "You probably can't even smell it because you're so used to it."

"But what is it?" I asked. I knew I didn't smell like sugarplums and Christmas after running around and sweating, but it wasn't even hot outside.

"Fiends are warm-blooded—way warm-blooded. Their body temperatures are much higher than a human's. That smell, the sulfur, that's their version of sweat. So when you get overheated you sweat like normal, but . . ."

"So does he," I finished. "Awesome."

I smell of conquered kingdoms and doom and despair, Alastor cut in, proudly. *Unlike you paunchy, knotty-pated maggot pies.*

"So basically I'm going to smell like a stink bomb until we get him out, or he worms his way out?"

"Well, if that second thing happens, at least you'll have bigger things to worry about," Nell offered in a weak voice.

I followed her up the path to the library, where my study hall was being held. "Maybe I could just get out of PE—"

"Yeah, good luck with that," she said, holding the door open. "Remember, stay here until I come get you after school. We'll take the bus home."

"*Your* home," I corrected, with a pang.

"If you need anything, I'll be in the theater," she said. "And, *Ethan*? Don't be an idiot, please."

"It'll be a challenge," I told her. "But I think I'm up for it."

The library was empty except for a few kids at the row of computers in the center of the stacks. A half dozen more were hunched over tables, scribbling away at their homework. The librarian glanced up at me as I walked through the security thing, giving me the once-over.

"Are you new?" The woman wasn't old, but she wasn't young either. Her brown hair was streaked with rivulets of silver. A deep crease marred her forehead as she frowned at me. "You look familiar, but I can't seem to place your name."

Crap.

No—there was no way she could recognize me as Prosper Redding. Nell's glamour spell was still in effect. *Stop making dying-animal noises. You are fine. You. Are. Fine.*

I could feel myself start to shrink back a little from her intense stare, but I forced myself to stand up straight. "My name is Ethan White. And, yeah, I'm new."

The woman seemed to measure me with a single look. "All right. Library closes at five. No monkey business on the computers, understand? Let me know if you need help finding a resource."

I took a seat at one of the worktables, fully intending to ignore the rest of my homework in favor of planning out my project for Mr. Gupta's class. It was just that the computers were so close to me, whirring, breathing out their hot air as they loaded and printed and processed. They were ancient compared to the thin screens and wireless keyboards that we had at the Academy.

Lucky us, I realized for the first time. I'd just taken them for granted.

I took a seat as far away from the other kids as I could, glancing over at them while I waited for the Internet to load. The librarian left her desk, pushing a cart of books needing to be reshelved into the stacks.

My fingers hovered over the keyboard for a moment, itching to type REDDING FAMILY into the search bar. I took a deep breath and shook my head. The most important thing was keeping Nell's spell intact and lying low. If everything went according to the plan, I'd see my family soon. Right now that had to be enough for me.

But it didn't mean I had to sit there idly and just stay safe, like Uncle B had instructed. If they didn't have a computer at home to research, I could do it here for them.

I typed GETTING RID OF DEMONS into the scarch bar and leaned close to the screen. Instead of pulling up the search page, a white one with a huge red stop sign appeared.

YOU HAVE BEEN DENIED ACCESS TO THIS SITE AS IT HAS OBJECTIONABLE CONTENT. ETHAN WHITE, YOUR INTERNET USAGE IS MONITORED AND LOGGED.

"*Craaaaap,*" I whispered, clicking back. I tried again, this time searching for EXERCISING A DEMON.

I believe the word you are looking for is "exorcising," Maggot, Al said, sounding bored.

But I remembered the subject that definitely had not bored him. A DEMON—I deleted that. Something told me *demon* was a word the school blocked for very obvious reasons. TRUE NAMES AND MAGIC.

Search results finally loaded. I scanned through them quickly, scrolling down. Most of the pages had to do with Dungeons & Dragons or video games. There were a couple of sites dedicated to Wicca, and a *Wikipedia* page dedicated to "True Names."

Interesting. *Many cultures possess a secret, sacred language from which they derive names which express their true nature . . .* I scrolled down farther. *In certain folktales, there is a tradition that if one possesses someone's true name, that person or being can be controlled or affected magically.*

Rubbish, Alastor declared. Which made me instantly print out the page to show Uncle Barnabas and Nell later. There were even a few academic papers linked as references at the end, which I added to the print queue so I could read them later, when I wasn't scared of someone looking over my shoulder.

NAMES OF EVIL CREATURES. The same *blocked* page came up. And then again when I tried to search for FIEND CURSE, REDDING FAMILY CURSE MAGIC, and HOW TO KILL THE DEMON INSIDE OF YOU.

I let out an annoyed groan and slumped back in my seat.

"Something I can help you with . . . Mr. White, was it?" The librarian was standing right behind me, staring at my screen with an unreadable expression on her face. My hands slapped against the mouse, exiting the page and logging out entirely. I stood, grabbing my bag and almost tripping over the chair.

She held out a stack of papers, still warm from the printer. "Here you are."

"Oh, um, thanks, sorry, just, gotta—do my work. Yup, ooookay, bye—"

I all but ran back to the worktable, nearly dropping the papers in the process. One kid looked up and shushed me as I let out a small noise of frustration.

I tucked those printouts back into my notebook and flipped it open to a blank page. I was halfway through my list of ideas for the Greek mythology project when two guys—friends of Parker's I recognized from PE—sat down behind me.

"It sounds like it's broken," one of them whispered, trying to hide his phone beneath his desk. "He doesn't need surgery, though. That's good, I guess. Maybe he'll be healed in time for track season?"

"He's definitely not going to be able to do the play. I don't think the drama teacher is going to let him onstage with crutches. And didn't the understudy get mono? What are they going to do?"

"Maybe the girl with the glitter glasses will try to audition for the part again."

Glitter glasses? As in . . . Nell?

I turned around in my seat to ask them about it, but as I did, I saw the aforementioned glitter glasses and the girl wearing them slip past the library's window, glance back and forth, and then bolt for the side entrance of the school.

I was on my feet before I remembered standing, scooping all of my things into my backpack.

"Hey, isn't that the kid . . . ?" one of the guys started to say, but I was already leaving, keeping my head down. The librarian had her back to me as she reached up to replace one of the books on the shelf, and I took my chance to duck outside without her noticing.

"Where did she go?" I muttered, looking around. Nell wouldn't leave class without a good reason, not unless something was happening.

As soon as the thought floated through my mind, I spotted her, running through the trees on the east side of campus, heading for the side street that ran alongside it.

What is the meaning of this, Maggot? Al demanded as I ran after her. *Were you not told to remain here, in this place?*

I wove through the trees, my backpack and hair catching the golden leaves as they fluttered down. The faint green magic of the boundary came into view. It stretched like a ribbon as I struggled to push through it. With a *pop!* it spat me out and I was running again, following the purple of Nell's sweater like a star as she disappeared between two houses.

On the other side of them, just past the fencing of their backyards, was another small house, this one sitting between two empty maple-tree-filled lots. It looked Victorian, in contrast to the other homes' sturdy colonial style, with stained glass in the two bay windows on the main floor. A sign hung from the porch: ESSEX BOOKSTORE & OTHER ESSENTIALS.

I was close enough to hear the bell ring as Nell pushed the screen door open and let it slam shut behind her.

Here there be magic, Alastor warned, sounding uneasy.

I crossed the street, keeping behind the old trees weeping their leaves onto the front lawn. A lone swing swayed in the breeze. I cut around it, getting as close to the nearest bay window as I could.

Inside, piles of teetering books filled every corner of the shop, some stacked as high as the ceiling. Shelves were neatly labeled with their contents, and through the green coating of the glass pane, I made out an old-fashioned cash register and a neat pile of bags waiting to be filled with purchases. Behind them was a wall with a wood carving of the shop's logo, a few framed newspaper articles, and a photograph of Nell grinning between two women. One had dark skin like her, her warm, wide smile and the tilt of her eyes nearly identical—clearly, Nell's mom. Her hair was braided into a crown around her head and woven with flowers.

The other woman in the picture walked into the room, coming down the spiral staircase behind a grim-faced Nell. Unusually tall, she had long blond hair that poured down around her shoulders like moonlight. Her clothing was loose and silky, weighed down by the heavy silver necklace and earrings she wore.

"Nellie, please—"

Nell kept her back to the woman, stuffing her backpack with a white paper bag and a book.

"At least tell me everything in that house is okay," the woman continued. "Are you happy?"

Nell, finally, looked at her and said coldly, "What do you think?"

The woman tried to tuck Nell into a hug, but the girl pushed her back. "Thanks for the herbs."

"Come live with me here," the woman said, following her again to the door. "I don't care what your father says, what *anyone* says—"

"Like the way you fought to keep me before?" Nell shoved the door open, but turned back at the last moment, facing her. "The way you fought to save Mom?"

"You don't mean that," the woman said as they stepped out onto the porch. "Come back inside for a moment, we'll—"

I took one step toward them, meaning to make my presence known. But almost as soon as my sneaker sank into the wet earth and leaves, a nearby rosebush lashed out a thorny vine, snapping it around my ankle and violently jerking me back. I felt myself soar through the air, only to land with a cold, wet splat in the nearby little pond. A hurricane of tiny green frogs suddenly emerged from the muddy banks, their glossy eyes turned toward me.

"No—*no!* Missy, that's him! That's Prosper!"

Nell rushed up, dragging me away from the frogs and whatever else was in the water, slapping the thorny vines that were stroking the edges of the murky water, daring me to try to rush toward the house again. A short distance away, my book bag had split open, spewing everything—papers, notebooks, pencils—onto the ground.

"What are you doing here?" I asked. My ears rang like I'd been clubbed on either side of the head. A lone frog clung to the back of my hand. I felt my good arm start to prickle again.

Tiny, little, delicious, juicy frog legs—

"No!" I said, slamming my left hand down on my right to keep it in place.

"What are *you* doing here?" Nell demanded. "Why did you follow me? I told you to stay in the library!"

"I wanted to make sure you were okay," I said.

"A fiend," Missy said coldly from behind us. "Checking up on a witch?"

Her unusual violet eyes flashed in warning as I looked up at her. They only softened when she saw that the hem of my jeans had been yanked up during the tussle and a criss-cross of angry cuts ringed my ankle.

"Come inside, I'll clean those for you," she said finally. "Come in, come in, and let our work begin."

The barrier, including the vines, shrank back. The line of airy green magic I'd missed yet again fell to my feet, allowing me to step over it.

Nell said nothing as we entered the warm, cozy shop. She barely seemed to be breathing as Missy led me upstairs, to the second floor. There, behind the door at the top of the steps, was a room filled with light.

It was the opposite of the attic in every way. Book-shelves lined every side of the room, each painted a pristine, welcoming cream. The window was large, catching the golden afternoon light through the thinning tree branches. While there were plenty of books up here for purchase, most of the shelves contained bottles in neat rows, or had sachets of sweet-smelling herbs. Here and there, there were copper cauldrons, but they were filled with some of the same black soap I'd used that morning at the House of Seven Terrors, or tiny vials of green liquid for "Aches & Pains of the Heart."

So. This was the "& other essentials" part of the store.

Nell stood with her back to the door, keeping me locked in, or someone or something else out.

"Have a seat, Mr. Redding," Missy said, gesturing to a hand-carved stool.

"You know who I am?" I asked, but did as I was told. Missy was gentle as she rolled my jeans up away from my shoes and began to apply a peppermint-scented ointment.

"I know of you, yes," Missy said, with a look back over her shoulder to Nell. "As a witch, I can see through the glamour Nell placed on you."

The girl crossed her arms. Said nothing.

Though the cuts were already mending themselves back together, Missy still wrapped a loose white bandage around my ankle and tied it off—with maybe a *bit* too much force. The way she looked at me now, down the bridge of her nose, eyes never leaving my face, made me feel like I was a feral dog she'd pulled off the street and now had to watch nonstop to keep me from tearing her home apart.

"Don't come back to this place ever," she told me.

Dread-bolted flax-wench!

"Missy!" Nell hissed.

"This is sacred, protected ground," Missy continued. "I can't have any kind of fiend jeopardizing it, no matter who its host is, or how powerful his family might be. You have no business coming here and forcing Nell to care for you." She turned to the girl. "And you, as a witch, should know better than to believe whatever lies that man has told you—"

"All right," Nell snapped, coming across the room to take my arm. "Come on, Prosper, let's go." Then, glancing back to Missy, she added, "Don't worry. We won't come back here again."

Missy's face visibly fell, horror and sadness crashing over her features. "You know I wasn't talking about you—Nell, please—please, just listen to me. This is still your home."

We were already outside, Nell dragging me after her down the street, when I finally heard her soft reply. "No, it's not."

Cleaned Out

"What do we do now?" I asked, holding my torn schoolbag together. "Go back to school?"

Nell was pacing around the corner at the end of the street, just out of eyeshot of the bookstore, fuming so hard I thought I saw smoke escaping her ears. Every now and then, a car would whisk by us, but just as quickly, we'd be left with the silence and the darkening sky once more.

The houses in this part of town looked like they were burdened with centuries of memories. They were old, overrun with ivy and brambles, and despite being so close to the school and the center of life there, had faces that glowered at anyone who passed them by. I hadn't minded the way Missy had treated me, or the odd feeling I'd had in her shop. But these houses seemed to whisper warnings in the clattering of their old shutters and the squeaking hinges of their gates.

"The buses have already left," Nell muttered.

"What should we do, then?" I asked. "Should we call Uncle B? Call for a driver?"

"We do what *normal* people do—we're going to walk."

So we did. Through the same streets we had passed on the way to school, around the same gas station, and through a few pockets of trees (that might have been considered trespassing if it didn't feel like everyone who lived in the town had such firm ownership over its empty places).

"So . . ." I began, reaching down to pick up a single maple leaf that showed nature's ombré in full effect: yellow at the tip, red at its heart, green at the stem. I let the wind snatch it from my fingers and carry it off toward the gray sky. "Who's Missy, exactly?"

Nell's hands were jammed into her pockets, her forehead creased in thought. After a long while—long enough that I didn't think she was going to answer—she said, "Missy was my mom's girlfriend. Her fiancée. They were a few months shy of getting married when my mom got sick."

I didn't know what to say to that, so I just nodded. Maybe there really *was* nothing I could say. Like the haunted house, it was another dream interrupted. And, sometimes, we just had to live with those disappointments and wait for their sharp edges to dull.

"The commonwealth said I had to live with my father,

even though I hadn't seen him in years," Nell told me. "They claimed that was what was right."

It clearly wasn't.

Despair, I thought. That terrible word. The terrible, consuming world of it.

"Is that why you left school? To visit her?"

"I had to pick up a few ingredients for your spell," she explained. "And a few other things we're going to try in case the fiend grows more powerful and starts to make his will known."

"Oh. Thanks."

She spun on me so suddenly I backed myself into a tree to avoid her. Nell took another challenging step forward. "If you tell Barnabas that I left school and stopped by Missy's, I'll curse you so fast you won't even know what's happening until your nose is suddenly on your butt and you're forced to breathe in *every. Single. Fart.*"

"Okay, okay," I said. "I wasn't going to tell. Jeez. You really are a good actress—I had no idea you were even planning on leaving until I saw you go."

Nell's lips twitched, just for a second, into a small smile. Soon enough, her usual scowl was back. But it was a better opening than I could have hoped for.

As we passed by a garbage can on the street, I glanced at the front page of the newsletter shoved into it, and the bright orange headline screaming across it: SALEM HAUNTED BY A PUMPKIN THIEF?

"Did you hear about Parker?" I said, trying to keep my voice casual. "I guess he broke his ankle. Some kids were saying that he might not be able to perform his part in the school play."

She rolled her shoulders back, straightening. "I guess."

After a full half hour, we finally passed through tourist Salem, the part of the city with all the witch shops and ye olde buildings and the common. The salty smell of Salem Sound hit us first, even before we saw the old wharf.

"You're in theater class, right?" I asked. "Are you playing one of the other parts in *The Crucible*? That's what I heard you rehearsing in the house, right? Lines from the play?"

"I'm just on crew," Nell said, her breath frosting the air. She pulled her jacket closer to her center. "I only wanted one part, and the teacher wouldn't let me audition for it."

"Parker's part?" I pressed.

She nodded. "John Proctor."

Otherwise known as the male lead.

My eyebrows rose at that, but the more I thought about it, the fewer reasons I could come up with about why Nell couldn't play the part. The fact that the drama teacher didn't even let her try out for it cranked up the temperature of my blood until it was near to boiling.

"Things don't tend to go my way," Nell explained quietly as we started up the path to the House of Seven Terrors' front door. "Even magic doesn't really let you make your own luck. Not white magic, at least."

I nodded, but my attention was quickly dividing between her and the clean yard around us, which only a few hours ago had been littered with trash from visitors and dead overgrown grass. Nell seemed to notice it at the same moment I did, her feet dragging to a stop.

"Wow, Uncle B must have gotten home early to clean things up for the tour-group audition tonight," I said. Weird that he couldn't keep a space as small as the attic clean, though.

Nell's chest was rising and falling in faster bursts. She dropped her bag on the path and ran toward the door, muttering something under her breath. It flew open without her touch, banging against the wall.

"Nell?" I called, chasing after her. "Nell, what's wrong—?"

She stood frozen in the middle of the entry hall, her face turned toward the zombie operating room. Or what had been the zombie operating room.

The wall that was once drenched with fake blood had been scrubbed clean, leaving only a faint pink stain behind. The gooey guts previously dribbling out of the fake corpse's body had been pulled up from the floor. They were now neatly coiled on the dummy's stomach, wiped clean. Everything was. The metal gurney and fake silver knives and saws were sparkling. Not even I could have done a better job.

"He *didn't*," she breathed out. "I can't believe this—"

Nell bolted up the rickety staircase. The whole house

groaned under her pounding steps. She hit the second floor and flipped on the overhead lights.

The giant spiders were stacked neatly in the far right corner. All the fake cobwebs had been yanked down from the trees, the leaves littering the ground had been swept up, and the stuffed werewolves had been shoved out of sight in the hallway closet.

Every room was the same: the fake blood vanished, the creatures piled up, the guts and gore and mummies and axes and swords—all of them organized, dusted, brushed, polished. All the scrubbing I had done up in the attic was nothing compared to this. It was nothing compared to what the house looked like now. The floor and walls were practically three shades lighter.

"Would someone steal all your garbage and decorations?" I asked, my mind suddenly spinning with the investigative crime shows I sometimes watched after school. "Do you think it was a rival haunted house? Someone with a grudge against shrieking children?"

"No! No, that's not what I—" Nell was shaking. "Don't you get it? Whoever did this messed *everything* up. There's no way we can get the rooms back in shape before the run-through tonight—and all of the spells my mom used to enchant everything, they're—"

Gone.

Everything she and her mother had made was gone.

"Why would he do this, tonight of all nights?" Nell said, her fingers clenched in her hair. The lights over us, all throughout the house, began to flicker dangerously, the electricity surging until the bulb just over my head burst with the force of it.

"Uncle B?" I asked. "What does he have to do with this? Hasn't he been at work all day?"

Nell was fighting so hard—*so* hard—not to cry. I saw it in the tightness of her face and the way her hands clenched and unclenched at her side. The room began to take on a gray, silvery tint, as actual storm clouds formed over our heads.

"He never wanted to run the House of Seven Terrors," she said. "He only saw it as a temporary thing, a place where we could hide out with you when the time came." There was no anger in her words, but I winced all the same. "But he's been talking about selling it. I bet he even canceled the tours tonight without telling me. All I wanted was to show him that we could turn a good profit—that we didn't have to sell the house."

"I'm sorry," I said. "What can I do to help?"

She sucked in a deep breath through her nose. Her posture straightened as slivers of electricity crackled over her curly hair. When she looked at me again, her eyes were glowing—not literally, though. Just with determination.

"You can stay here," she said. "And not leave the house. I'm going to talk to Uncle B, even if it means interrupting one of his precious historical lectures."

"I don't know if that's"—the front door slammed behind her—"a good idea."

Why does the witchling cry? Alastor asked, sounding flabbergasted.

"It's a human thing," I said as I started the climb up to the attic. "You wouldn't get it."

No, Maggot, I ask: Why does the little witch cry when you could easily set it to rights?

The attic looked perfect to me. Clean. Fit for human habitation. But if Nell had been here, I knew all she would have seen was what was missing: the plants, the pots, the cobwebs.

"Me? What in the past forty-eight hours has got you convinced I could put the house back together that quickly? And why would I, if Uncle Barnabas is so against it?"

But I already had three reasons: Because it was important to Nell. Because Nell had saved my life more than once. Because Nell, like me, wasn't one of life's lucky ones.

Okay, four: Because it would make her happy.

How often did I really make people happy in my own life, never mind proud? My parents said I did, but what else were they supposed to do, lock me in the dungeon whenever I fell asleep in class or was overheard by an undercover reporter suggesting my grandmother was a lizard alien wearing human skin?

My stomach rumbled, so I wandered over to the refrigerator. There were still a few bottles in it, but not much else.

Ketchup, maple syrup, soy sauce. I grabbed a half-empty bag of chips from the top of the microwave and sat down on my couch-bed, sick to my stomach.

As bad as things were for me now, I never had to worry about stuff like this. About empty refrigerators or jobs or losing the things I cared about. At least not before the malefactor.

"You've been pretty quiet, Alastor," I said around a mouthful of chip crumbs. "Did *you* have something to do with this?"

Even as I asked, I knew it was stupid—impossible. Where I went, he went. That was part of the whole deal. Also, the stupid parasite had no limbs. Well, except mine. But I think I would have remembered him taking over.

You insult me. Alastor's voice was thin. *I would never lower myself to such a baseless act as cleaning human filth. I would, however, consider helping you put things to rights.*

"In exchange for a contract," I said. "Yeah, no."

Not for a contract, simply a favor, and the promise that you will do nothing to endanger us before I am able to ascend out of the prison of your puny body.

"What kind of favor is this?" I asked. "If it involves my death, destruction, or mayhem, that's an even harder *no* from me."

I would like for you to ask the witchling what news she and the coven of this town have heard about the state of Downstairs—in particular, the fiend on the throne there.

"Isn't that your dad? Are you worried they've redecorated your palace in your absence?" I asked. "Gave away some of your human heads mounted on spikes?"

Consider this carefully, Prosperity Redding: I am confounded by your inclination to help the witch and her dimwit, snaggletoothed father. I can only assume you feel a debt, or this is a passing disorder of the mind.

"Or, you know, compassion, but go on," I said.

I have the strength, the speed, and the resilience you need to work quickly. I have memories to show you of my breathtaking home of terrors Downstairs, of which this is a mere shadow. You seem to possess some . . .

"Come on, pal, you can do it," I said. "It's just one compliment. Just one. I seem to possess . . . ?"

Some . . . He nearly choked on the words. *Artistic ability. If they desire this decrepit hut to be a fountain of wealth, then I will show you what I know of such things, teach you how to present it, and it shall be so.*

"And, in exchange, I ask Nell your question," I finished. "What's the catch here? How do I know I'm not accidentally agreeing to a contract?"

Because, Maggot, he said, *when we form our contract, it will be because you've asked for it yourself.*

Set Up

I began to suspect that Nell was right about Uncle B being behind the housecleaning when I found the bulk of the materials and props piled in the overflowing garbage can in the side yard. Whatever couldn't fit inside the canister had been piled up neatly beside it, waiting for trash day.

"All right," I said, after I'd dragged it all back inside to assess the situation. "You ready, Al?"

Who is this "Al" you address? Surely not myself, a noble, malicious prince of the Third Realm—

"Sure, Al pal," I said, feeling the first trickle of hot needles rushing through my good arm and legs. Something sparked at the center of my chest, spreading its heat out through my blood. When I closed my eyes, the glimpses I'd had of each room in the house slid into place. I began to sort all the supplies by the rooms they belonged to, lifting enormous, hulking piles of fake tombstones and trees as easily as if they were rolls of old parchment. My hands were blurs as they jammed everything back into its right place, strung up the blackout curtains, stretched and draped what had to be miles of cobwebbing. I found a shovel leaning against the side of the house and began to dig up fresh dirt and grass to pile onto the floor of the graveyard on the second story, using the empty trash can to haul it all up the stairs.

No, Maggot, she had it arranged like so.... Al used my hand to tilt one of the crumbling headstones back up. ***By the realms, your brain is the size of a mouse's. I can see it quiver with effort.***

The only other part of the room that was missing was the blood shower. I glanced up at the ceiling, trying to find the sprinkler system they must have used, only to see a pale, translucent face staring back at me.

I jumped over the nearest gravestone, tripping over my feet until I backed straight into the wall.

The ghostly woman—*the ghost*, I realized—leaned down farther through the ceiling, examining my work. With a long, delicate arm, she pointed at the fake bats I'd pinned to the ceiling, and then pointed a short distance to the left of them.

A shade, Alastor confirmed. ***Likely bound to the house, by choice or by magic.***

"Oh, right," I managed to say. "Um, thanks?"

With the room finally back in order, the woman drifted down through the air, her old-fashioned white dress fluttering as though it had been cut from fabric, not moonlight and mist.

The shade reached out her arms. *"My sweet boy—"*

"Okay, bye!" I shut the door firmly behind me, leaning back against it. Something rotten wafted up to my nose, and I didn't need to lift my arm to know that it was me. Upstairs, whatever creature was behind the locked door on the right began to pound against the door and yowl.

Funny. Whatever it was, it almost sounded like my furry friend Toad.

Wait.

"Toad?" I'd been so distracted by Nell and the house itself that I hadn't realized the changeling hadn't made an appearance since leaving that morning. My feet pounded out a steady, quick clip against the old wood, until I gripped the banister just a bit too tight to keep my balance and splintered the wood.

"Whoa," I muttered. "Settle down, Hulk."

The chains on the door were gone, but someone had wedged a doorstop under it to keep it firmly shut. I kicked it away and threw the door open. "Are you—?"

With a ferocious, hair-raising screech, Toad flew out of the room, his tiny paws raised like a boxer's gloves. I ducked, narrowly missing a claw to the eye as he took an indignant swipe.

"Are you okay?" I asked. Toad ignored me, his wings slapping at the air as he darted past, inspecting the rooms before zooming downstairs. All the while, he sniffed and sniffed and sniffed, like he was trying to track or find something—or someone. "Do you know who did this? Was it Uncle Barnabas?"

Do not trouble yourself, Maggot. The changelings have brains smaller than even your own.

But the CatBat shook his head. He let out a low, mournful noise as he looked around the half-finished zombie-hospital floor, finally landing in the middle of the room with a dejected *thump*. The edges of his fur began to shimmer and I let out a yelp as the creature dissolved, splashing against the floor as nothing more than a puddle with big, green eyes.

"Holy crap!" I dropped to my knees beside him, trying to scoop him back together. "I'm working as fast as I can, but I need your help, okay? We won't finish setting up in time for the run-through without whatever spells Nell's mom used. Can you go find her and bring her back?"

With a loud *pop!* the changeling shifted again, this time into a large, green-eyed raven. *Caw-caw!*

He agreed, Maggot, said Alastor, who, apparently, also spoke evil bird.

Toad flew to the door, his wings beating against the wood until I opened it for him. Leaving a window open for his eventual return, I set to work finishing the first floor, ignoring Al's suggestion I use my own blood to splatter the walls. Instead, I used a mixture of what was left in the ketchup bottle in the refrigerator, flour, and water, smearing the fake blood on the plaster and scratching a message into it with my own hands.

I didn't know what to do with the ghost room upstairs. I turned the house and backyard inside out looking for whatever machine they had used to chill the room so brutally and make it feel as though you were standing over a crack in the earth that sank as deep as the underworld.

A witch would never dare to open the realm of shades, for fear of unleashing the unhappy dead.

So it must have been an illusion, then.

I have another thought about this room.

I saw the thought as clearly as if I had slipped inside a memory. The hazy film that seemed to cover my vision lifted, revealing a dark, damp stone room. A *drip, drip, drip* set my hair tingling against my skin. Layered just beneath that sound was a faint clicking and clattering—no, a scrabbling. Almost like . . .

A thousand insect legs. The walls crawled with spiders, some as small as my pinky, others bigger than my head. I tried to lurch back, only to bump into something heavy, something sticky. Whirling around, I came face-to-face with a long, shimmering white cocoon and whatever poor creature was wrapped inside it. When I took a step back, two glowing red dots appeared through the webbing. *Eyes.*

The spiders swarmed my feet, crawling up my legs, into my hair. "Get me out of here!"

I slammed back into the reality of the empty room, still breathing hard. "What was that place? Where you hide the bodies of your enemies?"

No, you tickle-brained canker blossom, Al said. *That was a malefactor nursery. My own!*

"Eesh. That explains a lot." I shivered, patting at my hair to make sure it had all been an illusion. "Wait. I thought you *ate* spiders? You mean they raise you, and then you eat them?"

Only the small ones. That is beside the point.

Downstairs lie witch dolls and other beings, Al continued, *as well as an obscene amount of useless spider-webbing.*

"All right," I said, turning around, trying to picture it. "I can see it. It'd be easy enough for someone to hide in here and make the spider noises. I just need to find some paint—"

There was a cabinet full of black and white paint downstairs, hidden behind where the cleaner had tried to fold and store the zombie victim's gurney. A few brushes too, which was more than I'd hoped for. I hesitated, wondering if it would really be okay to paint the spiders and stones on the wall, and then just went for it.

Al was mostly silent as I worked, occasionally weighing in on the design with his usual bluntness, but mostly I just felt the hum of power and happiness buzzing through my veins as I painted and painted and painted. Leaving my work to dry, I went down to wrap the stuffed witches and one of the skeletons in the webbing.

I flipped the first witch over and fell back onto my bottom with an embarrassingly loud gasp. Her plastic face, from her black eyes to her wart-covered chin, had been mauled. It looked like a claw had torn through it.

"What the . . . ?"

Fiends and witches are enemies. Nell had said that, right? Whoever—or whatever—attacked the witch mannequins clearly hated them. It looked like they would have set them on fire, if they'd had matches. Something heavy settled in my stomach.

"You *do* know who did this," I said out loud. "Don't you?"

Alastor said nothing, but I felt the slightest tremor of fear ripple through my heart.

When the front door finally opened, I shot up to my feet. "Nell, I'm in—"

But it wasn't Nell. It was Missy.

She was wearing a long black overcoat with a high collar, her braided hair falling down her back like the knobs of a spine. Toad, back in CatBat form, was perched happily on her shoulder, chewing on a loose strand of her hair. Under one arm was a heavy, leather-bound book.

I stared at the changeling in confusion. "You get lost, little buddy?"

"He knows to come straight to me if there is trouble."

Missy glanced around quickly, her lips pressed in a tight line. "Nell isn't here, is she?"

I shook my head, unsure of what to say. Alastor only hissed at her sudden appearance, making Toad's ears stand straight up.

"I'll work quickly, then," Missy said, opening the book and flipping through its coarse, yellowed pages. "Nell's father won't like it that I've come. I encourage you not to say anything, if you value your short, doomed life."

That was a new one. I didn't know Missy well enough to know if she was making a joke or a prophecy. "Nell already threatened to rearrange my body parts, so, believe me, your secret's safe with me."

"Good," she said, then, finally, looked up at me. "This looks different—did something happen to the house?"

I quickly explained.

"And you did all of this yourself?"

"Yes," I said.

Ahem.

"Er, mostly. Nell went off to find Uncle Barnabas, so I tried to restore the house the best I could. The tour groups are coming tonight to do a walk-through and I knew it was important to her, so I just—"

"You did all of this for Nell?"

"Well, yeah. And Uncle Barnabas. There were a few things I couldn't replicate because of, you know . . ." Magic.

"Yes, I know," she said absently, violet eyes fixed on

the pages as she turned them. "I helped Tabitha—Nell's mother—and Nell enchant them. Oh, here we are—she did write it all down."

"What's that?" I asked, leaning forward to get a better look.

Missy jerked the book away. "Do *not* touch it—not even for a moment. It's enchanted to destroy itself before falling into a fiend's hands."

Just like Goody Prufrock's book had. "Is that Nell's grimoire—her book of spells and notes?"

"Her mother's," Missy said. "All right, Prosperity Redding. I'll finish what you've begun, but I'll need your help, if you're willing?"

"Yeah, of course," I said. "Just tell me what to do."

"Right," Missy said. "Then your first task, young man, is to go up to the attic, open every window on your way, and take a nice, long shower."

"That bad?" I asked.

The woman gave me a pitying smile. "Worse."

By the time I finished showering and dousing my clothes in air freshener, Missy was nearly done with her work, and all that was left was for me to dutifully hold a candle with her as she added a touch of tiny spiders to the room upstairs, all spun from smoke and shadow.

"There's one more thing," I said. "If you have time . . ."

Earlier, Al had made a good point about the House of Seven Terrors being a business, and one that needed to be taken seriously. Whether Nell wanted to actually use it, I thought it would be a good thing to have a real logo for the business. Something she could put on a sign outside or in flyers.

I brought Missy up to the attic, where I'd pulled one of the white curtains off the window. Missy's face went pinched as she looked around, the whites of her eyes going pink at the edges.

I had already painted a black version of the tree out in the yard, along with the many little roofs on each level of the house. All I needed was to write the words *House of Seven Terrors*.

"Missy," I said. Then I said it again, louder.

She turned toward me, startled. "What is it?"

"Is there any way to . . . Do you remember what Nell's mom's handwriting looked like? I wanted to try to copy it for the sign."

Her eyes widened. "There's a spell for that. Here, may I have the paintbrush?"

I dipped it into what was left of the black paint before handing it over to her. She flipped the grimoire open to a page and began to whisper to herself, moving her fingers along the handwriting on the page. The words began to swirl, then flowed toward the paintbrush, being absorbed into it. When she brought the tip of it to the curtain, the brush seemed to move on its own, the words she'd lifted from the book spilling out onto the fabric.

After we hung the sign up over the porch, I walked Missy to the back door. Toad took it upon himself to climb her ropelike braid to lick her cheek.

"I know, old friend, I miss you too," she told him, scratching him beneath the chin. "Come see me when you can, but only when Nell is safe at school and under Eleanor's watch. Remember your promise to Tabitha to protect her."

I tried to fade into the background to give them their moment, but I couldn't help but ask, "Eleanor? The spider? That Eleanor? She's, what, another changeling?"

"My own," Missy said.

No wonder Nell hadn't wanted to use her during the spell to get Al out of me.

The witch smoothed her hair back, taking a moment to consider her words. "Prosperity, perhaps . . . I misunderstood your situation. I did not think anyone controlled by a malefactor would be capable of such a kind act. But I need to warn you—"

The front door slammed open, and Nell's shocked gasp carried through the house to where we stood.

Quickly, I turned back toward Missy. "Warn me about what?"

But the witch was already across the yard, disappearing into the woods.

"—didn't do it, Nell, I don't know how many times I have to tell you that," Uncle Barnabas was saying as he stepped onto the porch behind Nell. "I would never disrespect your mother's memory in such a way."

"So you say, but you never wanted the responsibility . . ." Nell's words trailed off. A second later, I heard her footsteps pounding around the corner. "Prosper! Did you do this? *How?* The magic—"

Uncle Barnabas, as pale in the face as I'd ever seen him, appeared behind her.

"I know, right?" I said, quickly, shooting her a look. "*You* did a great job with it *before you left*."

"I did?" she said. "Oh—*I did*."

I followed her upstairs, bracing myself for her judgment. Uncle Barnabas and Toad trailed behind us.

When she reached the new spider room, the words "I couldn't put it back exactly right, I'm sorry!" sprang to my lips.

Nell whirled in its threshold, pointing a finger at me. "*Skúffuskáld!*"

"*Gesundheit?*" I offered back. Just to be sure, I reached up and touched my nose, to make sure it was still in the right place.

"No, no," she said, laughing. "It's Icelandic. It literally

means *drawer poet*—someone who writes poems but tosses them in a drawer before showing them to anyone. The painting in here is *amazing*. Why would you hide something you obviously like and are really good at? Because, Prosper, you are really good. Trust me."

Uncle Barnabas looked around, scratching at his pale hair. "So I suppose this means the run-through's back on for tonight, then. Nell, why don't you go give the agencies a call and let them know? The Witch's Brew Café will let you use their phone."

Nell's eyes were narrowed as she looked at him, and was silent, as if still waiting for him to confess.

"I can do it," I offered. "You two have to get ready, right? And it's just down the street. What's the worst that could happen two doors down from here?"

After a beat of silence, Uncle Barnabas relented. "All right. Be quick about it."

"But—" Nell began, looking between us.

He fished out a crumpled sheet of paper from his pocket and handed it to me.

I knew Nell was watching me from the front door as I ran down the street. Al's power was still moving through me, swirling just beneath my skin. I reached the café in no time, almost flinging the door open in the face of its owner.

"My goodness!" She looked like a storybook grand-mother, all softness and silver hair.

"Can I borrow your phone? Just for a second?" I said in a rush of breath.

"O-of course, dear, it's behind the counter," she said, pointing. "I'm closing up, but let me know if you need anything else."

The landline phone looked like it had time-traveled out of the 1950s. I smoothed the paper out over the counter, scanning down the three numbers. When I reached the last one, I startled—it looked like—

No. It wasn't Mom's cell-phone number. Hers ended with a 5, not a 2. But it was close enough to make my stomach twist.

"All right," I said, dialing the first number and leaving a message with the tour group's receptionist to confirm. The second call went the same way, and I was told by the woman who answered how excited she was and how she loved haunted houses and how—

"Okay, see you soon, bye!" I hung the phone up quickly, glancing around to make sure the café's owner was still busy sweeping. I punched in the third and final number and sat back on my heels, eyeing one of the carrot cakes in the café's refrigerator case.

"Hello?"

That was—that was Mom's voice.

Crap, crap, crap, crapcrapcrap—I punched in the wrong last number.

I choked on my spit, my hand gripping the phone so hard the plastic handle cracked. I released my grip and, with a deep breath, forced myself to hang the receiver up just as I thought I heard her say, *"Prosper?"*

Oh no.

Oh, well done, Maggot, Al said, irritated. ***Now you've done it!***

I started to make a run for the door, only to realize I hadn't actually called the third tourist office. I concentrated so hard on inputting the right number this time I almost gave myself a headache. The woman I spoke to happily confirmed her group would be there as sweat soaked through my shirt and my stomach began to roll.

I messed everything up, I thought, hanging up the phone. No. No, I was okay. I didn't reveal myself intentionally, right? And I definitely hadn't confirmed who I was. Mom would just think it was a random wrong number. In any case, the owner of the Witch's Brew didn't give me a second look when I thanked her and stepped out. My breathing was finally under control by the time I made my way back over to the House of Seven Terrors.

Stopping under the sign that Missy had helped me hang, I couldn't stop the warm curl of pride that wound its way through me. Nell's voice drifted down to me from the attic window.

"Everything good?"

"Yup, everything good!" I called back.

And that was the truth. It was a small thing in the grand scheme of life, but I finally felt like I had returned the favor for Nell and Uncle Barnabas's help. Alastor's influence was slipping away, and my limbs felt suddenly heavy, making me so exhausted it was a struggle to get up the few porch steps. I sat down instead, trying to catch my breath, wondering at how easy everything had felt only a few minutes ago. How *good*.

My parents ran Heart2Heart but sat on a dozen charity boards, struggling to divide their time and energy among them. It would make things so much easier to have a life spilling over with luck and strength and fortune, and turn around and share it with others. I could do more. Be better.

As I sat there, watching the sun set and the moon rise, I could almost understand why Honor Redding had made a contract, thinking he could do real good and help his family in the process.

Almost.

Something Dark and Dreadful

The boy fell asleep far faster on the second night than the first. It irritated Alastor to no end to have to suffer silently through the ridiculous game of pretend one more time. Well. Truthfully, it was a bit hilarious too. Watching the little witch's face as she went through the pocket spell again, "binding" him back, feeling the boy's smug satisfaction. By the realms, humans truly were the stupidest species haunting their world.

No wonder Alastor's great ancestors had thought to bring their worthless spirits Downstairs and put them to work doing tasks appropriate for the size of their miniature brains. The boy's head was so empty Alastor was convinced he could hear his own voice echoing inside his skull.

He sat the boy's body up, folded the blanket back, and

escaped to the hallway. There was much to do tonight, and so few hours to accomplish it.

Nightlock awaited him on the other side of the window. He panted with excitement, fogging up the glass with his breath and saliva. The hob's face split into an enormous, crooked grin at the sight of Alastor. He wasted no time in scratching at the window, as if the malefactor could have possibly missed him.

"My lord and master!" Nightlock was balanced on the top rung of a ladder, but risked releasing one hand to scratch a pointy ear. Alastor merely took this as an opportunity to flick him between the eyes.

He heard the hob's startled shriek of surprise as he tumbled onto the grass, but was not concerned. If Alastor actually had a heart, it might have broken at Nightlock's huge, glowing eyes. The hob's rotting pumpkin cap lay a few feet away, smashed beyond recognition.

"What have you to say for yourself?" Alastor asked.

Nightlock's forehead wrinkled. "Banana?"

"Pardon me?"

Nightlock's face screwed up, as if the hob was capable of deep thought. "Pigeon?"

"What are you on about?"

"Wind?"

The boy's hand shot out, easily closing around the small fiend's neck. Its already bulging eyes seemed in true danger of popping out.

"Master did not specify what he would like me to say," the hob choked out. "What word would please you? What has Nightlock done to displease you?"

"The house!" Alastor wanted the words to roar out of him, but had to settle on a whisper. "You cleaned the house and nearly exposed us!"

At that, the little hob gathered himself up, the snot and tears literally sucked back up his bulbous nose. He looked indignant. "That house was not fit for my lord and master! No, this hob would not stand for it, not Upstairs, not Downstairs, not anywhere in between! My prince must be cared for, and not live with the filth of sickening humans— pwah!" The hob launched a blue-tinged wad of snot at the ground to emphasize his disgust.

Alastor sat back, releasing him slowly. Thinking. "You did this for me?"

"Only ever for you, My Eternal Prince of Nightmares that Lurk in Every Dark Sleep."

The boy's wounded arm flopped around useless and unfeeling as Alastor forced his body to rise.

"You must take my other horn." Nightlock was rambling. "You must, you must, you must—otherwise there will be no forgiveness, you will look at me in despair, Master, you must! I am a stupid, stupid creature. I do not deserve to bear horns!"

In truth . . . Alastor had always been silently disgusted by the practice of taking a hob's horns. Perhaps it had to do with the way they screamed and thrashed around as it was done. But then, it was almost worse to watch them suck up all of their tears at the task's completion and pretend nothing had happened. To see them immediately go back to work, fighting through the terrible pain. He had seen his own father maim countless hobs—and all for trivial things, like a spilled glass of troll milk. Sometimes, it was done out of anger when tasks did not turn out the way the emperor had hoped.

The worst had been when their father had forced Alastor and Pyra to watch as their nannyhob's right horn was sliced off, all because of something *Alastor* had done. An order *he* had disobeyed. As the eldest of five brothers and a single sister, Alastor should have known better than to sneak off to the human world.

He had only wanted to prove himself to his father; his brothers were constantly trying to get him to stumble on his path to greatness. He only meant to bring a human spirit down for eternal servitude—but he had left the gate between the worlds open by mistake. A witch had come through and nearly murdered his father. A single, filthy human had nearly destroyed their empire, and yet, to Alastor, his nannyhob losing her horn had been the hardest fact to bear.

Alastor glared down the boy's nose at the groveling servant's small body and sighed. "Do not touch the humans' possessions again unless I ask it of you. Do you understand?"

Nightlock nodded, clutching his clawed hands together under his chin. Alastor thought he was about to start crying again, this time with tears of joy, and so pressed onward.

"You found the fiend you spoke of this past night?" Alastor had made a hollow bargain with the boy, giving him the illusion it was a fair trade rather than a trap for his heart. He was curious to find out if the witchling had heard anything about what might be happening Downstairs, but he would not hold the boy's breath waiting to find out. No, Alastor always had a second plan.

Nightlock nodded. "Yes, yes, I found him. He will speak the truth of our world to you. He is not under the curse; no, he is not. He is beyond the black throne's reach."

"How is this possible?" Alastor asked. No fiend was beyond the black throne's influence. His family was the most powerful in the realm.

The hob trembled slightly, the knob in his throat bobbing as he swallowed.

"Because, my lord and master," Nightlock said, "he is not a fiend at all, but an elf."

Alastor could not decide whether or not he was annoyed or disgusted at the thought of dealing with an elf. In truth, he had only ever met one of their kind, and that had been when he was very young—only 103 years of age. The elf, with its humanlike form, hunched at the shoulders, had come to the

Dark Court to speak with his father on behalf of the fiends that had been banished from Downstairs.

Elves were neither human nor fiend, but something far more gentle and quiet and tender—in other words, utterly repulsive. They were smaller in stature than men, their skin green and mottled with sprouts and leaves. If superstition was to be believed, the elves began their existence in the innermost of the four realms—the realm of Ancients.

The mysterious elves did work with great creativity and craftsmanship, but they refused to use their natural gifts to do something useful. Something such as creating a deadly blade with which to stab one's enemies.

This was likely also the reason the elves had been foolish enough to choose to live in the realm of humans over that of the fiends. Their own innate magical gifts allowed them to use a glamour when they wished to pass as men or women, but they more often seemed to live just at the edge of mankind's awareness and sight.

The elf that arrived at court that day was advanced in age, well into his tenth century, by the look of his skin. As elves aged, it became rough, thick. Their hair darkened to a forest green. And when it was their time to pass on to the next life, they found a parcel of open land and became what humans called trees.

The whole notion of dying to become something useful to the humans made Alastor want to vomit.

"This way, this way, this way," Nightlock said, scampering ahead on all four limbs. Alastor forced the boy's body into a run to keep up with him, choosing to ignore the strange decorations and sights that had baffled him the night before. It seemed that they were heading straight for the section of the village that the little witch had called some sort of trap—a tourist trap?

Worse yet, Alastor had seen grown men and women who were dressed in ridiculous imitations of witches and monsters that did not, in fact, exist. For the life of him, he could not figure out why a village that had once prided itself on hunting and killing witches should now display their image everywhere.

If this elf was here now, Alastor could only imagine the green sprouting from his head, and the scratchy skin, and the creaking joints that slowly were stiffening into timber. His brain would likely be just as useless.

Alastor slowed his pace as he rounded a corner, darting through the flickering streetlight's orange glow. Nightlock had all but faded into the shadows. Every now and then the light would catch his eyes and set them ablaze.

"Who is this elf," Alastor whispered, "and what business does he have with the humans?"

"Oh, Master"—the hob said the word like a sigh—"he is an elf of rare talent, oh yes. He sells his jewelry wares on the street—the likes of which will never be duplicated. He has promised this hob a crown worthy of you when you are rid of the human boy's skin!"

A crown made by elf hands? Why would an elf ever agree to such a thing when their kind loathed fiends as much as they adored humans? Alastor would rather melt the gold down and fling the boiling liquid at his own face than wear a crown that came from such disrespectful, disgraceful, disgusting—

He heard their mindless chattering only moments before the boy's dull nose picked up on their rancid, sweet scent.

"Faeries," he warned the hob. "Step lightly, man—it seems as though there's a cloud of them."

Their smell was . . . different, somehow. It had been several hundred years, but Alastor was sure he would have remembered a stench so sweet, touched by a hint of sourness. Already, he could feel the boy's stomach churning.

Downstairs, the faeries fed on other small creatures—like three-headed lizards or fire-horned beetles. Pests controlling the population of other pests. When the faerie infestations became too large, they began seeking larger prey. They gnawed on the bones fiends used to build their houses and shops. They left their droppings all over the streets and on the fine hats of lordly fiends. Really, they were flying rodents, and they reproduced with the same ease as hay catching fire.

Nightlock brought him down one final backstreet, toward the rear entrance of what looked to be some sort of shop filled with sweet confections, frozen and baked. He looked at the hob for confirmation.

"Oh yes, it is what the humans be calling 'ice cream.' Much milk. Much sugar. Blegh!"

Alastor had to agree—there were few things more poisonous to his delicate, refined innards than sweets. The only thing he liked iced were the guts of dragons—but only with a hearty side of nymph blood, and served from a bowl carved from the skull of an imp.

The faeries, however, did not share his refined taste. A cloud of them clung to the clear sacks of garbage. If it hadn't been for the rapid fluttering of their wings, they might have looked to the human eye like a skin of thick moss. Their paper-thin black wings were coated with white dust and splotches of sticky drips of brown and gold. Each had a gray body that normally had a velvet sheen, two sets of stick-thin arms, and frail, spidery legs.

They were no bigger than the boy's hand—or, at least, they should not have been. These faeries were twice as wide as they were long. They slurped and sucked loudly with their whiplike tongues. Their faces, closely resembling those of miniature cats, were as bloated as their bellies.

"By the realms . . ." Alastor breathed out, horrified. The rodents could hardly *fly*. He watched as they bobbed under their own weight, crashing to the ground with loud splats, wheezing farts, and deep-bellied burps.

"Choco–cho–cho–choco–coco–chocolate—"

"Flavor, special flavor. Tuesday pumpkin, spicy pumpkin—"

"Orange-ysicle, creamsicle, orange-y dreamsicle—"

The faeries had brains as small as specks of dust. Unfortunately, they were capable of speech. Perhaps even more unfortunately, they were limited to repeating back only what they had overheard. Many secrets plots and devious schemes that had been passed in whispers in the Dark Palace had been regrettably announced to the entire realm by the unseen faeries clinging to nearby rocks and statues.

Nightlock had clearly visited this place before and had come prepared. He reached into the pocket of his drooping, brightly patterned shorts. He whipped out a half-eaten bar of chocolate the little witch had abandoned the night before. It was as though he had cast a spell of his own. The chattering fell silent and each and every tiny head swiveled toward the hob.

Alastor found himself taking a step back. Their eyes were huge with hunger and shot through with red. Nightlock threw the candy as far as he could down the alley, grunting with the effort. The cloud of faeries crawled, fluttered, and buzzed their way over to it.

"Shame," Nightlock said. "They have become addicted to the humans' evil sweets. Evil, evil, evil. It gnaws at their minds, poisons them, makes them hungrier."

With the swarm of faeries occupied, Nightlock turned toward the metal garbage container. Alastor stepped aside, allowing the hob to pass. He watched as the little fiend knocked once, twice, thrice, against the side of the bin. The sound was like thunder.

"Elf, His Highness is here—make haste," Nightlock said. He knocked again, this time harder and faster. "Do not keep my lord and master waiting. It is a school night, and he has a bedtime."

"Silence," Alastor hissed, feeling his face flood with heat. Princes of the Third Realm did *not* have bedtimes. If he hadn't been trapped in the boy's body—

The wind shifted, cutting a path straight up the alley. It lifted the boy's dark mop of hair off his forehead. Just for that moment, the sickening syrupy smell lifted away; now he smelled iron. Sticky, hot iron with the faintest touch of damp earth.

Nightlock, though an inferior creature, must have scented it too. His huge eyes seemed in danger of popping from his skull.

"Open it, servant," Alastor managed to squeeze out around the lump in the boy's throat.

The hob squared his shoulders and used every ounce of power in his squatty legs to huff, puff, and drag the bin away from the brick wall. He revealed a wall of climbing green vines, where no plant should have been able to grow.

Alastor followed the unnaturally bright trail of green down the rain-slicked wall. Down to a second, narrower alleyway that had been masked by the bin. Down to the source of the vines—a pool of dark emerald-green elf blood.

Nightlock shrieked and scampered behind him, clinging to the boy's leg. Snot streamed out of his nose as he shook.

"Master, Master, *no!*" he moaned as Alastor dragged them both forward to peer into what had been this elf's home.

The alley was only feet deep, but was kept impossibly clean and tidy. Stretches of shining fabric were draped overhead, likely to keep out the rain and snow. There was bedding for sleep and a worktable and bench. Half-finished pieces of jewelry and precious stones were abandoned, untouched. They gleamed, calling to Alastor. That was the elves' true magic: everything they touched became irresistible.

This was not a robbery, he thought. If it had been, they would have taken the gold. He let his vision fall back upon what was left of the elf's body.

Its long, pointed face had been slashed nearly off. Ribbons of bloody cuts ran down the creature's body—the deepest in his chest, where his two hearts once beat.

Alastor felt ill. Beyond ill. True, in the past he had seen battles, ordered the death of criminals Downstairs, and he had tormented his own brothers with their worst nightmares. But this . . . this was brutal. This violence was frightening, even to him.

"What could have done this?" Nightlock moaned. "By the realms!"

The shadow beside them dove forward with a ferocious roar. Alastor was all instinct, swinging the boy's arm around, sending a white-hot surge of power rippling up to his clenched fist. The blast connected with the ghoul's jaw, snapping it hard to the right. Its face, all twisted and wrinkled green flesh, was nearly all teeth, its mouth enormous enough to fit the boy's head inside.

Eight eyes rose through the flaps of skin where a man's eyelids might have been. Stringy black hair slapped the boy's face as the ghoul tried to land a blow to his stomach.

"You attack *me*?" Alastor growled, sending another surge of pure, crackling power to the boy's fist. "You *dare* to challenge me?"

The ghoul stood nearly two heads taller than the boy; its limbs could stretch and contort on demand, which was the only reason it was able to reach behind itself and pull a jagged blade from the belt draped over its wrinkled, pocked skin. Alastor caught the hilt and let his magic pour from him, melting the metal down until it disintegrated entirely.

"Return to Downstairs," Alastor commanded, pouring his crackling, rageful power into the ghoul, "and—"

For the first time, Alastor noticed that the ghoul's control collar had been removed. That explained why he had become vicious enough to attack, he supposed. Under his brother Bune's herding and influence, the ghouls were nothing more than collectors of the magic that came from young humans' fears. He searched for the bottle they used to store the energy, hoping to drink it to replenish what he had used tonight, but there was none.

Curious.

The ghouls sent children dark dreams, or, when the malefactors were in dire need of magic, were allowed to pass through the mirrors to hide beneath beds or in closets. They did not attack malefactors. With or without their collars, they did nothing without the command of one fiend— Alastor's brother, Bune.

"Who do you serve?" Alastor asked, shifting the boy's hand until it closed around the ghoul's neck, which was splattered with emerald elf blood. "Why have you come here?"

The ghoul leaned forward, meeting Alastor's gaze in an outrageous show of impertinence.

"I serve," it gasped out, "the true, worthy heir, my master—"

Bune.

One last surge of power burst through Alastor and out the boy's hand. He held on to the ghoul as it screamed, burning from the inside out until there was nothing but ash floating in what had been the elf's home.

"Bune," he whispered, scattering the remains of the ghoul with the boy's feet. He had not been Downstairs when the curse was cast—at least *he* could name the villain. What was this feeling inside of the boy's chest—this unbearable tightness? "I knew it would be so."

"My lord and master!" Nightlock said, crawling out from

under the workbench. "How—how fearsome! This hob did not know you possessed so much power, that you h-had recovered so much of it already."

He had. Human "junior high," as it were, was an excellent breeding ground for misery. Alastor had feasted on the feelings of frustration, anger, and hopelessness he'd felt there. But he did not tell the hob that he had used too much of it. Already, he felt his grip on the boy loosening in a dangerous manner. Now, unless the boy signed a contract, there truly would be no escaping until the night of his thirteenth birthday.

He could not let Bune defeat him.

His brother had always gone two steps beyond cruelty. Alastor believed that humans deserved whatever ends their foolishness brought to them, but Bune believed that they should be destroyed, and their realm and its magic claimed once and for all.

He had been the one to lock Pyra inside the tower for not being able to manifest her animal form. Bune had taunted her, bruised her, told her that it was only by their father's mercy she was still alive. As their father's heir, Alastor had been able to swear to her that he would free her once he had the throne.

But he did not have the throne, Bune did.

Which meant that Pyra was in far more danger than he ever imagined—if his sister was still living at all.

A Kind Heart, a Sharp Knife

On the third night, the dream returned.

The panther with its gleaming black coat and sinewy limbs did not make an appearance, but the vision was scorched with fire. It lit something beneath my skin until even my nostrils were drenched with the rotten-egg smell of sulfur. Its words seemed to stroke down my spine like its soft, silky tail.

Do you hear the singing bone? Do you hear the singing bone?

Heading to school that morning, just before the bus turned into the drop-off lane, I finally built up the nerve to ask Nell about it. Ever since the tour groups had enthusiastically agreed to work with the House of Seven Terrors on a regular basis, she'd lost that pinched look on her face whenever she spoke to me.

As I said, to win favor from others, you must grant them a favor.

I brushed Al's words aside, waiting as Nell thought it over.

"A singing bone . . . that's something from folklore—fairy tales," she said. "My mom told me about it once, and I think there are a couple of variations of it. It usually goes something like, a jealous brother or sister will kill one of their siblings and hide their bones. But when the bones of the victim are found, they sing the truth of what happened."

"Ugh," I said. What did that have to do with anything in that dream, though? What was my brain trying to get me to figure out?

"Why do you ask?" Nell said as the door swung open and we made our way down the aisle. I caught her glancing around as we passed some of the other kids, but they hadn't said a word about her or to her since we got on the bus.

"Just something I read when I was doing research on . . . well, you know," I said, lowering my voice. "By the way, I think we should look into the whole name-of-fiends thing. . . ."

Nell stopped so suddenly I accidentally walked into her back. "You think we haven't? Trust me, the spell is the only way."

"I know, but—"

"Uncle Barnabas checked on his source for the . . ." She dropped her voice to a whisper. "For the toes. He thinks he'll be able to get them by the end of next week. He has some way of shipping them to us without customs freaking out, apparently."

Somewhere inside me, it sounded like Alastor let out a tiny gasp of alarm.

I knew it was an option—the only real plan that we had—but something still made me wonder about the name thing, if only because of Al's reaction to it. If Nell and Uncle Barnabas had given up on that line of thinking, I'd pursue it myself. Just in case we needed a backup plan.

"Hey . . . one more thing," I said quietly. "Is there anything, you know, amiss Downstairs? Have you heard anything about something going on there?"

You remembered. Al sounded genuinely surprised.

Nell stared at me. "Why would I have heard anything at all? It's not like I have a pen pal down there."

I tried, I told him. *I could maybe ask Missy . . .*

You would?

I was still thinking about those words, and the malefactor's surprise, as we arrived at school and left the bus behind. I didn't shake them off until it was time to put my plan into play.

"Aren't you coming?" Nell asked when I started to turn down the wrong corridor.

I glanced at the clock in the hallway. I had less than ten minutes to do this.

"Just—bathroom," I said, giving her a small wave. "Be there in a few."

Once she headed toward homeroom for announcements, disappearing around the corner, I took off at a run, bursting back outside into a drizzle of rain cold enough that it probably should have been snow. The clouds were enormous, twisting around the sky, making me feel like I was standing at the center of a whirl of mist.

What are you doing, Maggot? Alastor asked, curious.

I'd never been in the theater building, but Nell had pointed it out to me in passing. It was attached to the art studios. Inside, the hallways were covered with cast and crew photos, more than half of them *The Crucible*. Spaced between them were large theater posters, all featuring the same woman in different roles and big seventies hair: Anna Drummer. Otherwise known as Madam Drummer, the theater teacher.

I found her in her office, her head of frizzy purple-red hair bent over a costume that looked older than her, carefully stitching the frayed ends back together. To her right, a big backdrop was partially unrolled, exposing some of the artwork.

I'm not one to criticize another artist's work, but . . . yikes. Making the sad depiction of the forest even worse was the odd ripple at the base of it, where it had clearly been damaged by water.

"Madam Drummer?"

The woman jumped about two miles in the air, clutching at her chest.

"Sorry! I didn't mean to startle you," I said. "I just wanted to ask you something, if you have a second?"

"Well—my goodness, let me catch my breath," she said. "Are you here about the auditions for John Proctor?"

The one thing Madam Drummer, wearer of three scarves at once, had in common with my grandmother was that they both tried really hard to make normal words like *auditions* sound French, even with her New Jersey accent.

"Not for me," I said. "For my cousin Nell Bishop."

Madam Drummer stared at me. "I'm not sure I follow . . . ?"

"She wants the part," I said. "She has everything memorized—and she's *good*. I don't get why you won't even let her audition."

"Because she is a girl," she said, speaking slowly and clearly, like I was a child.

Preposterous. Al sounded surprisingly indignant on Nell's behalf. *As if your poor excuse for a bard, Shakespeare, did not have men play women all the time.*

Good point.

"Didn't Shakespeare have men playing the female characters?" I asked. "I know it was a different time, you don't have to explain that, but . . . it just seems unfair."

Many humans do not care about what is "unfair," for it varies so much between them. They are, however, highly motivated by the promise of wealth.

"The script, you see, it's very specific on the matter—"

It took me a second to understand what Al was trying to say. "But think about how much publicity and exposure you'll be able to get for this—I mean, come on, aside from the fact it's just the right thing to do to give everyone a fair shot, haven't you done the *exact same* version of this play every year? With the same backdrop, and the same costumes?"

Her expression narrowed unpleasantly. "What are you suggesting?"

"What if—I don't know, isn't the whole play about unfair persecution and how easy gossip and lies can spread?" I said, mind racing. "Isn't that just like . . . isn't that just like middle school? What if you used the script but changed the setting and characters, just a little bit?"

"Young man," she began, drawing in a deep breath. "The play debuts *next Wednesday*. Today is *Friday*. Even if we worked through the weekend, do you think I have the funds to simply purchase new costumes and backdrops? It's not like I can ask the parrot-brained art teacher for her help."

"No, no—but—if it's set in modern times, the cast can just wear their own clothes. You can use desks and props from classrooms. *I* can paint the backdrops for you for free.

Please just consider it. She's such a good actress. She can't prove you wrong if you don't even give her a chance."

The warning bell rang, interrupting the long silence that followed.

"I'd need to see your artwork," she said slowly. "Your ideas."

"Okay," I said. "I'll sketch some at lunch. They'll be great, I promise. But does this mean you'll let her audition?"

Madam Drummer flicked her hand at me. "Yes, yes, now get to class."

I didn't bother to hide my grin as I took off at a run, bursting outside and pounding through the mud to get back into the main building.

Why did you do this? Alastor asked. *What are you hoping to trade the witchling for?*

Nothing. Not everything is a transaction, I told him.

Did you engage this plan because you wished to feel better about yourself? The malefactor was clearly flabbergasted by the concept of friendship, never mind kindness.

I want to help my family. I thought you'd get that, since I'm guessing what you really want me to ask Nell is what's going on with your family, not your realm.

Such presumption, he sputtered, *such impertinence—*

Out of the corner of my eye, I saw Parker coming up the ramp next to the staircase on his crutches, trying to keep up with his friends. I shoved through the door, flinging rain and mud everywhere, including on the ground the janitor was trying to mop up.

"Hey!" he barked after me, slamming his HALLWAY CLOSED sign down. "Freaking kid!"

I glanced back, just as Parker and his goons tried to approach the janitor.

"Go around—I don't care if you're late, the floor is too wet to be safe—"

I all but slid into first period, shoes still squealing as I hit the carpet and ran to my seat next to Nell. The tardy bell rang just as I collapsed into it. She looked at me, alarmed. Mrs. Anderson gave me a raised-brow look from where she was writing out the day's earth science lesson on the whiteboard.

It wasn't until after the announcements had finished that Parker finally limped his way in, looking rain-soaked and irritated.

"You're late, Parker," Mrs. Anderson said, pointing to a stool at the front of the class. "You know the drill."

"But I had to go around the long way," Parker said, leaning against his crutches. "And it's hard to get around in these things—"

The science teacher put her hands on her hips as the rest of the class squirmed uncomfortably, trying not to laugh at the faint squeak in his voice. I cringed on his behalf.

He does not deserve your pity, Maggot.

"Unfortunately for you," Mrs. Anderson said, "I saw you

chatting with your friends in the yard this morning. You had plenty of time to get here before the warning bell, never mind the tardy bell."

Man, Mrs. Anderson was *stone cold.*

"What's happening?" I whispered to Nell as Parker assumed his seat on the stool, balancing against his crutches.

"Pop quiz," she said. "If he gets the question wrong, he gets detention."

"Now," Mrs. Anderson said, facing him. "Your question is: How many interior layers does Earth have?"

Parker flinched, his face falling, and I knew he didn't have the answer. I made four fingers and started to lift them just above the edge of the raised table that served as our desk, but Alastor seized the arm and drew it back down.

"Um . . . five?" Parker guessed. I sighed.

Mrs. Anderson shook her head. "Four. Looks like we'll be eating lunch together, then, Parker."

His crutches clicked against the tile floor as he sat down heavily in his seat, burying his head in his hands.

Do not pity him, Alastor said as Mrs. Anderson instructed us to open our textbooks. ***He received what he deserved, and a soft heart only makes it easier for a knife to slip in.***

During humanities, Mr. Gupta pulled me aside and told me that he had spoken to the art teacher—weirdly enough, another Ms. Drummer—and that I was welcome to join her last period to see if I wanted to sit in going forward.

There wasn't a big enough word to describe my excitement, so I ended up accidentally screaming a *Yes!* directly into Mr. Gupta's face. I hadn't felt like I could take any of the art classes as Redhood Academy, not without people judging me or mocking whatever I was working on. But here I was *Ethan*—and, awesomely, no one cared.

I'd made it two steps inside the classroom when I was met at the door by another purple-red-haired woman with curly hair exploding from the fabric she'd wrapped it in. All I needed was one look at her familiar face to know why there were two Drummers in this school.

They were twins, like me and Prue.

I blew out a sigh from my nose, trying to push the thought away.

Ahhh, Alastor cooed. **More sadness, more loneliness, Maggot, please. Delicious.**

"You must be Ethan," Ms. Drummer said, smoothing her hands down her paint-splattered apron. "It's nice to meet you. I loved the sketches Mr. Gupta showed me—you have a real talent for playing with light and shadow. Have you taken an art class before?"

I shook my head.

"That's not a bad thing, but even innate talent needs some guidance to reach its full potential. Hopefully we'll be able to share some useful skills and ideas that will help you push yourself to grow and develop your vision and style."

I couldn't form a word. A high, happy noise escaped my throat like a squealing balloon.

"These are my eighth graders, but that doesn't really matter," she said, guiding me out of the doorway so the kids waiting behind me could come in out of the rain. "The only real difference is the techniques I teach, but you clearly have a handle on the ones I'd teach to my seventh graders."

She walked me around the cavernous space. It looked almost industrial: wide-open, with metal shelves of paint and supplies. At the center of the room were big tables with wood tops, tattooed with carvings and stains and drawings. The class was small, only two dozen kids or so. While they were retrieving their canvases from where they'd been stored in large, flat lockers, Ms. Drummer introduced me.

"There's an open seat here," a girl said, raising her hand. She moved her bag as I sat down. "Hi, I'm Lizzy. That's Cody and Brayton on the other side of the table."

"Pros—um, Ethan," I said. "Thanks for letting me sit with you."

She gave me a strange look. "Of course. Why wouldn't I?"

Because in Redhood, kids I didn't even know would get up and move to a different table or desk if I tried to sit down next to them.

The huge windows behind Ms. Drummer let in a ton of light, even with the rain sheeting down on the school.

"All right, a few announcements before you dive into

your projects," she said, making her way over to a freestanding bulletin board. "I'll give you the bad news first: the school is officially out of walls they're willing to allow us to cover with a mural. We'll have to think of a different graduation gift."

The class booed in disappointment.

"So it's back to the drawing board!" she said with a wink. "Good thing that we're all creative types and we're good at reworking ideas. Take the weekend to think about it. Remember, it has to be something we can work on together, and it has to be of use. Now, on to good—and I mean *great*—news." Ms. Drummer brandished a sheet of paper. "Our very own Lizzy has won second place in the statewide art contest for junior high for her piece *At Home in the Harbor!*"

Next to me, Lizzy froze, turning bright red as the class cheered.

"Well done, you," Ms. Drummer said. "They're sending me your plaque and the information about the award ceremony."

"Wow, thank you," Lizzy managed to get out, looking overwhelmed. She stared down at her oil painting of a nighttime sky until the attention of the room shifted onto their own projects.

As Ms. Drummer went around to critique everyone's work, I opened my notebook and tried to plan a few ideas to present to the other Drummer.

"I forgot to explain; I'm sorry, Ethan," she said when she finally reached me. "Our project for the week is depicting our favorite aspect of nature through oil painting. I'd love to see what you come up with—just let me show you where to pick out a canvas."

"Actually," I said, looking at the supplies around me. "I was wondering if I could maybe join your class for the full week and a half and work on a project for Madam Drummer?"

Ms. Drummer's face went carefully blank at the mention of her twin. "Oh?"

"She needs new backdrops for *The Crucible*," I explained. "I don't have a space big enough to try to paint them anywhere else."

"Oh yeah," Cody said from across the table. "Didn't one of the water heaters in their storage closet explode? All of the backdrops are probably a wreck."

"Really?" Ms. Drummer said. Then, muttering to herself, she added, "Why didn't she say anything about it?"

I didn't want to tell her it might have had something to do with her sister calling her "parrot-brained," which now seemed totally uncalled for.

"Could *that* be our class project?" Lizzy asked. "Creating new backdrops of different scenes for them to use in upcoming plays and sketch shows?"

"Not a bad idea," Ms. Drummer said, putting a hand on my shoulder. "I'll ask my sister about it and have her come up with a list of scene possibilities for us to create. Thanks for bringing it to our attention. In the meantime, I'll show you where the canvases are. . . ."

I shrugged and followed her over to another rack, listening to her explanation about which sizes and materials to use for different projects. By the time I made it back to my worktable, Lizzy had retrieved the notice about the art contest off the bulletin board.

"Who won, though?" Cody asked as I sat back down and laid out my paint.

Lizzy looked down at the sheet of paper, and then laughed. "I should have known. It's a Redding."

My whole body went rigid.

"Figures," Brayton said. "That family is unreal. Can I see the piece?"

She slid the paper over to him. My heart was beating so hard in my chest it felt bruised.

"*A View of the Cottage* by Prosperity Redding," he read.

"*What?*" The word was out of my mouth and echoing around the art room before I could catch it.

Cody blinked, sliding it back over to me. "Yeah, check it out. It's not bad at all—at least we know the win came from talent, not from someone buying off the judges."

"There are so many of them, though," Brayton said with a laugh. "The judges were probably all related to them in one way or another."

My hands shook as I looked down at the announcement.

But there it was. My name. A photo of the small painting I had done of the Cottage to give to Prue for our birthday. Instead, I'd been too embarrassed to actually gift it to her and had hidden it under my bed.

Prue. It had to have been her. She had to have found it and sent it in on my behalf.

Oh no. My eyes were itching, burning, and I felt like I wanted go hide outside for a few minutes to get a grip. But . . . I'd won. Not Ethan White. *Prosperity Redding.*

"Do you know the Reddings, Ethan?" Lizzy asked. "You seem surprised."

"No," I said truthfully, setting the paper aside and picking up a brush.

If the past week had shown me anything, it was that I didn't know my family, never mind my twin, at all.

A Too-Close Encounter

Nell met me outside of the theater, bright-eyed and out of breath.

"I got the part!" she said. *"I got the part!"*

"Which part?" I asked, playing dumb.

She punched me in the arm. "You know."

"Cool," I said. "Congratulations, you deserve it—I'm so glad Madam Drummer changed her mind."

Will you not take credit for your work? Al asked, curious.

No, I thought back, *there's nothing to take credit for. Nell's talent got her the part. I just pointed out to Madam Drummer that she was missing what was right in front of her.*

It happened. Sometimes when you get so stuck in a routine, lost in an idea, it can feel frightening to start over or rework it. And I firmly believed that even if I hadn't gone to see the theater teacher this morning, Nell would have found a way to audition.

See how many doors open, Alastor said, *when someone with influence and ideas comes along with a key? Fortune can be hoarded, or it can be shared.*

And a bad thing like a contract could be used for real good . . . like helping people achieve their dreams. Helping them feel more accepted, and less alone.

Indeed, Alastor purred. *All of that and more.*

I shook my head, trying to clear the thought away. It stuck to my brain, unwelcome.

"All of a sudden she started talking about changing the setting and the characters to modern-day," Nell continued as we made our way to the bus. "It was so random, but everyone's really into the idea, and we're going to run through it at rehearsals this weekend. The blocking is pretty much all the same, and we all know the script—it's just a matter of getting the set in order. The old backdrops were trashed anyway, so I guess it's not a bad thing."

"Yeah, Ms. Drummer—art teacher Drummer— mentioned that the eighth graders might take on the backdrops as their school gift this year," I said. "Starting with a few for *The Crucible.*"

"Oh, that's right! How was art class?" Nell said, forcing herself to slow down her happy, skipping steps.

"It was fine, but the weirdest thing happened—" I began, only to be interrupted by a familiar, gravelly voice somewhere behind me.

"Can you tell me if you've seen this boy . . . ?"

I swear, it was like the guy took a baseball bat and slammed it into the back of my head. My eyes went all wonky and out of focus. My throat tightened with panic— my whole body felt like someone had stretched it to the point of snapping in two.

I knew that voice. I knew whose face I would see if I turned around.

Rayburn.

For a moment, I just stood there, wondering if I had ever seen his hunched form outside of the Cottage. In the natural daylight his skin looked as thin and pale as white silk, and the ring of fluffy white hair around his head had been groomed and awkwardly slicked back.

Of course. If my grandmother couldn't come, she *would* send the only other person who despised me as much as her. He was the only unofficial member of the family who wouldn't be recognized by the general public.

I glanced back, just to confirm it. Rayburn's cane thumped against the winter grass, rising slightly, as if to strike, as a few kids ran past him. He shook himself, his mouth twisting and face graying with disgust at the laughter around him. Clearly out of practice for anything that wasn't unlocking, opening, and shutting a door. Beside him, one of the vice principals had a photo in his hand and was showing it to one of the janitors.

Flee, Maggot! Flee!

Nell glanced behind me. "Who is that?"

"Butler," I whispered back.

"Okay, stay calm," she murmured. "Walk fast, but not too fast."

"How fast is that?" I whispered, hating the tremble in my voice. It was too soon—they couldn't take me back, not before we got Alastor out and proved to them I wasn't wandering around with a fiend bent on their destruction inside me.

I closed my eyes, and all I could see was the silver knife in Grandmother's hand, glowing in the candlelight. I stumbled through the mud.

"I see hundreds of kids every day," the janitor was saying.

Nell hooked her arm to mine, forcing me to match her pace.

Flee! Alastor was shouting. *He comes for us!*

"Nell? Cornelia?" the vice principal called, fiddling with his ghost-themed tie. "Can you come here for a moment and speak to this gentleman?"

"I'm going to miss the bus—" Nell protested.

"They've been instructed to wait ten extra minutes," the vice principal said. "It'll just take a moment."

"Stay here," she muttered under her breath. "Don't forget the glamour. He won't know it's you unless you reveal yourself."

As I watched her walk over to them, I realized that while I hadn't revealed myself, I'd given the other family members who weren't Mom or Dad a possible lead. Uncle Barnabas was right—my grandmother had enough tricks up her sleeve to find out about a wrong-number call made to Mom's private, fiercely protected cell-phone number. One of their security guards must have reported it as suspicious to Grandmonster, and she'd sent Rayburn here on the chance it had been me.

Sorry, Mom, I thought. I'd almost ruined their plan in a single moment of carelessness. At least the glamour was still in place.

For now, Al said helpfully.

"Nell and her father run a haunted house that sees many tourists and guests," the vice principal explained. "She might have seen the boy you're looking for."

The vice principal held the photo out for her to see, and she made a big show of looking it over, considering my face.

But the butler was only looking at me.

"Mr. Matthews!" the vice principal called, stalking over to where a kid was about to break his neck skateboarding down a wet rail. He turned around only to hand the photo back to Rayburn. "Do *not* attempt that!"

Rayburn pointed a bony finger at me. I could barely hear him over the rain. "—boy matching his description . . . phone . . . Witch's Brew . . ."

Sweat poured down the back of my neck with the rain. I knew I was panicking, even with the magic mask Nell had placed over me.

"Child, yes, I am speaking to you!" One wraith-like hand reached out and gripped the collar of my fleece, turning me back around with surprising strength just as I started to run. "What's the hurry, young man? Is there something you wish to hide?"

I shook my head.

"The owner of the coffee shop told me about a young guy matching your description making a few phone calls. Did you, perhaps, accidentally use a wrong number?"

Behind him, Nell looked both angry and exasperated.

I shook my head.

"Is that so?" Rayburn asked. "And are you sure you weren't hired by another child to place a call? Say, this one?"

He held out my horrible fifth-grade portrait. I tried not to wince.

"Young man," he said, letting go of my collar. "This child may be in danger. If he asked you to make a call for him—"

"I didn't do *anything*," I interrupted.

In all of Nell's warnings about not revealing myself

to anyone, in all of her explanations of how the glamour worked, I had never once thought to ask her if the glamour also changed my voice.

Now I had my answer.

Rayburn's face fell, then screwed up in confusion. He turned me back around, leaning in close. "Pros—?"

Nell was suddenly next to him, reaching into the outer pocket of her bag. She gripped his arm to get his attention, and the second he looked down at her, she blew a small burst of pink dust in his face.

Rayburn coughed and tried to wave it off, but it was no use. I stood frozen until I saw that his hand had gone lax and I could finally pull away. Eventually he just sort of . . . stilled. His whole body relaxed as his shoulders slumped.

"You didn't find anyone here," Nell said, rubbing the dust off her palm against her dark pants. "Prosper wasn't here. Go back and tell them that."

She didn't wait for him to respond. He stood there frozen as she shoved past him to get to me. "Let's go."

"Why didn't you tell me about the voice thing?" I demanded as we left. "Nell? What gives?"

Perhaps she was hoping you might reveal yourself after all? This time Alastor only sounded as confused as I felt.

"I—I forgot, okay?"

"What was that stuff you used on him?"

"It's dizzy dust," she whispered, yanking me along after her, dragging us through the mud to the waiting buses. If she had slowed down for even a second, I might have run for the nearest garbage can and thrown up everything in my stomach.

"What's dizzy dust?" I dared to ask.

"Herbs and crystals and a bunch of other stuff," Nell said, finally letting go of my arm. We slid down a hill that was slick with orange and red leaves and weaved through the trees, running to the bus just as its doors were shutting. She and I took the only available seat left.

"My mom created it. It disorients a person and lets you influence their memory," she whispered, resting her forehead against the seat in front of us. The windows were fogged over with condensation, hiding us from view. The whole town was wrapped in thick, churning mist. "But—don't tell him, okay? Don't tell Barnabas I had it, or what happened. If he knows, then we'll have to stay in the house. He won't let us leave."

Dread ran a cold finger across my throat. "He wouldn't."

She turned slightly, looking up at me through her fogged-over glasses. "You don't know him. Just promise, okay?"

"Okay," I said, hating that it felt less like a secret and more like a lie.

Alastor, Interrupted

There were a number of things to consider as the day wore on, and Prosperity and the little witch ventured home. Alastor stayed silent, considering how close he and the boy had come to being returned to Redhood. Playing the scene out in his mind again and again.

This close. He had come *this close* to being taken back to Redhood.

It was fear that had made Alastor yell for the boy to flee. Pure, disgusting fear for his own life, which was tied to the boy's. He hated it, every bit of it. The feeling that he was still far too weak. The smell of the boy. The knowing that if they were to return to Redhood now, before Alastor regained his full powers and cut himself free, anything the

Redding family did to the child would affect him.

And, knowing the family as he did, Alastor didn't doubt the grandmother would kill them both to prevent Alastor from finishing the curse he had begun centuries before. They would do anything to protect their fortune, even destroy one of their own household. Honor Redding had proven as much.

But, still . . . the boy refused a contract. Alastor felt as though Prosperity Redding had been on the cusp of saying yes several times, but something—*something*—always held him back. The fiend was confounded. Shown just the edge of what he might achieve with the aid of Alastor's influence, the boy backed away from greatness every time. He was either a coward, afraid of such attention, or . . .

No. All Reddings were alike. Even Honor had begun with the purest intentions, only to discover that success tasted best with a dash of power. Once you craved it, you required more and more to satisfy your ravenous heart.

Alastor reclined against the crumbling tombstone, digging the boy's hand into the squirming bag of spiders Nightlock spent the day collecting for him. He popped one in his mouth, letting it crawl up the tongue. That was better. His sense of himself expanded, filling the boy, as if threatening to burst his skin at the seams to escape.

"Can you . . . pick up your pass, wretch?" The modern phrase sounded wrong to his ears. He had absorbed much by way of this century's language simply from listening to the boy and with the hob's diligent, if not humiliating, instruction.

"Pick up the *pace*," Nightlock said, with a small bow. "I shall do my best, my lord and master."

"I think we're beyond such formality now," Alastor said with a fond smile. "You may call me Your Highness, Dark Prince of the Third Realm."

The fiend beamed with pleasure. He was still busying himself arranging the shards of the broken mirror over a nearby grave.

"Are you sure that's a witch's final resting place?" Alastor asked, reaching over to pluck a stray leaf caught between the stacked stones of the nearby wall. "A true witch's grave? This will not work otherwise. The moon will be far too weak without the added power."

Nightlock merely bobbed his head. "Oh yes, oh yes, oh yes. A true witch—only a true witch. This hob has seen other fiends moonbathe upon this earth."

The moon was the source of the witches' power. The legends of it stemmed back thousands of years, to the pesky ancient Greeks who worshiped the moon goddess Artemis. The lady hunter.

Alastor knew, however, that the moon's power was a gift from the Ancients, who sought to maintain the balance in the realms. To keep each species in its rightful place.

The Ancients had created the witches just as they had created the fiends and the humans. Alastor had them to thank for this. Those women were like a sore on his behind that refused to heal.

A witch merely needed to spend an hour in the moonlight to absorb its full magic and use it throughout the day as she saw fit. The only danger to them came on those nights of a new moon, when the milky-white face was hidden entirely from view.

But this was not one such night. No, indeed, the silky white face was half-hidden in the darkness. And for the fiends who knew such tricks, it was a gift to *them*. Because on this night, any fiend could absorb the witches' magic and make it their own—so long as they had the proper tools.

The final resting place of a witch. That is, a grave. Upon this grave, the shards of a newly broken mirror—aged a hundred years or older, preferably—were scattered in a circle. At midnight, the witching hour, all Alastor needed to do was lie down in the center of the circle, on a mound of damp earth. The power would fill him like the cold air in the boy's lungs.

"Your Highness," Nightlock began, taking the bag of spiders and sealing it. "Perhaps . . . there is another way? Is it not dangerous for us to use a mirror for such purposes? Will you not call forth beasts from Downstairs who hunt for power like your own?"

"Do you believe I could not protect you from my brother or any who serve him?" Alastor asked, trying to stomp out his irritation.

"It's only . . . the boy's flesh is so soft, so thin—and his bones are like straw!" Nightlock clutched at his pointed ears, sniveling and sniffling. "Not suitable for Your Highness, no."

Alastor dismissed his concerns. He had chosen the Old Burying Point Cemetery for this rite, near the row of shops and the courthouse. The two fiends had waited impatiently as the last of the curious humans were led out by law enforcement officers. Now they had the secluded section of the grounds to themselves.

So no, Alastor was not worried as he forced the boy's body down at the center of the ring of mirror shards. As he felt the moon's first kiss of cool magic, he told himself that the wild call in the distance was merely a wolf, and not a howler risen from the realm below. Some lonely beast.

But he was surprised—quite surprised, in fact—when the boy woke himself up.

Prosper, Awakened

"What . . . the . . . *crap?*"

I shot up off the ground, slipping over—what was that, glass? A broken mirror? And that was dirt and grass and a tombstone—

That is a grave. I am in a graveyard. I am outside. I am in a graveyard. I was on a grave. Why-why-why?

"Al!" I barked. "What did you do?!"

I could hear the fiend sputtering in shock—screaming in anger, **What have you done?** Over and over again.

"I asked you first!"

"Your Highness?"

The graveyard was almost pitch-black, and totally empty. If I squinted, I could see the lights from the nearby strip of brick-fronted shops, where the Bazaar of the Bizarre street fair had been. A few tourists were stumbling around aimlessly, heading toward the train stop. I spun around, looking for the source of the voice. It had a weird accent, almost like you'd expect out of a leprechaun.

I felt a tug on the edge of my witch boxers and looked down.

"Milord?"

Big, buggy yellow eyes were staring up at me, unblinking. I thought it was a dog. I seriously thought it was one of those little French bulldogs standing on two legs. Its face was kind of smooshed, and its nose was round and red and shiny, almost like a blister. Then I blinked, and I saw the one horn that spiraled out from the top of its head. The creature was the size of a toddler—it came up past my knee.

It was sniveling and sniffing around. The noise almost sounded like a low purr, until it sucked the dripping blue snot back up into its nose.

I stared at it. It stared at me. I felt my right leg jerk and fill with a hot, stinging rush. Alastor's scream of frustration tore through my brain. I tried to press my hands over my ears, but it was pointless.

He tried everything—moving my head, my fingers, my good arm, my toes—but I was too awake. I wasn't even scared looking down at the freaky little mutant at my feet.

All of a sudden I was just . . . *angry*. I couldn't tell where my anger began and where Al's ended.

"Not milord." The creature's eyes got wider, if that was

possible. He seemed to shrivel and shrink for a second like crumpling garbage. Then he bolted.

That should have been my cue to head screaming in the other direction, but I leaped superhero-style over the nearest tombstone and tackled the thing to the ground. He squirmed and shook and shrieked like my grandmother when she found litter, but I had him. Even when he sank his teeth into my arm and I howled in pain, I didn't let go.

"Release this hob! You will release him at once! Milord, oh, Your Highness, oh, this hob has *faaaailed* you, he has *faaaailed*—"

"Shut up!" I hauled him like a sack of potatoes out of the cemetery and started heading back to the house. "Stop it—just—!"

It's funny. In the back of my mind, I had been thinking it would be pretty awful to run into a cop right now. Not even just a cop, but any adult who could then call a cop on me for breaking curfew. That had been the worst I could think of, especially with Nell's warning to not tell Uncle Barnabas about trouble that could get us locked away in the house.

Your brain just isn't programmed to guess that the broken mirror shards around you would start to shiver, then seal their jagged edges back together. You just don't think to imagine a huge shaggy dog the size of a small cow, with teeth as long as your fingers, digging its way out of a small shard of glass.

I couldn't even choke out a whimper.

The dog smelled sour and sharp all at once. It reeked like it was rotting from the inside out—its hot breath fogged the air around its head in swirling clouds, turning my stomach as it drifted past me. But worse—even worse than all that—were its eyes. They were red, red, *red*.

"Nice . . . doggy?" I tried, backing up. The creature in my arms went boneless, fainting with a wheezing gasp of terror.

As if that weren't enough, the monster opened its mouth, the words dripping from its mouth with its acid drool. *"Find Alastor. Take Alastor. Find Alastor. Take Alastor."*

Run.

I took a step back, the dog took one forward—all the way back onto the sidewalk and out of the graveyard. Yellow drool slipped between the gaps in its teeth, foaming as it hit the ground. The pavement sizzled as it burned. The air filled with the stink of rotten eggs, but I wasn't sure which one of us it was coming from. There was a warm, damp patch on my shirt where the little creature had wet himself.

Awesome.

"What . . . what is that?"

A howler. You will not escape.

"Thanks for that vote of confidence!" I wanted to look around to see if there were other people watching, but the street was deserted. The giant dog came one step closer, its nose turned up to sniff the air.

I will run us back to the house and the witchling. We will only escape if I am at the helm.

"No way," I choked out. The dog arched its back in a leisurely stretch. Black, gummy lips pulled back, almost like it was smirking at me.

Prosperity. Alastor sounded calm, but there was a sharp edge to his words. The fact that he used my name only made my heart lurch. *We shall work together, or we shall die together.*

No contract?

You think I have time to draft one? Zounds, Maggot—

The dog sprang forward, its jaws snapping open with a howl that tore through the moonlight. *"Find Alastor! Take Alastor!"*

And I was running.

The tingling heat filled my legs like a rush of pricking needles, but the night was cold against my skin. It smeared past me in a dark blur. My feet flashed under me, faster and faster until I wasn't even sure they were touching the ground. I wasn't even sure we were headed back to the House of Seven Terrors. I just gripped the ugly little creature in my arms and let Alastor pump pure rocket fuel through my system. The dog's paws slapped against the sidewalk, kicking up sprays of mud and water. Two drops of its acid spit flung against my neck, and I almost stumbled at how bad it hurt.

Something sharp caught the back of my shirt and tore

it across the back. I felt the pinch of that same sharp thing against my skin and let out a cry of my own.

I am going to die. I am going to die. I am going to be eaten by a Godzilla dog, and no one will ever know what happened—

SILENCE!

Alastor forced me to take one last leap off the sidewalk before my whole body launched into the air. I was flying—well, technically falling. I arched up over the two neighbors' lawns. Their Halloween decorations seemed like tiny toys, I was up so high. I heard the hound snarl and snap its teeth, clipping my heel, and risked a look back.

The monster fell to the ground in a twisting bundle of dark fur. It whimpered like any dog would when it hit the gnarled bushes and flattened them. It thrashed against the pumpkin lights that were tangled around its neck, until it finally yanked itself free. The cat that was sitting on the porch, its tail swishing back and forth against the welcome mat, watched the whole thing happen without so much as a blink.

I didn't look back again to see if it was following us. Not when I was the one that was suddenly taking a swan dive.

Alastor tucked my body in on itself just before I hit the dead grass with my shoulder and rolled to safety, narrowly missing the stained cement path. The ugly little nugget of a fiend I'd had in my arms went flying clear across the way, landing up on the porch with a *thump.*

It was such a weird sensation to be tired down to my

bones but have someone else prop my legs up and move them along. I slumped forward against the porch steps, crawling the rest of the way.

Into the house, Maggot. Do not forget my servant.

"What if it comes after—"

Look. It stays at the fence, do you see? But why . . . ?

Some part of me recognized the sound of the stairs creaking overhead. The front door was still wide open, giving me a picture-perfect view of the big shaggy black dog prowling back and forth on the sidewalk in front of the lawn.

The black puffball that was Toad had shifted into an even bigger dog than the one outside of the gate, and he was growling with anticipation of the fight. I wouldn't have even recognized the changeling without its bright round eyes. He took off with a roar, chasing the other dog down the street until it was yelping in fear.

Note to self: do not upset Toad.

"Prosper?"

Nell's already frizzy hair was sticking up every which way from sleep. She wiped at her eyes and suddenly jumped when her brain finally woke up the rest of the way at the sight of:

1. Me sprawled out in the front hallway with my legs twitching.
2. My pajamas hanging off me, totally shredded.
3. The bloodthirsty dog that had been staring the two of us down.

"What did you do?" she demanded. "Did you sneak out with the fiend to summon the howler? Did you make a contract with him?"

"Don't—" I warned. "Don't come any closer!"

Nell didn't understand. I couldn't get the words out fast enough. Before I could push him back, Alastor had my arm, he had my hand, and he was wrapping it around Nell's neck.

Secrets and Slobber

"No—*no!*"

The words ripped out of my throat. Nell's eyes bulged as she tried to push my arm away. Her lips were moving, but the blood was thundering too hard in my ears, the fiend was laughing too loudly for me to hear what she was saying.

You understand now what I am capable of. Al's voice sounded unnaturally high. I felt his fear and desperation like it was my own. *You claim to only wish to save your family. Your only hope for her survival is to sign a contract with me. Agree, Maggot—agree!*

"Screw. You," I gritted out. *No contract now, no contract ever!*

She will die, just as your whole family will—

A burst of warm energy struck me dead center in the

chest, shocking my entire body into numbness as it shoved me back down the steps and across the yard.

No, I thought, still feeling dazed from the blow. *You don't know Nell.*

"I've got more of that, you parasite!" Nell was saying as she advanced toward the gate, one glowing fist still raised. The howler let out a tooth-snapping growl that was met in kind by one from Toad, who launched off the porch like a bolt of lightning.

A hot rush of pins and needles filled my limbs. My hand twitched closer to a sharp rock, and I could see it so clearly, how Alastor would use it to hurt Nell or Toad.

"No!"

It felt like jamming a cap back on a bottle of exploding soda. That horrible fizzing sensation eased up, and Alastor's cries of frustration started.

"Are you okay?" Nell asked at the same time I said, "I'm sorry! I'm so, so, so sorry!"

"What's going on?" Nell looked like she wanted to punch me. "How could you be so stupid as to leave the house?"

The truth exploded out of me: "It wasn't by choice!"

She took a wide-eyed step back. "What do you mean?"

"He's been . . . he's been taking my body out for a ride at night," I admitted. "I had no idea."

"Obviously," Nell said, pinching the bridge of her nose. "Okay . . . okay . . . we'll figure this out. . . ."

I almost forgot about the ugly little gremlin I had carried

back with me. Nell couldn't see him sprawled out on the porch, but she heard him snarfing, sucking up his dribbling electric-blue snot and drool.

"Slip from the shadows into sight," Nell whispered, "reveal yourself in the light."

A ball of light tracked over to him, hovering no matter how far away from it he tried to get. I knew when she finally saw him. She shook her head, but didn't look all that surprised.

"A hob?" she asked, looking straight at me. "You couldn't survive a few weeks without a slave to attend to you?"

"Hey, I would never—" Oh. She was talking to the bratty malefactor. Not me.

I will not dignify that with a response. I am a Prince of the Third Realm.

"We need to get Uncle B," I said, finally feeling strong enough to push myself off the ground.

"No!" she whispered. "No! We can't tell him about this—not the malefactor taking over your body, not the howler you saw. I told you, we'll be trapped in the house—"

"What does that matter if we're dead?" I asked. "Is this about the play?"

A hurt expression flashed on her face. "Of course not. But if I can't leave the house, I can't . . . get to some of the things Mom left me to take care of. Things I could use to protect us."

She looked so upset that I believed her. "Well, what are

we going to do about . . . *that*?" I nodded to the little fiend and his round belly.

Nell bent over and picked him up like an oversize stuffed animal. "Can you walk?"

Not super-steady, but yeah. Instead of going upstairs, she took us down. It was my first time being in the basement, and right away I knew I wouldn't be back. It was cramped, filled with barrels of salt, cardboard boxes, and mostly broken furniture.

She moved to the other side of the room, where something long and rectangular was hidden beneath a dirty bedsheet. The little fiend—the hob, or whatever—was left stretched out on the top of a dresser at the other end of the room.

"Tell your fiend friend we need to talk," Nell said, whipping off the bedsheet. A long, elaborate gold mirror was hiding there—very fancy, very old. Very forbidden.

"Uncle Barnabas said to destroy all the mirrors," I said. "That howler came through *shards* of one. Isn't this dangerous?"

She hesitated for a moment.

"If the malefactor is powerful enough to control your body, he's strong enough to hold back whatever tries to come through to get him. We'll break the connection at the first sign of trouble," she said. "I'm going to get a candle—don't move."

Like her wish could be command enough to stop me.

The prickling, tingling sensation raced along my good arm. All I had to do, though, was picture Nell's face when Alastor forced me to attack her, and I shut it down. I guess my anger was stronger than whatever powers he did have.

Al didn't have a comeback to that one. He didn't want to talk at all.

I don't know how long the three of us stared at one another in the mirror. Long enough for the white wax to start dripping down onto my hands. I held the candle tight between my fingers, trying to push away the uneasy feeling I got when I noticed the white fox had grown. It wasn't a fuzzy little cub anymore. Even though his voice sounded young, Alastor looked . . . older.

"What were you doing?" I asked, finally. "Out in the graveyard?"

Nell's head whipped toward me. "Which one? Describe exactly what was happening."

So I did. And I watched Nell's face go from white to pink to a furious cherry red in seconds. "You were trying to swipe witch magic. You thought it would work for you? You thought you could just use our gift, and that would be enough to fully awaken yours?"

The fox only stared. One blue eye. One black. Neither of them blinking.

"Well, it wouldn't have!" Nell said. "Witch magic and fiend magic don't mix. I don't know where you got your information from, but they lied."

"I do not know who told you that we cannot harness your power under special conditions," Alastor said, and it was nice to hear his voice outside of my head for once. *"But they are the ones that lied."*

"How many times?" I asked. "How many times have you slipped out of the house?"

The fox licked its paw innocently.

"Once? Twice?" I tried. "More than that? Since the beginning?"

Alastor's little chin nodded, just slightly.

"Holy *crap.*"

"You have no memory of it?" Nell asked. "You haven't been feeling tired?"

"I mean, I have a few more bruises and cuts, but I feel fine. I felt fine."

"You could feel better than fine. I've tried to make a contract with you. I tried to reason with you. You could have power of your own. All I would have asked in exchange—aside from your spirit's eternal servitude, of course—would have been the freedom to do what I must to understand what is happening."

"What do you mean?" Nell asked. "What's happening?"

"His Highness, Dark Prince of the Third Realm, refers to the mysterious, oh yes, mysterious happenings of the human realm and our own," came a shaky voice behind us.

I spun around. The little fiend was sitting upright, his stubby legs dangling over the edge of the dresser.

"Be silent! It is not the business of humans!"

"When I come *this close* to getting mauled by Fido the monster, then yeah—I'd say it's my business!" I hissed. "Tell us what's going on. If it gets me killed, it gets *you* killed too, remember, buddy?"

The fox leaped to its feet and began pacing the length of the glass. The hob's eyes lit up at the sight of it. "Your Highness, my lord and master, your form here is of great beauty, the greatest beauty. It surpasses that of your brothers—the hare, the feline, the crow, the snake, the lizard, and the hedgehog. Blegh! Nothing compared to you."

"Hedgehog?" Nell repeated. "One appears to humans as a hedgehog?"

"*Quiet, little witch. Do not strain your inferior mind to speak of things you do not understand. We did not choose our forms. Our father chose them for us.*"

I raised an eyebrow. "He must not have liked you very much, fur ball."

Apparently it is possible for a fox to look totally outraged. If it hadn't been for the hob going up to the glass and making grabby hands at the fuzzy little animal, he probably would have launched into another tirade.

"Can you . . . not?" I asked, trying to pull the hob back from where he was slobbering over the glass. Nell had vaguely explained that hobs were servants of the Downstairs realm, but this one either had a serious case of separation anxiety, or he was obsessed with cute animals.

Nell disappeared for a second, rummaging through the

nearby boxes. She opened up one labeled NELL'S TOYS. She dug around until she pulled out a stuffed gray cat and a fuzzy pink bear.

Judging by the way the hob flew across the room to try to tackle them out of her hands, it looked like he was just obsessed with cute animals. We'd have to hide Toad.

Nell held the stuffed animals just out of his reach, trying not to laugh as the hob jumped up in the air for them. His long ears flopped back and forth, and his snot went flying.

"Give them to me, give them to this hob!"

"Tell me what you guys found out, and you can have *all* of them," Nell wheedled. "Look how *cute* they are. Look how *soft*."

"Don't you dare!" Alastor warned, his face smooshed up against the glass. *"Nightlock!"*

"Is that your name?" Nell asked in that same, sweet voice. "Nightlock, don't you want Miss Kitty and Growley the Bear?"

The hob nodded, his eyes wide and wet. "Please," he whimpered.

"Tell us what's going on."

Alastor let out a defeated sigh as the hob spilled his guts.

"My lord and master is trying to figure out which of his siblings betrayed him to the Reddings, yes," Nightlock said. "One of them, his rival and brother, must have given the witch Prufrock his true name. This is the only way to control a malefactor—oh yes, the only way. She would have needed his name for the spell to bind back his power, to bind it back and destroy him."

"Traitor!" Alastor hissed.

I whirled toward Nell. "I *knew* it! You guys were wrong!" Nell paled.

"Oh yes, a traitor indeed, but which brother, which brother, or the sister?"

"Sister?" Nell and I said together.

"It was not Pyra!" the fox continued. *"My sister is innocent and far too young for such trickery—too young to even gather souls. She would never harm her own blood, nor is she able to inherit the realm. It was one of my brothers—I am the rightful heir of the Third Realm, of Downstairs, and he could not stand this."*

"Your sister can't inherit?" Nell asked. "What kind of crappy rule is that?"

We were getting a little off topic. "So you've been meeting to try to absorb power from the moon?" I asked. "And to try to investigate who might have betrayed Al? Did you find anything?"

Nightlock finally looked away from the stuffed cat. "No. Alas, no. The ruler on the Black Throne has cast a curse. All fiends banished and escaped from Downstairs, including this hob, may not speak the name, or they will be struck dead instantly. Instantly!"

"You know who it is?" I pressed. "It's not Al's father? Is he dead?"

The hob was shaking, just a little. "I cannot speak the name, I cannot. I have tried to find an elf for Master to speak to, but the howlers—the howlers killed the elf first. I have sought out nearby trolls, a White Lady, a banished dwarf, but none can speak the name. It is protected. It is protected."

I shared a look with Nell. This was so much worse than even I imagined. "The howler that chased us here was after Al? And there are more of them?"

"Yes, and yes," the hob said. "Now—Miss Kitty and Growley the Bear, wretched witchling. Give them to me!"

Nell rolled her eyes. "Since you asked so nicely . . ."

Nightlock pounced on the stuffed animals before they even hit the ground. He scooped them up and cuddled them close to his chest, rocking them back and forth even though they were almost as big as him. He cooed and dribbled blue snot all over them in delight and started sucking on Miss Kitty's paw.

"Al, you're in way deep," I said, turning back to the mirror. "And you're taking me down with you. It wasn't just Honor that wanted you dead, it was someone in your family. And between my family and yours, if we don't work together, we're screwed."

"Prosper . . ." Nell warned.

"I can help you get out of me, or at least try to stay safe until you can do it yourself, but in return you can't take control of me without my permission, and you *can't* hurt my family or friends."

"Are you proposing a contract?"

"No!" I said. Why did eternal servitude or whatever always have to factor into everything with him? "I'm trying to call a truce to keep us alive as long as possible. I can be your friend."

"Friend?" Al was disgusted. *"A malefactor has no friends, least of all humans, who are lower even than worms. If you will not sign a proper contract, then I owe you nothing. If you will not sign a contract, then we are at war."*

Nell blew out the candle in my hands at the first sound of footsteps from above. Al's image vanished with the rising smoke.

"Help me!" she whispered, tilting the mirror and lowering it so that it was facedown. We covered it with a sheet for good measure.

"Cornelia?" Uncle Barnabas said, yanking on the light cord hanging above the steps. "What are you doing down here? And at this hour?"

I looked to Nell, uncertain. How could we fix anything without his help?

"The malefactor is keeping Prosper awake, so we were trying a few spells," she said. "We didn't want to wake you up."

Uncle Barnabas's eyes narrowed to thin, pale slits. His hair was glowing under the old lightbulb. "He's getting more powerful, isn't he? I told you that pocket spells wouldn't be enough. Perhaps this will inspire you to remember where your mother placed her grimoire."

But . . . Nell knew exactly where the grimoire was. Missy had told me it was at her shop. Why not go get it and see if there was a spell in there that might actually work, if she really meant to help me?

I shook my head. No. She must have already checked and found nothing. Nell said that grimoires weren't just spell books, but served as private journals. Even if she was protecting her mom's privacy, she could tell him that.

But Nell clearly had no problem lying to her father, or at least keeping secrets, did she?

An excellent point, Maggot. I wonder, how can you entrust your life to two people who endeavor to keep secrets from each other? Because surely if they lie to each other . . . they lie to you as well.

Bells, Books, and Candles

It got bad. Real fast.

What I learned right away was that I could push back against Alastor and regain control of my body—when he was tired. And pretty much only when he was tired.

After trapping Nightlock downstairs and locking the basement door, Nell and I went back to the attic. She stayed up the rest of the night making sure Al didn't try anything. I was too exhausted to try to play it cool and stay awake too. I passed out the second my head hit the couch pillow.

But I had nightmares. Horrible, horrible nightmares. The kind that show you, in gory detail, your family dying. Your house burning down to little piles of ash. Falling off the side of a tall building. Being chased by red-eyed demons and fiends, feeling them tear you apart. It made me miss the prowling panther and its singing bone.

Nell and I went to school on Saturday and Sunday for play rehearsal. The art class rotated each day, coming in to finish each other's work. Once, my hand "accidentally" jerked and nearly knocked over a whole can of paint onto the newly finished classroom backdrop we'd spent hours on. After that, I had to suck it up and lie, pretending I was sick and needed to sleep it off in the audience, which made me feel both useless and lazy. And, on Sunday, I stayed home with Uncle Barnabas and listened to the many, many ways Alastor was going to tear my family apart like confetti once he was free of my body.

Monday arrived like a snake, silently slithering up to us before we were prepared for it. Frost coated the world, and what leaves had managed to hang on to the trees dropped overnight with the sudden spike of cold temperature. I couldn't shake the feeling that this was some kind of ending.

I tried to keep my spirits up, knowing that fear and hopelessness only fed the malefactor. Failure couldn't be an option when my family's lives were on the line. But I couldn't shake the shivers of dread that were working through my blood.

"What if I hurt somebody?" I whispered as we waited for the bus. Alastor was silent, but not sleeping. It felt like he was . . . waiting.

"I'll be there," Nell promised. "We have almost every class together. If it seems like it's getting too bad, let me know. We'll ditch. Everything will be okay."

Everything was not okay. That much was clear from homeroom, when Mrs. Anderson stood at the front of the room and began to cry because Eleanor, the classroom tarantula, had gone missing.

"Please, if you find her . . . if you took her, just return her, no questions asked . . ."

I turned to look at Nell, but she only shrugged. Maybe the changeling had finally gone back to Missy. Still, it seemed weird that she would just leave when the point of her being there was to keep an eye on Nell. But, clearly, the witch herself didn't seem to think so.

In math class, Alastor made me kick the girl sitting in front of me until she cried and the teacher sent me out into the hall for being "rude and disruptive." And because Nell couldn't go with me, I ended up spending the rest of the hour slamming my good hand into the side of the building until the knuckles bled and I was sure it was broken. Nell was horrified, but there wasn't much she could do beyond take me to the nurse's office.

Alastor still wasn't done.

Mr. Gupta gave us a surprise pop quiz on the Greek gods in humanities. I was tired and felt a little fuzzy, but I knew all the answers. Or, at least, I thought I did. At the end of the class, the teacher waved me over. His dark eyes narrowed as he looked at my twitchy, bandaged hand. Which I'm sure seemed even worse when I used my other already bandaged arm to hold it down.

"I didn't realize you could speak Greek," he said.

The sinking, sick feeling was back in the pit of my stomach. "I can't. . . ."

"Oh, really?" Mr. Gupta asked, holding up my sheet. "Then, in that case, please don't waste my time or mock me. If you don't know the answer, just leave it blank."

I squinted at my first answer. It was my dark, smeared handwriting all right, but . . . it was definitely not in English.

My answer is perfectly correct, Alastor said. *I don't see what he's so upset about.*

"I'm impressed you know this many Greek letters," Mr. Gupta said. "I suppose I should give you some points for creativity."

"I'm . . . sorry, sir?" I said, because I had no idea what else I could say.

Nell was smart enough to separate us from the rest of the kids at lunch. We ate out on the basketball court, then moved onto the nearby field when other students wandered over to play a quick game before the bell went off again.

"Nell!" We both turned at the sight of Norton, dressed in head-to-toe red, jogging toward us across the dead grass.

"What's got you mad today?" I asked, eyeing what looked

like a red puffy snowsuit. To be fair, he looked the warmest out of everyone sitting outside on that icicle of a day. Behind him, one of the basketball players was so distracted at the sight she threw her pass too hard and it hit Parker square in the head from where he was watching from the sidelines.

Norton raised his eyebrows. "What makes you think I'm mad? Red is the color of *passion*—oh, never mind. Here! I remembered."

In his hand was an old, beat-up iPod.

"*Thank you!*" Nell threw her arms around him, and his face suddenly matched his suit.

"N-no problem," he said. "It's yours. I got a new one for my birthday a few weeks ago."

I waited until Norton wandered off at the warning bell before asking, "What's that for?"

Instead of answering, Nell shoved the earbuds into my ears and began scrolling through the menu to find what she was looking for. But she wasn't in the music section—Nell was in the alarm one. Before I could repeat my question, the sound of bells—big, metal, hearty bells—were clanging in my ears.

Al shrieked. Legitimately *shrieked*.

I pulled out the earbuds, enjoying his pathetic moaning maybe a little too much. "Wow, he's not a fan."

Nell pushed the alarm again and turned down the volume. "I totally forgot about this trick, I'm sorry. Fiends hate the sound of bells. The sound is too pure and beautiful. Every time he does something, just give him a blast of this. At night, we'll put it on a loop so he won't be able to sleep. That'll keep him too tired to do something during the day."

It was like a little electric zap. I could feel Al's entire spirit clench and shudder when the bells played. The pressure in my legs and good arm released, like he had lost his grip.

"And if he can't sleep at night, he'll have to sleep during the day, or he'll be too exhausted to take over," I finished. "Nell, that's genius."

"The class bell made me remember last week—it's just too bad it's an annoying beeping and not a true bell sound." She grinned. "Anyway, it's just a temporary fix for now. Be careful a teacher doesn't catch you with it, or they'll take it away."

Hey, I wasn't going to complain about a temporary fix. Even a little bandage can stop a cut from bleeding.

The day got *so* much better once I knew I could give Al a friendly little jolt. I slipped the bud in and out of one ear when I saw the teachers weren't looking. In between classes. When I just wanted to feel him squirm.

The only class I begged out of was PE, which Coach didn't really appreciate. But how could I run with my injured hand? Nell had asked. What if his future track star never fully mended? What if he couldn't run come spring? (Nell was really good at acting.)

I sat beside Parker on the sidelines in awkward silence before working up enough nerve to ask, "How's your ankle?"

The other kid grunted. "You care?"

"I just . . . never mind. I just feel bad, okay?" I said, watching the other kids run by. "I feel like it's my fault."

It is.

Those two words from Alastor came like a kick to my chest.

"Nah," Parker said with a long sigh. "It's not. I knew it was stupid of me. Just trying to prove something, I guess. But it's just the latest in a long string of bad luck."

Hmm.

My heart was in my throat when I asked, "What do you mean?"

"My dad lost his job, my parents are divorcing, I might have to get surgery on my ankle, which means I might not be able to run track for a few months," Parker admitted, his voice tight. "But it's fine. It will *be* fine."

Al. I could barely get the thought through my mind. *Did you do this?*

Of course I did, Maggot, as did you. Luck isn't infinite. Even in this form, even limited to your body, I can manipulate those close by. To gift you luck, it first needed to come from someone else.

For a second I was sure I was going to throw up.

I didn't ask you to do that! I thought, furious.

But you enjoyed it, didn't you? Al sounded almost wistful. **Tell me, do you think you truly are a good artist, or that I helped to align the right pieces to convince other people they were seeing something great when it was only truly mediocre?**

I stood suddenly, feeling like my entire face was on fire. I mumbled some excuse to Parker and the coach about needing to use the bathroom. Once I was in the empty locker room, I collapsed against the nearby wall, shaking.

Stop pretending to feel sorry! Al hissed. **Stop pretending to be anything other than another Redding wretch!**

"I wish I had a singing bone," I muttered. "So I could figure out when you were telling the truth—"

What did you just say? Alastor's voice jumped in pitch again, alarmed.

Singing bone? I repeated. *What about it?*

No, nothing—nothing at all. He sounded relieved. **But where did you hear such a thing? A . . . dream, perhaps?**

Now it was my turn to be alarmed. *Yeah. You didn't already know?*

I cannot see your dreams when I, too, sleep.

Wait—what was it that Uncle B and Nell had told me about fiends and their realm? That they traveled between mirrors . . .

And used dreams to communicate.

"Do you think it was one of your siblings?" I whispered.

"Trying to tell me something? Something like, oh, I don't know . . . *your name?* Do I need to find a singing bone in order to reveal it? I'm sure that Nell and Uncle B could help with that too—"

Rather than wind him up, my words only seemed to deflate that anger and glee I'd felt running through my veins and nerves all day.

Prosperity, he began, taking on an even more formal tone. *There is something I wish to say to you. I ask for a moment of your consideration, for I believe we are in grave danger.*

It was hard not to roll my eyes at that one. *Are you asking for a truce?*

Alastor snorted. *If you wish to call it such. A temporary understanding.*

Fine. What is it?

The malefactor took his time making sure his words were as dramatic as possible. *As both of our lives depend upon it, I must ask you to reconsider the trust you have placed in the little witch and your uncle. I do not think their aim is to help you.*

Well, it's definitely not to help you, I shot back. *Why am I supposed to trust you over them?*

Because our lives are tied together. What befalls me, befalls you. I speak to you now in all honesty, as if you were my own brother.

"You hate your brothers," I muttered.

Well. We cannot choose our family, as you yourself are well aware. Last night proved my suspicions to be true—as I said, I do not think they wish to help you. I think they mean to keep us imprisoned here in this city, while they wait for someone—or something else.

"What makes you think that?" I whispered.

The howler. They are controlled by whoever sits on the Black Throne. Did you not notice that we are still alive? The fiend repeated its command to find and take me. These beasts are trained to kill or retrieve wayward fiends who have snuck into the human realm and threatened the balance of life.

The balance of what? How was it possible this kept getting worse and worse? Wasn't there a limit to how awful things could get? A rock bottom we could hit before heading back up?

Each kind of creature—human, fiend, specter, and Ancient—is bound to its own realm, for if too many of one kind pass into a realm that is not their own, the balance is thrown, and the realms collapse on themselves. This is the one law we are all bound by, and the sole reason for the howlers' existence.

That dog could have easily killed us last night, I thought. *Or dragged us back to the fiend realm, right?*

The moment we passed the threshold of the house, it backed away, even before the changeling, yes? It has been ordered not to attack us while we reside there. This only proves the witch and your uncle's involvement to me. If they themselves cannot control it, then they are allied with the one who can.

"They're my family."

Ah yes, family. You and I both know how dangerous a family can be.

The Dread of the Dead

After PE, Nell went to her last class, theater. But instead of heading to art, I returned to my old friend, the library.

"Singing bone," I muttered, sitting down at one of the open computers and logging in. "Singing bone, singing bone, singing bone . . ."

Stop this at once, Maggot. You meddle in matters you do not understand.

Why would one of your siblings try to contact me? Why would they use that phrase?

It's as I've told you: my brother, the one who betrayed me to the witch Prufrock, is determined to make sure I do not return Downstairs to reclaim my throne.

So they are *trying to lead me to your true name.*

Alastor, as expected, said nothing. But I could feel his own thoughts spooling as I loaded the Internet browser.

So. Three people—well, living creatures—knew Alastor's true name. His brother, who then gave it to Goody Prufrock. And Alastor himself.

And my mother, Maggot, who whispered it into my ear as a child. She's been gone for centuries, however.

And the only other person who knew Alastor, or at least *of* Alastor, in our realm was . . . Honor Redding.

If I couldn't get access to Goody Prufrock's grimoire in the Cottage, then maybe Honor's journals were the next-best thing.

I quickly typed in the address for the Redhood Museum, clicking over to their special-collections section. My great-great-grandfather had bequeathed Honor Redding's journals to the museum to keep and preserve, and the museum staff had taken nearly a decade to scan and enhance them enough for visitors to read. I'd never looked through them, mostly because I hadn't cared enough to try.

Someone, at least, had taken the time to transcribe the faded, tiny cursive writing from the scanned pages into normal text below. *We arrived in America this day past, and already trouble is upon us. . . .*

I skipped ahead, through a number of entries charting rampant sickness, cold, and the colonists' inability to grow the crops they'd brought with them. The first mention of the tide turning was a hastily scribbled *Fate has brought us a boon, we shall survive, we shall survive, we shall survive!*

And then four weeks of entries were missing. If that "boon" was Alastor, then the details of his contract with them had been torn out of the journal, if it had ever been noted at all.

What was he like?

You speak of Honor?

I was a little surprised Al answered.

Yeah. He must have been a terrible person to do the things he did.

The malefactor was quiet for a long time before he finally said, **The man was a fobbing plume-plucked hedge-pig, but he . . . When we first met, I . . . liked him fine. I respected his ambition and the way he led the settlement—these are not easy things, you understand. But he turned out to be the same as all men. His taste for power turned into a hunger, and he was not strong enough to stop himself. It is the nature of human hearts to be weak.**

Were you friends? I asked. The portrait of Honor Redding at the Cottage showed a glowering old man, but it had been painted almost a decade after his death. He looked like the kind of guy to go around stomping daises. I couldn't imagine him having heart-to-hearts with a fluffy white fox.

No! This time, Al answered a little *too* quickly. **I do not form lasting bonds with my future slaves.**

"Yeah, yeah," I muttered.

Prosperity, it is not too late for us to leave this place. In four days' time, my power will be at its peak, and I will be free—which means that whoever is trying to kill me, and therefore you, will show themselves before that. I am willing to make an agreement with you—not a contract in the strictest sense, but a gentlemen's agreement. If you are willing to escape this village and these people, I will grant your family one year to enjoy their power before I send it crashing down around their ears.

"There you are!"

I quickly closed out the browser before turning in my chair toward Nell. She was panting, her shoulders heaving as she tried to catch her breath. I opened my mouth to ask her what was wrong, but she knocked the words off the tip of my tongue with a swat to the back of my head.

"I've been looking all over for you!"

"Don't you have theater?"

She turned my head toward the clock on the wall. For the first time, I noticed that the library was empty save for me and a librarian reshelving books.

"I lost track of time," I said.

"No kidding," she said, grabbing my bag. "Come *on*— we have to run to catch the bus."

But the buses, every last one of them, were already gone. The sky itself was darkening quickly, and the only brightness was my white breath fogging the air.

"Okay . . . I know you said you'd never call for a car . . ."

I started, arms crossed over my chest. I only had on one of Nell's old fleeces, and it was just barely keeping me warm enough. "But what about calling Uncle Barnabas? Or Missy? Or Mrs. Anderson?"

"He doesn't have a car," she said. "We had to rent one to go rescue you."

Mrs. Anderson had, of course, gone home. And Missy didn't pick up any of the times we called her.

"We'll just walk far enough to take one of the city buses," Nell said.

If she could tough it out, then so could I. It also helped to remember, after walking a few blocks from campus, that I had a built-in internal furnace with Alastor inside me. He might have stunk to high heaven, but at least I was radiating enough heat that none of the snow falling from the trees stuck to me.

We stopped at a corner, waiting for the light to change. A few cars zipped by, two slowing to turn left into a nearby parking lot. And when they did, it gave me the perfect view of the snarling black howler waiting for us across the street.

An Escape in the Night

By the realms . . .

The walk signal flicked to the white guy and Nell stepped off the curb. My hand shot out and caught her arm, hauling her back onto the pavement.

"Hey! What are you— Prosper?"

Run, run, run, run! Al chanted. I barely heard Nell's gasp.

"What do we do?" I whispered.

The walk signal began to flash orange, chirping in warning. A line of cars was building up, waiting for the light to turn red. I started backing away from the sidewalk, taking Nell with me. There was a roar of an engine as the white car in front jumped forward with the green light. And by the time the last car cleared, it wasn't just the one howler that was waiting there for us. It was three.

They all charged at once, ignoring the cars blitzing past. The drivers couldn't see them as the howlers clawed and climbed their way over their roofs. The people in the cars were freaking out as the dogs' bodies slammed into them, denting the metal and sending them spinning like toy cars.

That's when we started running.

Let me—let me take control, Prosperity. I can get us out of this again. Give it to me! Give me control!

"What about Nell?" I gasped out.

"What about me?" she shouted.

The first dog was almost on us, snarling. I felt its acid spit spray the back of my shirt. Nell had wanted it to get that close—she turned, reached into her pocket, and threw a huge handful of dizzy dust right in its eyes.

It skidded to a stop, shaking its huge head and rubbing at it with its paw. The others tore past it and got the same treatment, but they weren't down as long.

"By my flesh and by my bone, turn this creature to living stone!"

If that was supposed to be a spell, it didn't do *anything*.

No spell will harm them, they must be banished back to the Third Realm! Tell her!

"You . . . believe him?" Nell was panting hard. "We need to get back to school or get home—or Missy's? Anywhere that has a protection spell!"

"Missy's is closest!" I shouted, dodging through the trees.

Let me run! Let me run! I can save us, just—

"Okay, okay," I said. "Nell, get on my back!"

She shot me a strange look. "Excuse me?"

"Piggyback! *Now!*"

It was awkward considering she was two inches taller than me, but the second I felt her arms around my neck, Al was ready.

I wasn't about to ask any questions, and neither was Al. It was like being at the wheel of a speeding car. He was the engine, and I was the driver, and somehow we were working together perfectly.

I didn't look back when I heard the howling start. The second my feet hit the next street, I launched into a jump. Al knew what I wanted to do and kicked in the power I needed. We went soaring over a house and people shoveling snow in their backyards, arcing across the moon itself before landing on the other side of it.

Everything looked different in the dark. Nell pointed us in the right direction, through the right cluster of trees. I tore through them, letting the branches snap against my face. The old Victorian house was a glowing blur in front of us, getting bigger by the second.

The windows were lit but the curtains were drawn. I leaped up the stairs, grateful that Missy's protection spell let me pass without trouble. We went crashing through her front door, spilling into a heap amid the stacks of books.

"—dare tell her, I will destroy you—"

"Destroy *me*? As if you could—"

That sounded like . . .

"Barnabas," Nell muttered, closing her eyes.

But instead of hearing the whimper of a big, ugly dog getting thrown around by Missy's rosebushes, there was a heavy *click, click, click* of claws against her porch. When Nell and I looked back, we could see one of the howlers standing on its hind legs, peering down at us through the glass of her front door. Another one of them pushed the first down to get a look into the shop.

"Who's there?" a woman called. "Nell, is that you?"

Nell darted forward, turning the lock. The howlers banged their heavy bodies against it, splintering the wood.

They are here for me.

"For us," I muttered.

I was right—it was Uncle Barnabas. He stormed down the stairs after Missy, his face red with fury at the sight of us there, in her shop, where he'd expressly forbidden Nell to go.

"I can . . . I can explain," I tried. "But—"

The glass door shattered into a million pieces when the first howler crashed through it.

Make haste! Alastor yelled. *Leave this place!*

Uncle Barnabas threw himself against the wall, nearly falling over himself to get back upstairs. Missy dove forward, reaching for Nell as she all but climbed a mountain of books, knocking over a pile of them. "Nell!"

"*Here!* Missy, I need your help! I can't reach it—"

The howler growled, pawing at the glass. The other two followed it inside, all slinking muscles and moon-white teeth.

"Nell . . ." I called. "Whatever you're doing, can you please hurry it up!"

"*Distract them!*"

"Seriously?" I said. "*Seriously?!*"

I did the only thing I could—I started throwing whatever was in reach, which happened to be books, and lots of them. I might as well have been tossing feather pillows. The books whacked into their skulls, all right, but the howlers didn't even flinch. In fact, I kind of thought they were . . . laughing at me. They made this awful *chu-chu-chu* noise, tossing their heads. One even caught a book between its teeth and snapped it clear in two.

The leader of the pack went stiff, its ears perking up. Then it pounced. My skull knocked flat against the tile, making stars explode in front of my eyes. It didn't matter. All I could see were teeth—hundreds of sharp, slobbering teeth. The howler's claws pinned me where I was, sinking into my shoulders until I couldn't hold in my cry.

"*Those who trespass in our land*"—Nell's voice rang out clear behind me, along with the older woman's—"*now be blocked by my hand.*"

I craned my neck back, trying to see what was going on. The two of them stood there, Missy with a silver hand bell, Nell with a big leather book open in her hands.

There was a pause as a bell rang three times. Alastor groaned in my ears, but that was nothing compared to the dogs' reactions. They howled and yelped like they were being beaten. Even the one on me backed away. Nell wasn't finished, though.

"I bind you back to your realm, I send you back to your realm, I banish you to your realm!" The bell rang three times, and it was like a tornado dropped on my head. A black wind whirled free and wild, tossing books around, lifting the howlers off the ground, and sucking them down, down, down, into a thick blackness I wasn't awake long enough to see.

I drifted in and out of sleep, too exhausted to open my eyes, when I heard Nell and Missy whisper to one another.

"While he's still upstairs, please, let us leave, it's not too late. The coven will protect you. We can end this now—"

"You wouldn't do anything, you refused to help, this is the only way—"

"If you're afraid of that man, then *leave*. Come to us, we'll care for you—"

"How could I? You know . . ." Nell sounded like she was in tears. "You know who he is. I have to stay."

"And this boy," Missy began, her voice shaking. "This is not what our magic is meant for. How can you possibly untangle yourself from it all?"

"I can't," Nell said. "It's already too late."

Locked Up, Locked Out

Nell was right. Once Uncle Barnabas found out what was going on, everything changed.

"You betrayed my trust! Not only that, but you have endangered yourselves and everything we've been working toward! How dare you? *How dare you*, when you know what the consequences are?"

Since we'd been sneaking around behind his back for the last week, it only seemed fair that we let him spend a few hours lecturing us about it. I probably would have felt a little better about the decision if my skull wasn't pounding so hard I thought it would explode.

"Do you know what went through my head when I learned you'd been visiting that witch in secret? When I saw you pursued by the howlers?" he continued, pacing in front of us. Nell and I were slumped on the couch, looking like we had been dragged through a field of mud before being tossed out into a thunderstorm.

"I'm sorry," Nell said for the tenth time. "We're both so sorry. You just have so much on your plate, and we didn't want to worry you. We didn't expect—"

"You didn't expect to be attacked by fiends? You didn't expect anyone else to come after the malefactor? After *Prosper*?"

We hadn't even told him everything, and he was already this mad. Nothing about Rayburn, or Al taking control of my body, or the hob.

Nell flinched, rearing back.

"What are we going to do now?" I asked, trying to change the subject.

"If you had taken care to get yourselves safely home, you would already know this." Uncle Barnabas went to the desk, which had quickly regained most of its clutter after being ruthlessly cleaned. He retrieved a small cigar box and opened the lid, revealing three small, shriveled prunes.

Not prunes.

Toes.

"Dead man's toes?" I leaped up, taking the box from him. "They actually made it here?" Knowing my luck like I did, I hadn't expected the toes to arrive within the month, let alone by my thirteenth birthday on Friday.

Nell hung back on the couch, tilting her head to look at the ceiling.

"Yes, well, it seems like fate is on your side," Uncle Barnabas said, plucking the box out of my grip and placing it in a soft cloth. "We'll take the next few days to make our final preparations."

Final preparations?

I didn't like the sound of that either.

"I have rehearsal for the play tomorrow night, and the show starts on Wednesday. I can't miss it without upsetting everyone," Nell began.

"I don't want to hear another word about this *stupid* play of yours, Cornelia." Uncle Barnabas whirled on her, throwing a finger in her face. "And we'll be closed for business until further notice. From this moment on, neither of you leaves this house."

It was another few hours before I realized what—or rather who—was missing.

"Where's Toad?" I asked. "I haven't seen him since . . . the first howler."

Nell sat up from where she'd been stretched out on her bed, her face buried in her pillow. Her dark, curly hair was standing up around her face like a full halo, bouncing as she quickly searched the room.

"Huh," she said, sitting back down. "He sometimes

wanders off to visit with Missy or go hunting for his meals. I wouldn't worry yet."

Is not the other changeling also missing?

I was about to point that much out to Nell, but the look on her face, so tired and gray, made me bite my tongue.

The snow outside had melted as rain set in that night and continued into Tuesday morning. It made it seem like the whole world was weeping, awash in its own misery. It could only have been painted in watercolor. The edges of the streets and nature seemed to blur with dark lines.

On the other side of the bathroom door, the shower's running water continued to sputter and spurt. Curls of warm, wet air escaped the crooked cracks around the door.

"Prosper," Nell whispered. "Maybe you should go."

"Go?" I pushed myself up so I could see her more clearly over the top of the couch. "What do you mean?"

"Leave," she said, keeping her gaze fixed on the bare tree branches outside. "Go back to your family."

"The people trying to kill me?" I said. "Don't forget, *you* are my family too."

The shower cut off abruptly. The silence between Nell and me was so thick I could hear Uncle Barnabas as he dressed and quickly shaved. His glasses were still steamed over as he stepped into the attic, a large, familiar-looking leather book slung under his arm.

Nell's mother's grimoire.

He'd had it in his possession since we left Missy's, and

there hadn't been a second he wasn't watching it, holding it, reading through what pages weren't enchanted to disappear to maintain privacy. Several times, I thought Nell would snatch it away from him, but in each instance she stepped away and left him to it.

"Cornelia," he said. "I need to speak with you. Alone."

They made as if to go out into the hall. I stood up quickly, recognizing my one chance for air and a small bit of freedom. "I'll go check to see if Toad, uh, escaped into the backyard."

"I don't think that's wise—" Uncle Barnabas began.

"Just the yard," I promised. "You can watch me from the window."

"Then put on the iron bracelets before you go."

Something inside me recoiled, and I couldn't tell if it was me or Alastor. Missy had given Uncle Barnabas four old, rusted iron bracelets that she claimed would have the same effect as a cut from a cursed blade. They were thin enough to not be heavy or cumbersome, but locking them over my wrists and ankles made me feel more like a prisoner than I'd have liked.

I left them to their serious faces and conversation. I felt a nudge of guilt and worry over leaving Nell to him— not because I thought Uncle Barnabas would hurt her, but because I had a feeling he hadn't even given half the tongue-lashing he'd wanted to the night before. It was one thing to yell at a nephew, and another to discipline your own kid.

As I stepped outside, my feet sinking into the mud, I threw one look back up toward the attic window and saw nothing but the curtains.

You should not have agreed to leave. They could be engaged in nefarious plotting.

"It's called trust. You should try it sometime," I muttered, then cupped my hands around my mouth. "Toad? *Toad!* Are you back here?"

The snow and rain had turned an already hideous, overgrown yard into a swamp that seemed determined to suck me down into it. I made my way around the rocks and what was left of the lawn, checking the branches of the maple tree. Like a key inserted into a lock, each empty space twisted and twisted my heart.

Hopefully he was somewhere warm and safe—dozing in Missy's lap by a warm, crackling fire.

A rustling noise caught my attention. I spun around, back toward the trash cans that Uncle Barnabas had yet to remember to put out on the curb.

"Toad?" Another black thought crossed my mind. "Or is that you, Nightlock?"

We had fed the hob and brought him back down to the basement the night before, locking him in. I wondered what Nell was planning to do with him after I was back at Redhood and Alastor was gone.

You believe it will be as simple as that?

Ignoring him, I made my way over to the trash can, pulling up the black plastic bags to make sure Toad hadn't gotten trapped beneath them. And, because it's just my luck, one of them split open at the belly, pouring out garbage everywhere.

I turned my face up to the cold rain and tried not to groan in frustration. The only thing I could do was stuff the papers and wrappers into the other, less-full bags. I was nearly finished when my hand closed around an empty, beaten-up padded envelope.

It was addressed to Uncle Barnabas from someone named John Smith in Sydney, Australia.

It must have been the packaging the toes had arrived in . . . only, no, that didn't make sense. The CUSTOMS stamp from the United States said it had arrived on September 1, not yesterday. Maybe the package had gotten lost in transit to Massachusetts, or this was for something else. Those were the only options that made sense.

Because if Nell and Uncle Barnabas had all the pieces in place for the spell to remove Alastor this whole time, why were they pretending we needed to wait?

I warned you, Al said. And he wasn't even gloating. Fear passed through me like a shade, freezing my core. *There is still time. We can escape.*

And go where?

—

Hours later, Alastor lay awake, opening the boy's eyes to study the fattening moon through the window. The boy had not left the bells playing. There was no need. Every time Alastor tried to move his limbs, the iron bracelets weighed them down.

The boy's feeble heart was a thorny tangle of guilt, frustration, and longing. Alastor despised the taste of guilt—like overripe fruit, it was overwhelmingly sweet. Guilt was a sign of some goodness, however buried it might be, because it implied a human could still recognize right from wrong.

The malefactor released a long, long sigh through the boy's mouth. He needed to accept now that his conventional means of procuring a contract had failed, and would continue to fail. The boy's heart, it would seem, was a rare sort: incorruptible by greed, incompatible with jealousy. Unlike Honor, he saw the destruction that Alastor's good fortune wreaked on others. But *like* Honor, his one weakness, his truest wish, was nothing more than the survival and success of his family.

If Alastor were to make a contract, his last, desperate chance of getting out of the boy's body before the witch removed him by force and destroyed him, he would need to chase the tail of that lead. He would require somewhat drastic measures.

"Servant," he whispered.

Nightlock's eyes appeared at the foot of the couch.

"Take the boy's notebook," he said. "I've instructions as to whom, by hook or crook, you must deliver this book."

The hob's eyes glittered with excitement.

"Come closer. I'll tell you the way to Redhood."

Setting the Stage

In the end, Uncle Barnabas came around.

I'm not sure why that surprised me so much. After the lecture he'd given us yesterday about how it wasn't safe for us to leave before he and Nell could cast the spell to remove Alastor, I thought for sure we'd be stuck in the house for at least another day. But whatever they had talked about last night while they were downstairs, it was like Nell had flipped a switch in him.

"Good morning, good morning," he called as he came out of the shower. "I'm going to run out to grab some doughnuts, do you have any requests? Maybe you'd like some hot chocolate?"

Trying to smooth things over with a little sugar, huh? Well, I wasn't too proud to take a doughnut bribe.

"Man, forget doughnuts, I'd kill for a Silence Cake," I said.

His pale brows drew together in confusion.

"You remember," I said. "The pumpkin leaves?"

"Oh—oh yes. My word, I haven't had one in ages. Sadly they're not found outside of Redhood. What can I get you from the Witch's Brew instead?"

"I liked their glazed doughnuts," I said, "and I'll definitely take a hot chocolate. What about you, Nell?"

Nell was still in her pajamas. She had been working on her homework even before I got up, and hadn't moved an inch from her bed.

Uncle Barnabas grabbed his coat and a beanie, tucking his wet hair up inside of it. "While I'm gone, you can tell Prosper the good news."

The news couldn't have been that good. Nell cringed.

I waited by the window until I saw Uncle B head out the back door and down the street. The bakery was only a block away, meaning we didn't have much time to talk.

"What's going on?" I asked. "Why is he acting like he swallowed actual sunshine?"

Nell shrugged, keeping her eyes on her homework. "I explained to him last night about how important the play was to us. I convinced him to let us go to the performance tonight."

In exchange for what?

"In exchange for what?"

"Why do you think I had to promise him something?" she asked, her voice going high. "He said he would take us tonight, and I wasn't going to question it. It's not like he's making you go to school today. You should be happy about that."

Was I happy about that? I kind of liked this school.

It's not your school, I reminded myself. This isn't your life either.

"He's even going to watch the performance," Nell continued. "He was just . . . out of sorts. They're making cuts at one of his jobs."

So Uncle B really had just been in a bad mood after all. The poor guy probably wasn't sleeping well, and knowing there was a fiend lurking less than five feet away from him wouldn't help much on that front.

Nell slammed her science textbook shut and jumped off her bed. She didn't even look at me as she passed the couch. The bathroom door slammed shut behind her.

Sensing she hadn't already fed the hob, I pulled together a plate of potato chips and a banana to bring down to him. Only, when I opened the door to the basement, he was gone.

"Nell?" I called through the bathroom door. The shower was running, so I had to shout. "Do you know where our little friend is?"

"No," she yelled back. "Why?"

Alastor was quiet. Which meant one thing.

"Where is the hob?" I asked. "Al. Seriously. Where is he?"

But all I got was silence. That, and the horrible feeling all the players were stepping onto the stage, but no one had ever bothered to give me a script.

Uncle Barnabas had arranged for none other than Madam Drummer to swing by and pick us up that evening.

"I just have a few errands to run for our adventure tonight, but I'll meet you there," he said, when I made a face. "Buck up, Prosper. This will all be over in a few hours."

Sooner than that, if I didn't jump out of the van to escape Madam Drummer's long, poetic speech to Nell about how *special* this night was, and how we all had to *cherish* it and the memories we'd make, and also, don't mess up the lines, but really, don't miss your mark either, and don't improvise, all right?

It was a huge relief to finally be able to escape and head inside the empty auditorium. We were two hours early. That had felt ridiculous when we left the house, but seeing Madam Drummer on stage, waving her arms, screaming for "lights, more lights, *dramatic lights*!" made it feel like not enough time. Nell turned to say something to me, a weird expression on her face, but one of the crew members dragged her off to go get her stage makeup and hair done. I tucked the iron bracelets more firmly beneath my sweater sleeve, hoping they weren't noticeable under my socks and pants.

I kept myself busy helping the crew run through one last practice of switching the sets out between scenes. There wasn't really a reason for me to be there other than to watch the show, but I felt myself sucked up into the world onstage anyway. People were laughing and talking in nervous voices, drifting back and forth across the stage.

A few girls waved to me and asked about where Nell and I were the past two days and why we missed school. Even Norton came and sat with me at the edge of the stage, trying to catch me up on what I'd missed in class, offering his notes. The other students noticed me. They wanted to talk about my backdrop—they acted like I'd been going to school there for years instead of a few weeks.

Which is why it sucked so much that they thought I was Ethan White, not Prosperity Redding.

You could stay here forever. It could always be like this....

Yeah, yeah, I thought, rubbing the back of my neck. *Still not buying what you're selling, buddy.*

"Who's that?"

Norton's soft voice made me look up. There was a flash of red at the back of the theater—copper red. I would have recognized that hair anywhere.

It felt like my heart was going to jump out from my chest and escape out of my open mouth.

No.

No.

NO.

I knew the second Prue spotted me. The determined look on her face as she scanned the stage turned into one of total annoyance.

That is your sister, is it not?

"What did you do?" I whispered.

I believe the true question is, Maggot, what will you do to her? What shall I make you do?

The horrible memory of my hand closing around Nell's throat flashed through my mind.

I scrambled back onto the stage and bolted for the right wing. My hands shoved aside the black curtain and anyone who stepped in front of me. I fought the rush of prickling through my limbs, slamming my good arm down to my side to keep Alastor from moving it. It struggled against my grip.

All you have to do is make a contract, Maggot, and you both will walk out of here alive.

"I thought . . ." I squeezed my eyes shut, trying to steady my breathing.

You thought what? That we were friends? That I had forgotten my original purpose? You will make this contract, Maggot, or you will lose her once and for all. Do you not remember that sheet of paper, the one you found in your father's desk?

Of course he had seen it in my memory. When Prue was at her weakest, my grandmother's publicist had drafted a press release they could use if she didn't survive—so they "wouldn't have to think about it" during the worst moment of their lives.

"Why are you doing this?" I breathed out. "It doesn't have to be this way."

This time, I felt Alastor's anger and frustration detonate inside of my head. *Because it is the only way! If I do not feed off the energy of this contract, I shall never be strong enough to escape you in time!*

I stumbled forward, down the short hall connected to backstage. Alastor's words were still ringing in my mind as I found Nell applying her stage makeup with a small sponge.

"What's—"

I shoved through the other kids getting ready around her and hooked my arm through hers.

"Prosp—*Ethan!*" she hissed as I dragged us out of the room. "Stop—are you listening to me? Hey!"

We passed the greenroom, which, unfortunately, already had crew gathered there. I tried the other doors frantically. Nell gripped my shoulder, forcing me to stop. It was dark back there, but I could still see her wide eyes behind her glasses.

"It's Prue, she's here," I tried to explain. "I saw her! Al brought her here to try to force a contract—"

Nell didn't react like I thought she would. Instead of the panic I felt, her face seemed to harden into a mask. She glanced back over my shoulder. My eyes went to where her hands were fisting the fabric of her pants. "You . . . I think . . ."

She walked a few steps down the hall to the last door, an old dressing room that we'd used for temporary storage. Nell retrieved a silver key from her pocket and shoved it into the lock.

I let her push me inside the dark room. "Nell, what if Prue gets close? What if something happens to her and she—"

Nell shut the door behind us. I heard a *click* as it was locked again.

"Wait." My heart was beating so hard I thought it would bruise against my ribs. "What's going on? Nell?"

"Prosper . . . I wish . . . I wish things had been different. I wish it didn't have to be this way. I just . . ."

Her voice was quiet, shaking around the edges. I felt against the wall for the light switch. Nell snapped her fingers, but the overhead lights didn't come on. Instead, a ring of small white candles in a perfect circle flared to life.

There were mirrors *everywhere*, across both the front and back walls. They caught the candlelight and lit the entire room.

Prosperity. Get out of here. Get us out of here now.

"Nell . . ." I began, backing up toward the door. She beat me to it, holding it shut with her hand.

"Just go sit over there, in the center," she said. When I didn't move, when I tried to pull the door open by force, she threw out a hand and sent me skidding to the back of the room. As I slammed into the ground, all the air blew out of my chest. My vision blanked out for a second as my head hit the title.

"Tell me what's going on!" I demanded. "Nell!"

There was a sharp knock at the door. She scrambled to get it, letting two figures squeeze through. The door locked again, but she kept her hand there. The metal handle turned bright red-hot under her fingers.

"Prosper!"

Prue dropped the backpack in her hands onto the ground and rushed over to me. I pushed myself up just in time for her to throw her arms around my neck. "You're okay! We were so worried! What's going on? Who are these people?"

I pushed her back. "You can't be here, you have to leave!"

She looked hurt for a second. Then she just looked angry. "Are you kidding me? You're the one that asked me to come!"

"What . . . what are you talking about?" I whispered. "I never asked you to come!"

"Then what is this?" Prue reached into the front pouch of her backpack, pulling out my notebook—the one filled with sketches of the school, of the House of Seven Terrors, of me and Nell. Even the little one I did of the wharf.

"I found it wedged into my window," she said. "I recognized your drawings right away. I thought . . . you were trying to lead me to you. That you wanted me to rescue you."

"No!" I said. "You don't understand what's going on—Prue, you don't know what's inside of me."

"You mean the malefactor?"

Okay. Apparently she *did* know what was inside of me.

"Grandmother told me everything—they all did, everything about the curse and the Bellegraves, and what she was trying to do that night."

"All lies, I'm sure," I said, pulling out the last sheet of notebook paper. This one didn't have a drawing on it. It was a message, in the same smeared handwriting: *CohMe NohW. BRiNG Yoooous ONlY.*

"You thought I wrote this?" I asked. "Seriously? You don't even think I'm capable of basic English?"

"It was so fortunate that I was home when Prudence rang the bell," came Uncle Barnabas's rich voice. "She held up your school picture and asked if I had seen you. I'm glad I could reunite the two of you."

Nell stood silently at his side, staring hard at the floor.

"You already knew who I was?" Prue asked before turning to look at me. "Prosper? Who is this person? Who's that girl?"

"It's okay," I said, "Prue, that's Uncle Barnabas. You know, Dad's brother? That's his daughter, Nell."

Prue pulled away from me again, turning around. I scrambled up after her even though my knees felt hollow.

"This isn't Uncle Barnabas," she said. "I don't know who

you are, but our *real* uncle came to the Cottage last week to help look for Prosper. The whole family did."

"That's . . . impossible," I said, turning toward him. He leaned casually against the door, his arms crossed over his chest. Slacks and a loose button-down shirt—it was the nicest I had ever seen him look.

I warned you! Al roared. *I told you not to trust them!*

Why *had* I? It seemed enough at the time that he'd saved me, but then he'd shown me the letter from Dad . . .

And Missy had shown me how easily handwriting could be copied with a single spell.

Bile rose in my throat, burning.

"This is very unfortunate," he said. "This ruse would have been easier to keep up if the idiot had stayed in Las Vegas where he belonged. I suppose now is as good of a time as any to get things started. Cornelia, if you wouldn't mind . . . ?"

Nell looked like she wanted the floor to swallow her whole. She sat beside the cauldron that was steadily bubbling in the middle of the room. Around her were empty vials, the body of a dead eel . . .

Three toes of a man hanged for his crimes, a newborn eel's freely given slime, wings of a black beetle plucked midflight, two eggs of a viper stolen at night, a gleaming stone cast down from the moon, all boiled in a cauldron at high noon . . . The spell. Nell had started the spell, likely before we ever left school on Monday. If she'd had the key to the room, if she had reinforced it through enchantment, hardly anyone would have been able to disturb it.

"Who are you?" I demanded. "Answer me!"

"Typical. A Redding shouting and stomping around to get his way." The man I knew as Uncle Barnabas kicked himself off the wall. He gave a little sarcastic bow. "The name's Henry Bellegrave. My daughter and I are here to take back everything your family took from ours."

Bewitched and Betrayed

For a second, it was like my brain forgot how to work. Dark fuzz was crowding in on my vision, and I felt both dizzy and sick at the same time. I didn't snap out of it until I felt Prue's hand reach back to push me behind her. To protect me.

Not this time, I thought, stepping forward.

"You're a Bellegrave?" I asked Nell. My brain finally put together all of the little clues. I really was an idiot.

"No, I'm a *Bishop*," Nell said. "He . . . I never met him until my mom died."

"It was a fortuitous turn of events," Henry said. "I knew Cornelia's mother had . . . talents. I sought her out when I was doing my research for my PhD, lived with her, studied her. She herself had studied Goody Prufrock, and had ohared the ingredients necessary for Prufrock's spell. But

I needed the incantation, the words she spoke, in order to complete it. I left to do my own research, and, over a decade later, heard rumors that dear Tabitha had found a record of the incantation. By the time I returned to Salem for it, Tabitha had oh-so-sadly passed and her grimoire, where she kept all of her notes, was conveniently missing, but lo and behold, here was a daughter I never knew I had, just waiting for me. And she was *talented*, like her mother."

Nell turned back toward me, her voice breaking. "I couldn't . . . Prosper, they said if I helped them, I could have my mother back. The malefactor he contracted with would free her from the shade realm."

Oh, Alastor said. *Oh, these weak human hearts.*

What do you mean?

Tell Mistress Cornelia she has been lied to. The realm of shades can be opened, but not without throwing off the balance of life. Worse, it would not be her mother that returned to her. It would be a shade of her mother, a hungry ghoul who would haunt her forevermore. Tell her!

"They lied to you," I said. "Nell, I'm sorry, but it's not possible. Al says—"

"I don't care what he says!" she shouted. "They said I could have my mom back! Missy wouldn't help, and I couldn't do it alone. They promised! You have to understand!"

"Yeah, I understand all right," I said. "You really are a great actress. You had me stupidly believing we were friends."

"You were never friends," Prue cut in, giving the other

girl a look like Death itself. "They interrupted Grandmother in the middle of the ceremony to help you."

"How is trying to stab me with a knife *helping* me?"

"She had to cut each of your limbs to make sure the fiend couldn't control them or fight back—then she was going to finish the spell that witch—Goody Prufrock—started."

Wow. Okay.

"If that was her intention, then she's a bigger fool than I thought," Uncle—Henry Bellegrave said with a sharp laugh. "The intention of the original spell was to seal the malefactor inside of the servant girl, but it was also meant to strip him of his power and pass it to another. Of course, our friend Alastor cursed himself before that could happen and here we all are."

I understand now, Al said, sounding more furious than before. *If I hadn't done what I did that night, my brother would have stolen my powers and rendered me mortal. The flames would have taken care of the rest.*

"Start, Cornelia," Henry barked. *"Now."*

I stared at her as she came and picked up her mother's grimoire. Prue and I both tried to dive for it, but Nell threw us back against the wall with a wave of her hand.

Let me help you. I can get us out of this.

I don't *want your help,* I said, suddenly too angry to see straight. All of this, every single bit of this, was his fault. None of this would be happening—the attacks, the kidnappings, making me feel like I belonged here. My hands tightened into fists at my side. I couldn't hear the words that Nell was murmuring over the pounding blood in my ears. *Now, Prosper, NOW! She's summoning my brother— she'll bring him through and then it will all be for nothing. He will kill you to kill me!*

Prue screamed my name as I launched forward, knocking candles over and spraying hot wax everywhere. Henry knew what he was doing, though. He had his arm locked around my throat, and one of mine pinned at a painful angle behind my back.

I can get us out of this! Take the iron bracelets off! TAKE THEM OFF!

"Watch now, malefactor," Henry whispered in my ear. "I've made a contract of my own. Everything you helped the Reddings take from my ancestors will be mine once more."

He pointed me toward the nearest mirror and held me there. Prue took a step forward, raising her fist. All Henry had to do was twist my arm and get me to scream for her to back off.

"Dude," I said, struggling to pull away. "Get over it! It's been three hundred freaking years!"

"And yet I live with the consequences every day!" he said. "Of what *your* ancestors did! It's a miracle that I'm here today."

Yes, Al agreed. *Clearly I didn't do as thorough a job as I thought. I wonder which Bellegrave escaped the colony before I got my claws into him?*

The floor shook under our feet—one solid pound, and then another, and another.

Oh, Al said simply, *crap.*

"What was that?" I heard someone say outside the door. "Did you feel that?"

I opened my mouth to scream for help, but Henry laughed. "She's enchanted the door. No one will get in."

"What . . . what *is* that?" Prue's voice shook. I followed her pointed finger to the large mirror again, trying to ignore Nell's voice as she repeated, *"Come forth, come forth, come forth, and pass into our realm."*

It started as three blurry lights in the mirror. They bobbed up and down a little bit—one white, the others a wicked green. And then they got bigger. And bigger. And bigger. Until they weren't just little lights, they were . . .

Ogres, Alastor said. *They're dumber than fen-sucked louts, but they're bonny fighters.*

What does that mean?

Allow me to put this in a way you'll understand: it means WE ARE DOOMED.

They were ugly—skin like old, rotting frogs, with razor-sharp beaks that were already dripping with yellow foam. The stink of rotten eggs filled the small room, but it wasn't coming from me. The ogres' ears were long and pointed, jutting out from an otherwise smooth, grayish-green skull.

I've never seen eyes that shade of burning gold before. The two of them stared hungrily at us through the glass.

One raised a big beefy hand and knocked.

Prue screamed.

They weren't done. The same ogre pressed its huge clawed hand up against the glass and pushed. The mirror stretched and stretched and stretched like it was made of rubber. But even rubber has a snapping point. When it happened, it sounded like a gunshot. The ogre's hand smashed through, slapping against the ground for something to grip.

"Nell! Stop! *Stop it!*" I yelled. It was already too late. The first ogre pushed its wide shoulders through the gold frame, grunting with the effort. The metal bent and cracked, warping to give him and his identical brother enough room to duck through. When they finally stood at their full height, they towered over all of us—seven, eight feet tall. And almost just as wide.

"Keep going," Henry growled to Nell. She had stopped, staring at the fiends with total terror. "You're not finished yet!"

Nell glanced at me and then away, back at her mother's grimoire. Her hands were shaking so hard she could barely hold the heavy book up.

"Come forth, come forth . . ." she whispered, *"and pass into our realm."*

The final light began to take shape. It was a white light that quickly turned into a big black cat—a panther.

The panther from my dream.

Its silky coat flashed as it stepped through the mirror, slinking forward until it came to a stop between the two ogres and sat. One bright blue eye and one black eye.

One eye that allows us to see in this world, and one to see Downstairs.

I knew Nightlock had mentioned what form they took in our world—there was a snake, maybe. All I could remember was the poor one that got stuck with being a hedgehog. So who was this?

Before I could stop him, I felt the bubble rise in my throat. Alastor's prim voice burst out of my mouth. "Who are you? How dare you enter this realm and break the balance?"

The panther smiled. Actually smiled.

"Now, big brother," came a refined woman's voice, "don't tell me you can't recognize your own sister?"

What's Past Is Prologue

"Pyra."

The world seemed to drop out from under us.

Pyra? As in your sister, Pyra? As in your sweet little sister that, oh no, could never be involved in this?

The panther took a step toward us and nodded at Henry. The man released me and pushed me toward her. Prue got there faster, grabbing my arm.

"Alastor, how charming. You've made a friend," Pyra purred. "It pains me to see you in such a form, living with such creatures as these."

"What are you doing here?" I felt Alastor's words leaving my mouth, his words ringing in my ears. Prue looked startled, but didn't let go of my arm. "Have you come to take me home? You've finally manifested your animal form—how brilliant. I assure you the protectors will not be necessary once I'm free."

Al, I thought at him, *this is the creature I saw in my dreams—*

But I swear—I swear I felt Alastor swell with pride inside of me. My skin prickled, static racing along my arms, my neck, my face.

No! Al, think about this—if she's here, it means she's the one that's behind all of this! She made the deal with the Bellegraves, she betrayed you to Honor! Listen to me!

"Oh, my poor, stupid brother . . ." Pyra began to weave in and out of the candles, circling around the ogres. They stood like stone, guarding the mirror. The glass there rippled, signaling that the portal was still open. "I'm not here to take you home. I'm here to take what should have been mine over three hundred years ago."

If Alastor had been in full control of my body, we could have . . . I don't know, we could have at least made it harder for the ogres to swipe me off the ground and dangle me from my right foot like I was some kind of bug they were about to eat. I should have taken the iron bracelets off when I had the chance.

"Prosper!"

I forced Al back down. "Stay back, Prue! It's okay—just—stay back!"

For one second, I actually felt bad for Alastor. I could feel a storm of emotions raging in my chest, and all of them belonged to him. Blood rushed to my head, but so did anger, embarrassment, confusion—he was stunned. Too stunned to even speak.

"You must be asking yourself, *how?* How did it come to this?" Pyra circled back, her tail curling in the air and smoke. "It started when Father announced that you would be heir. When you allowed our father to lock me in the tower, in a *prison.* I was your shame, was I not?"

"Never!" Al said. "Never. I only agreed with Father for your protection—Bune and the others might have killed you otherwise!"

"It turned out well for me. There, I met a host of fiends, the kinds you scorned as servants and lessers for the roles our father had forced on them. The ones he'd enslaved to fight his battles and do his work. Do you remember our old nannyhob? Oh, how that hob grew to despise you. Without so much as a nudge, she revealed your true name, overheard at birth. At the time, I did not have the power to manifest my animal form because you and my other *precious* brothers would not allow me to make contracts. I thought if I could take your magic, *your* power, it would be enough to allow me to shift."

"Pyra . . ." Alastor sounded as though he was being torn in two. "You only needed to ask for my help, and it would have been granted!"

"Liar!" the panther growled. "It took time, what with you spoiling my original plan, but as soon as I'd enough power to shift, I'd gathered the other prisoners and unleashed them Downstairs. Under my leadership, the lowest of the low rose higher and higher, slaying all those who stood in our way. Not only is the Black Throne mine, but I've proven my might to our realm. They call me Pyra the Conqueror. I will do what all of you feared to."

"Congratulations, Pyra the Conqueror," I snapped, "but why go through all of this trouble *now*? If you have everything you dreamed of, why not just have Henry kill us from the start?"

"Because, human," Pyra said, stopping in front of my face. Her tongue darted out, licking the tip of my nose. "I had to wait for my brother to regain as much of his power as he could, otherwise there'd be no point in stealing it."

"The magic in the human realm is fading with each year. The fiends require a new, purer source of power, and she intends to unlock the gate to the realm of Ancients to get it," Henry said like a proud father would. "She required the sacrifice of all her brothers' lives and magic to form the necessary key."

I tried to right myself, but the ogre swung me around, still upside down.

"What are you talking about?" poor Prue asked. "What realm?"

"That's not what you said," Nell interrupted, "you said . . . You promised that she was just going to use the power to help the fiends Downstairs, to encourage them not to escape into our world!"

"Perhaps you should have asked to read his actual contract, witch," Pyra said. "Now get on with it. The full spell should be in that book, yes?"

"Did you send me that notebook?" Prue interrupted. Clearly she was adapting to the situation a lot quicker than I had. She hadn't even blinked at the talking panther. "You tricked me into coming here—why?"

"I did no such thing. My brother played a trick on you, likely thinking he could convince the human he resides in to form a contract with him—one last attempt to save himself, I'm sure. And now I can use it to my own advantage," Pyra said. "To strike pure fear in your own brother's heart, should he disobey me. Come out, dear friend, for you truly deserve the credit. Take a bow for this magnificent performance."

I saw the horn first as the hob leaned around one of the mirrors surrounding us. He had been tucked just out of sight, and now that he had shown himself, he was almost unrecognizable. His skin was clean, his claws filed, and his one horn polished. Nightlock wore gold silk robes that shimmered as he came toward the candlelight.

"You!" Alastor's voice ripped out of my throat. "You dare betray—"

"My lord and master?" Nightlock said. All of a sudden his voice was clear and almost refined. "My only lord and master is Her Majesty, Pyra the Conqueror. She bade me to watch your movements in this realm and report back, oh yes. How easy you were to fool, how quickly you assumed I was feebleminded. And yet you did not suspect that I told Her Majesty to send the howlers to keep you in check, to keep you from running away long enough to escape the boy. I removed each obstacle to her journey here, including the changelings."

No—what did that mean? What had happened to Toad?

Nell made a noise of distress, looking up from the grimoire again. I swung my loose foot at the ogre to dislodge myself, but it was like kicking a cement wall.

"You knew about Nightlock all along?" I turned back to Henry. Even Nell looked shocked by this turn of events.

"Of course," Henry said. "He removed his glamour for me months ago, during our preparations. Nightlock was meant to watch the two of you when I could not. To keep you close to the house. Everything was meant to frighten you into behaving—into believing the only way to stay alive was to stay with me."

"Imbecile!" Alastor wailed. "Filthy traitor! I'll have your horn for this!"

"Oh no," the hob said with a crooked little smile. "I think not."

"You may return now, Nightlock," Pyra said. "You have earned your place at the palace again."

The ogres let him pass. The hob didn't even look back as he stepped through the mirror and disappeared completely.

—

Okay, Al, what do we do?

I don't know—I just need a moment to think, to gather . . . to gather my thoughts!

We didn't have time for that. My head was pounding and it was hard to piece together thoughts when I felt so disoriented. The candlelight blurred. I blinked to clear my eyes.

Pyra lifted a paw, batting at my upside-down face. *Toying* with me.

"This spell," Nell continued, "what *really* happens during it? Is it even true that Alastor will be transferred to another living creature?"

"Not quite," Henry said. "It will remove Alastor's powers and bind him to Prosper forever. Remember what I told you, Cornelia—that our lives depend on this now too."

"But you said that all three of your brothers' magic *and* lives were needed . . ." Nell began, the candlelight reflecting in her glasses.

"Clever witch," Pyra said, turning back toward her. "Indeed it does. But since you've been so loyal, so very good to me, I will endeavor to make his suffering short. I take this claw and I gut him from here"—the panther pointed to my stomach, then my chin—"to here."

"Try it!" Prue snapped. "I'll turn you into a rug!"

"By the realms, that's terrifying," Pyra said, giving me— or rather Al—a wink. "Siblings who like each other. Can you imagine the horror of it all?"

The other ogre stomped forward, creating a wall between her and me. When Prue tried to dodge around his thick, hairy legs, the ogre caught her by the hair and held her. Prue yelped in pain.

I struggled against the ogre again. The fiend shook me out like a rug, but finally dropped me headfirst on the tile. I saw stars. A burst of black, black stars.

"Finish it, Cornelia," Henry said. *"Now."*

"My name," she said between gritted teeth. "Is *Nell.* Prosper—catch!"

My brain caught up two seconds too late to keep from catching the heavy book she threw at me. The second it touched my hands, the second it sensed that a fiend had it in its grasp, Tabitha Bishop's grimoire burst into flames and began to devour itself.

"NO!" Pyra shrieked, leaping toward it.

The book exploded into ash between my fingers.

"What did you do?" Henry roared at Nell. He raised a hand toward her, but Nell was faster. She threw him across the room, cracking against the opposite wall. Even Pyra was thrown back by the force of the windstorm that was building around Nell, whipping up the ash and smoke into a tornado around her.

"Those who trespass in our land," Nell was chanting, *"now be blocked by my hand."*

The ogres began to groan, stumbling around. They

clutched at their heads and knocked into one another. Instead of the floor opening like it had for the howlers, however, the mirror reached out with silver hands and grabbed them. They were squeezed back through the frame, one at a time, disappearing back into the black.

"Stop!" Henry begged. "Stop this! We must finish the contract! We have to see it through, or we'll lose everything! I staked your life on this contract, as well as mine!"

I scrambled back onto my feet. The air around Pyra wavered, smoke rising off her body. Then it wasn't just smoke—there was fire racing out under her claws, heading straight for Nell. I shoved her to the ground, knocking her out of the way. I hit the tile hard enough to rattle my brain.

Stop this! Let me speak to my sister, this must be a misunderstanding, one of my brothers has surely put her up to this.

"Shut up, Al!" I shouted. "Nell, finish!"

"I send you back to your realm, I banish you—"

"Nice trick, witch," Pyra growled, sweeping her tail against the ground. Fire followed. "It'll be the hard way for us, then, Alastor."

It was like watching someone else's dream. The air was burning hot in my lungs, warping and smearing the room in front of me. For a second, it looked like Pyra bit into Prue's arm. It looked like she yanked my sister toward the cracking mirror.

It looked like she pulled Prue into the dark.

Time sped back up and slammed into me. I knew I was screaming as I ran across the room after her. "Prue—*Prue!* Give her back! *Give her back!*"

I slammed my fists against the glass, and Prue did the same from the other side. I could see her shouting something, but only Pyra's voice came through.

"If you want her back, you'll have to come play in my realm," she said through the glass. *"What will it be? Her life, or my brother's?"*

Al's voice leaped to my lips. "Pyra! Stop this madness! Even if you opened the gate to the realm of Ancients, all you'd succeed in doing is collapsing all the worlds! It would be chaos and darkness!"

"We'll see about that," she said as the black came forward and devoured her and my sister whole.

"No! No, please! Bring her back! Bring her back!" I shouted, ignoring the flames licking at my shoes. "Prue!"

"Let me go!" Nell shrieked. I turned around, watching as Henry threw his daughter over his shoulder and rammed his way out of the room. "Prosper! *Prosper!*"

With the door open, the smoke filtered out into the hall. The fire alarms began to shriek, and the overhead sprinklers kicked in. I heard surprised yells from the auditorium—but people were already heading for the doors. The fire department would be here any minute.

I ran back to the dressing room, taking in small patches of flames that were still burning under the water, the field of candles, the drowned ashes of what had once been a witch's book of spells.

Despair. I finally knew what that word truly meant. It was smears of charcoal-like soot, the blue heart of a flickering flame. It was Prosperity Oceanus Redding standing alone, staring at a dozen versions of himself in the room's many mirrors.

Except . . . I wasn't alone, and suddenly I knew exactly what I had to do.

"Al," I whispered. "Are you still there?"

Yes.

His voice sounded heavy to me. Maybe he already knew what I was about to say.

"I want a contract." When he didn't answer, I continued, "Here are my terms: If you help me get Downstairs to rescue Prue, I'll help you take down *your* sister. I'll . . . even sign away my spirit to you, if that's what it takes."

I could feel myself shaking, but I forced myself to stand up straight. I thought for sure he would laugh at me, call me some stupid name, pat himself on the back for finally getting me hook, line, and sinker.

This is for Prue, I thought. Please, please, please don't let me be too late to save her.

"Al?" I whispered.

I felt him shift like a thunderstorm inside my chest.

Light a candle and step close to the looking glass. Time is short, and we cannot delay.

I took a step forward, my sneakers sloshing through the water on the floor. Alastor's power raced through me, and when my arm lifted and my finger touched the mirror's shimmering surface, I couldn't tell which one of us had actually done it. My image distorted, stretching and shivering as the glass suddenly rippled like liquid silver.

Maybe it was true that we never really escape our histories. That revenge is a poison that stays in the hearts of families, reborn with each generation. I was nothing like my family, but I was still a Redding. I didn't get to choose my family, or this curse, but I couldn't run away from them. Honor had tried to escape the consequences of his bad choice, and all it had done was hurt others by bringing fear and pain into the world. No more.

Warm steam belched out of the mirror as its surface parted just enough to see the darkness beyond it. The stench of sulfur and rotting garbage rolled out around me. I should have been afraid, but I wasn't. Instead, I kept thinking of the quote Nell had written on the gray bag she gave me, which now felt more like a warning than a simple line from Shakespeare: *What's past is prologue.*

The blackness beyond the glass gazed back at me like a moonless sky. I took a deep breath and stepped through.

It was finally time to write a new chapter of this story.

Turn the page for a sneak peek at

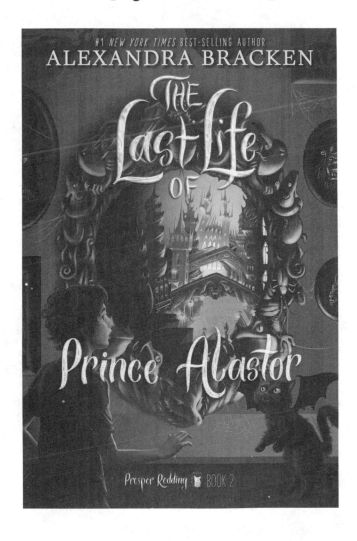

A Fiendish Arrangement

The mirror's surface rippled, exhaling a puff of warm, sour-smelling air. The overhead sprinklers were still putting out the last of the candles Nell and her father, Henry Bellegrave, lit to perform her spell.

The darkness inside of the watery glass glowered back at me as I took a step forward. My face distorted in the reflection, until it looked like I was snarling.

If only my family could see me now. *Poor little Prosper,* my aunts used to say, *scared of his own shadow.* They wouldn't believe for a second that I'd be willing to follow Pyra, or that I was capable of finding Prue, my twin, inside of whatever shadows were waiting Downstairs.

They didn't know me at all. I'd made mistakes, I'd been misled, but I wasn't some helpless victim in this story.

In that moment, the only thing I felt was anger. At myself. At my family. At Nell. At Alastor. At the fiends who couldn't leave the human world alone.

Wait.

I took a step back, frustrated. "What now?"

The deal. We must set the terms.

"*Seriously?* Now? We're going to lose their trail!"

Yes, "seriously," you craven rumpwart. An understanding up front will prevent later troubles. And, Alastor said, somewhat grudgingly, *I require the magic generated from the deal to open a direct portal to the mirror we'll arrive at. The mirror pathways have been cursed so that any humans who find their way inside will be trapped there forever, and I rather thought we had more important things to do than float around in perpetual darkness, Maggot.*

Okay. That was fair. "I want your help to save Prue from Downstairs, no matter the circumstances—"

That is acceptable.

"I'm not finished," I said. "I want you to also guarantee that you will help us get back to the human realm and not strand us down there or in the mirror pathways."

Well played, Maggot. You are learning the ways of a fiend.

I set my jaw hard enough that it was almost painful. "I'm *nothing* like a fiend. I won't ever be. All you do is hurt others and destroy good things. I just won't be your plaything anymore."

Alastor was silent.

"I also want you to end the grudge you have against my family," I said. "And leave them alone."

He sneered inside my head, making my skin crawl with the sensation of it. *No. I will grant your first two requests in exchange for the promise of your eternal servitude Downstairs upon your mortal death.*

I choked a bit at that. Forever . . . was a long time. It wasn't a long time, it was the thing past the standard of "a long time." My afterlife would consist of licking his boots clean and cooking him whatever disgusting things they ate Downstairs.

Oh no, Maggot. I have hobs to do such things. No, you would tend to my fireviper nests, and then, after you've proven yourself, you'd have the privilege of preparing my favorite fairy crisps. They screech and bite as you pluck off their wings, but the oven is always quick to quiet them.

I rolled my eyes, letting my hands curl into fists at my sides. The punishment wouldn't be doing any of those jobs. No, the real prison of misery was knowing that I'd be forced to listen to him going on about his "dark magnificence" until I'd probably wish I could die all over again, just to escape it for a few seconds.

I couldn't believe I'd ever been stupid enough to think, even for a second, that he might turn down my offered contract. Like, *You know what? I'll take the moral high road just this once and help you and your sister out of this dastardly situation I'm directly responsible for putting you in.*

But that was the difference between humans and fiends. Humans had the capacity for good. Fiends didn't.

How your courage crumbles at the prospect, Alastor said. *It is the only thing I ask, and yet you squander the passing seconds as though you have nothing to be concerned about. As if knowing for certain that your sister's heart is strong enough to survive the dark rigors of Downstairs.*

My own heart suddenly slammed against my ribs.

While she'd undergone several surgeries and had been given the all clear by doctors, Prue had been born with a heart condition that had nearly killed her. There was no telling if it was just the doctor's skill and her own innate strength that had helped her survive, or a touch of the unnatural, magic luck the Reddings possessed.

If it was the latter . . . what would happen to her if Alastor finally broke free from my body and took all of our family's good fortune away? What if it was so terrifying Downstairs—

No. I shook my head, flinging the horrible thought away. Prudence was strong. She'd always been the better of the two of us, in all the ways that mattered. She'd rescued me from any number of mess-ups. It was my turn to save her, and I would.

I will help you save your sister and ensure you return here together. In exchange, I'll have your shade. Do you accept these terms?

Wait. The thought of Alastor's vow of vengeance on my

family stirred up another one. Honor Redding had already promised all of the shades of his family and descendants centuries ago, including mine. I wasn't giving the fiend anything more than he already had.

Confound it all—Alastor spluttered, clearly hearing my thoughts. He'd been so in love with the image of tormenting me that he really *hadn't* realized it. This time I was the one smirking. *No! I require something else, then*—

A heavy pounding on the storage room's door startled me out of my thoughts. My head snapped around, stomach plummeting as someone called out, "Is anyone in there? Stand back from the door, we're coming in!"

"I accept your original terms!" I said. "Just hurry!"

A flash of green light gathered at the center of my chest, then billowed out in tendrils. I startled, jumping back from the mirror as the shimmering strands knotted themselves together over my skin and seeped into it.

I'd never seen a shade of green like this before, not in all of my paint sets or colored pencils; it wasn't one found in nature, that was for sure. It looked almost . . . electric. The last few traces of it floated around me like sparks, drifting into the mirror.

Fine, Alastor said, sulking. *Clearly my time inhabiting your puny mind has temporarily dulled my own. The sooner I escape, the better.*

Yeah. We'd see about that.

A surge of prickling heat went through my arm as he

took control of it. Somewhere behind me, the pounding on the storage room's door intensified like a booming heartbeat. I couldn't look away from the mirror, though, not when my finger touched its shivering glass and a spark of that same green magic leaped from it. I took a deep breath and closed my eyes.

Do you always close your eyes when frightened? Alastor asked. *Open them wide, stare down your fear until it obeys you.*

I gritted my teeth. "I'm not afraid."

Not yet.

By the time the door burst open and the firefighters spilled inside, the mirror had already closed behind me.

Where Fiends Dwell

Passing through the mirror portal was like being caught between one heartbeat and the next. For that single, disorienting second, there was nothing but pure black—no air, no light, no sound. You're not falling, or flying, or moving at all.

You're not even sure you still have a body.

And just when you know to start worrying, when the soggy edges of your thoughts start to make less and less sense, it all explodes.

Something reached out and gripped me by the throat, yanking me forward so hard that I felt my cheeks and lips peel back from my teeth. Rainbow prisms of light whirled around me, spinning faster and faster. My stomach heaved, and I couldn't close my eyes; tears streamed from them. A roar filled my ears, drowning out my thundering pulse and Alastor's gleeful laughter.

In the end, I didn't get off the ride—I got ejected.

My eyes and mouth snapped shut as all that spiraling air suddenly detonated, releasing me with a thundering *crack*.

"Al!" I managed to choke out. My knees hit wood and splintered it. When I finally landed, it was with a loud, queasy-making *splat*.

Brown mud and something that smelled suspiciously like what came out of the wrong ends of humans sprayed up around me on impact. It swirled around my waist like the most disgusting of swamps. I coughed and gagged. When my palms skimmed over the water, they caught on floating pieces of . . . something.

Ahhhhh, Alastor said wistfully. ***It is the essence of "home," is it not?***

It was the essence of puke, actually. Days-old puke, left outside in the heat.

Holding my breath, I managed to push myself fully onto my feet, closing my eyes as the watery, reeking substance dripped off me. The ground was compact beneath my feet, at least, and when I stood, whatever steaming poison was roiling around me only came up to my knees. Better. Ish.

I moved forward gingerly, craning my neck back to peer up into the shadows over my head. There was only a thin stream of green light illuminating the space, just enough to make out the basics.

We *had* fallen through some kind of wood bench. I held up the two biggest pieces of it, holding them together to reveal the telling circle that had been cut into it.

Oh.

No.

This was . . . Bile burned in my throat, on my tongue. I started to bring my hands up to cover my face, only to remember what was on them. I started to wipe them against my shirt, only to remember it was on that, too. And then, because the only other option was screaming, I took a deep breath.

"Al," I began.

Yes, Maggot? he asked, all innocence.

"Why," I said, the word tasting like vomit, "did you bring us through a mirror in an outhouse? Why? *Why?*"

Not that I must explain my every decision to you, but I brought us here because it is my private facility. It is cursed so that only I may open its door. It is the only mirror in all the realm that I could be sure was not watched by Pyra or her crew of filthy traitors, as no one else is aware that it exists.

"You put your emergency escape in your toilet?"

While many lesser fiends and peasants aspired to my station and adorably mimicked my finely tailored outfits and demeanor, no fiend would ever desire to look in here, would they?

There wasn't a lot that I could—or would—praise Alastor for, but I had to give him this: he could rival any cockroach for self-preservation.

"You really don't mind your subjects seeing you for the first time in over three centuries covered in . . . *this?*" I couldn't bring myself to say the actual word.

Fie, Maggot. I wouldn't dream of announcing myself in such a hideous and humiliating form as a mortal boy. No, I shall wait until I am free of your prison and in my true, terrifying form before I allow the realm to rejoice at my return. It will be soon enough.

"How soon?" I asked, unease prickling over my skin like thousands of spiders.

I felt the curve of his smirk in my mind and shook my head.

No—I had my own answer to my question. How soon? Not one second before I rescued Prue and got us back to the human world. Figuring out how to break my family's contract with him to save us all from his vengeance had to come second.

The Reddings: just your average all-American family who made a deal with a demonic parasite to destroy their rivals and pave their future with gold, and then were stupid enough to try to break the agreement to avoid its consequences. As much as I loved my parents and sister, the finger I was pointing at Alastor was crooked, and curled back at me.

If Alastor was a cockroach, then my ancestors had been the Black Plague. Alastor might have darted away from trouble to hide, but the Reddings hadn't been happy until they'd wiped out anyone who had dared to stand in their way.

"You better hope you never escape my head," I swore, "because the second you do, I am going to wring your fluffy white neck for all of this."

It would endlessly amuse me to watch you try, Alastor said. *Do you intend to stay down here and bask in the moist offerings, or shall I help you jump out?*

I don't need your help, I thought back. Eyes burning with the fumes, I stretched up, feeling for the ledge the seat had been balanced over. My fingertips brushed stone. Solid ground.

Now, how will you do this, Maggot? Alastor wondered. *I seem to recall your trepidation at the prospect of having to climb a rope ladder in—what do you humans call it? Ah yes. Physical Escalation.*

The soup of waste and mud shifted around my knees. My foot found a groove in the wall. I kept both hands up on the platform.

Physical Education, I corrected. I would have rolled my eyes, but they felt like they were on the verge of melting out of my skull.

Education? What is there to learn? Some creatures, like myself, are born with physical prowess, and others, like yourself, are not. You must accept your lot in life or make a deal with me to rise above your station.

That wasn't true at all. Even the best athletes had to build endurance over time. Like a lot of things in life, you worked hard, over and over again, to build up tolerance. You suffered through your extended family calling you worthless until it no longer stung. You learned how to stay silent as your teachers berated you for another failed test. You got used to a fiend talking inside of your skull enough to keep functioning and not curl into a tiny ball of torment.

I had a high tolerance for a lot of things. And I was *not* going to be the Redding Who Died of Starvation and Dehydration in an Outhouse, thanks.

My arms shook as I dragged myself up. The soles of my wet sneakers slipped against the wall, struggling to find purchase. By the time I finally flopped onto the flat, hard-packed dirt floor, my heart was pounding and I couldn't feel my fingers.

The outhouse itself was no bigger than a coffin. There was a small, crescent-shaped cutout in the simple wood door through which that eerie green light was filtering. I stood on my toes and peered out through it.

A long alleyway stretched before us, curving into darkness. Foul, pale vapor hissed up from cracks between the cobblestones on the ground. The walls on the buildings beside the outhouse seemed to lean over the pathway like vultures, waiting to see what prey might scurry by.

When nothing melted out of the nearby shadows, I slowly pushed the old door open. There was only one way to go—forward.

I stripped my sopping-wet sweater off and tossed it aside. By the time I reached what I assumed was the end of the alleyway, the smog thickened, glowing green under a nearby streetlamp that flickered with a magic flame. That electric shade of emerald fell over the whole realm like a coat of slime. They clearly didn't have real fire here, and I wasn't sure why that surprised me.

I took a deep breath, studying what I could see of the kingdom. Painting it would be simple. I'd only need three colors: sinister black, dull silver, and that fluorescent, unnatural green.

I don't think I ever truly appreciated how many bright vivid colors existed in the human world until I came here, a place stained with overwhelming darkness.

There's a stone at your feet, Alastor said. **Take it in hand and toss it against the wall to your right.**

I already knew I was going to regret it before the rock even left my hand, but I did it anyway. It clacked against the stones, and just like that, the structure dissolved into a thousand, inky bats.

"Gah!" I sputtered. Throwing my arms over my face and head did nothing. Their wings fluttered against my skin, prickling like cactus needles. "Why did you—why did you tell me to do *that*?!"

I bit back a small cry of pain as one of their tiny clawed wings hooked into my earlobe and tugged. "Get *off*!"

These bats made whatever we had in the human world look like flying mice. They were the size of hawks, and I could not have been less surprised when I felt a set of fangs puncture my arm and the drag as the bat pulled at my blood.

I gripped its squirming form with my free hand and wrenched it away, throwing it toward the others. The beat of their wings sent the vapors spiraling up, lifting its heavy cover to let me see what was beyond it. My eyes widened as I looked up.

And up.

Because of this, Alastor said, pride swelling in his voice. *Welcome, Maggot, to Downstairs.*